# QUANTUM WINE

A Novel by GREG MINCHER

Vintry Editions 2026

QUANTUM WINE SERIES · BOOK ONE: TERROIR

# QUANTUM WINE: TERROIR

GREG MINCHER

VINTRY EDITIONS

*To those who understand that truth, no matter how long suppressed,*
*eventually finds its way into the light.*

WINE, MEMORY, AND QUANTUM POSSIBILITY


## THE VINTRY, POKOLBIN

This novel began, as many wine stories do, with a tasting.

Not the fictional tasting at Pall Mall that opens *Quantum Wine*, but a real one: ten vintages of Tyrrell's Vat 1 Hunter Valley Semillon, tasted with Murray Tyrrell himself at the winery in 1995. Among those wines was the 1986—the vintage that would, thirty years later, become the quantum wine at the heart of this story.

I remember that 1986. The way it had transformed from tight citrus youth into something honeyed, complex, almost ethereal. The way Murray spoke about that harvest—January 1986, perfect conditions, the kind of vintage a winemaker waits decades to see. At the time, I understood it as great wine. I didn't yet understand it as memory preserved in glass.

But perhaps, on some level, I did. Because that tasting stayed with me through everything that followed.

## THE HUNTER VALLEY JOURNEY

I came to the Hunter Valley in 1994, already deep into a wine career that had taken me through various corners of the wine trade. By the late 1990s, I was working at Brokenwood cellar door, pouring some of Australia's finest wines—including the legendary Graveyard Shiraz— and learning from winemakers like Iain Riggs and PJ Charteris who understood that great wine is equal parts chemistry, terroir, and time.

The Hunter taught me things no other wine region could—the ancient alluvial sands, pale and austere, holding the fossilised secrets of a prehistoric sea bed. The way Semillon ages—not just survives, but *transforms*, developing over decades into something more profound than its origins suggest. The vineyard personalities: the Tyrrell, Drayton, Tulloch, Wilkinson, and Lindeman families who'd been making wine here since the 1800s, who knew their soil the way sailors know tides.

In May 1996, whilst visiting the Wine Society at Stevenage, I found myself in a pub in St Albans. Lower Red Lion, as it happens— the same pub name that appears in this novel, though the fictional version sits in London rather than Hertfordshire. There, in a moment of serendipity that writers dream about, I discovered the word *vintry*: the historical term for a wine merchant's house or storehouse, derived from the medieval wine trade along the Thames.

The word felt perfect. Historical, evocative, connecting wine to place to memory. I knew immediately: this would be the name of something I was beginning to dream about—a property in Pokolbin that would bring together wine, hospitality, and the stories that emerge when people gather over bottles that have been waiting decades to be opened.

## JANCIS ROBINSON: A MOMENT THAT MATTERED

Later that year—late 1996—whilst studying for the Diploma in Wine Marketing at Roseworthy (which later became part of the University of Adelaide), I attended a Jancis Robinson tasting and dinner at Bel Mondo in The Rocks, Sydney.

I brought my copy of *Jancis Robinson's Guide to Wine Grapes*—a hardcover published that very year, 1996—already well-thumbed despite being new. When the opportunity came to have it signed, I told Jancis I was changing careers into wine. A significant admission: I was leaving behind architecture and construction, committing to an industry that demands passion because it certainly doesn't promise easy money.

Her inscription was simple and generous. An encouragement to keep the passion I'd shown. A wish for luck on my wine journey.

That small moment stayed with me.

It nudged me deeper into wine study, towards the Wine & Spirit Education Trust (WSET) Diploma—the same path that had helped shape Jancis's own career decades earlier. It reinforced something I was beginning to understand: that wine, at its best, is a community of people who care about quality, integrity, and the patient work of understanding what happens in a bottle over time.

Jancis Robinson appears as a character in *Quantum Wine* not because of that 1996 meeting, but because there's simply no one more qualified to validate an impossible wine phenomenon. Her rigour, her scepticism, her absolute refusal to accept claims without evidence—these are the qualities that make her the world's most respected wine critic. If Jancis says wine can store consciousness, the wine world listens.

That 1996 inscription absolutely influenced how I wrote her. That moment of encouragement to a career-changer, that generosity towards someone at the beginning of their wine journey, is exactly who Jancis is. In this novel, when she agrees to taste quantum wine with Alex Hartley, when she takes seriously something that sounds impossible, she's being true to the person who signed that book in Sydney nearly thirty years ago: someone who evaluates wine on evidence, not on assumptions.

## CREATING THE VINTRY

In 2000, I began planting a Shiraz vineyard at The Vintry property on De Beyers Road in Pokolbin—rich red soils over limestone at the foothills of the Brokenback Range, distinct from the ancient alluvial sands where Semillon finds its voice. It was a deliberate choice, connecting my vineyard to Hunter Valley history, to the wines I'd poured and studied and loved, though I would learn that each site must find its own expression.

The planting took time—weeks of work in the Hunter heat, establishing each vine, understanding those red soils and limestone base, building the foundation for what would, in years to come, teach me the humbling truth: great wine comes from understanding your specific patch of earth, its unique character and potential, rather than trying to replicate someone else's success.

I finished planting on Tuesday, 2 October 2000.

That day, Murray Tyrrell passed away.

I didn't learn this until later, but when I did, it felt significant. Murray, who'd pioneered so much of modern Hunter winemaking. Murray, whose 1986 Vat 1 I'd tasted five years earlier. Murray, who proved that Hunter Semillon could age for decades when everyone else had abandoned it.

His passing on the day I finished planting my vineyard felt like a passing of responsibility. The old generation who'd built the Hunter's reputation, handing something forward to those of us who'd learned from them.

The Vintry opened as a deluxe accommodation and wine tourism destination in October 2005. The vision was simple: create a place where people could experience Hunter Valley wine the way it was meant to be experienced—slowly, thoughtfully, with time to appreciate what twenty or thirty or forty years in bottle can accomplish. Where guests could taste old Semillon and understand that wine is more than chemistry. It's memory. It's time. It's consciousness preserved.

I didn't know, in 2005, that I'd eventually write a novel about quantum wine. But looking back, everything was leading there.

## WHY THIS NOVEL?

*Quantum Wine* isn't autobiography. Alex Hartley isn't me. Elizabeth Chen is fictional. The quantum mechanism is speculative science, not established fact.

But the *feeling* of this novel—the sense that wine is more than fermented grapes, that great aged Semillon carries something beyond chemistry, that tasting a forty-year-old Hunter wine connects you to the moment of its creation—that feeling is real.

Every wine professional I know has experienced it. That moment when you taste an old wine and you're *transported*. Not metaphorically. Actually, viscerally transported. You feel the heat of that vintage. You sense the winemaker's decisions. You access something that shouldn't be accessible through chemistry alone.

Maybe that's just the power of great wine working on human psychology—sensory memory triggered by aroma compounds, the romance of wine making us imagine connections that don't exist.

Or maybe—just maybe—wine really does preserve something more. Some imprint of consciousness. Some quantum entanglement between maker and drinker, across decades.

I don't know if quantum wine is real. But I know that the *idea* of quantum wine—the possibility that consciousness can be bottled, that time can be tasted, that wine is memory made tangible—is a truth worth exploring.

And I know that in 1996, Jancis Robinson signed a book for a career-changer studying wine marketing at Roseworthy, encouraging him to keep his passion alive. That encouragement led, through years of working in Hunter Valley cellars, planting vineyards, opening The Vintry, and writing about wine, to this novel.

Maybe that's quantum wine too. A moment preserved across thirty years, influencing everything that followed.

## THE HUNTER VALLEY IN FICTION

This novel is set partly in London, partly in Bordeaux, partly in government offices and wine cellars and conference halls around the world. But its heart is here: Pokolbin, Hunter Valley, the rich red earth of De Beyers Road where The Vintry sits, where my Shiraz vines—planted in 2000 in soil over limestone at the foothills of the Brokenback Range—grow in earth that's been making wine for over a century.

I wanted to honour the real people who've made Hunter wine what it is. Murray Tyrrell, who pioneered Vat 1 Semillon and proved it could age for decades. Iain Riggs, who understood that great wine comes from respecting terroir and time. Jancis Robinson, who showed a nervous career-changer in Sydney that the wine world rewards passion and rigour. The generations of winemakers, vignerons, and wine professionals who've dedicated their lives to this valley.

They're not characters in this novel, but they shape every page. The integrity to make wine for thirty years rather than three. The patience to trust that terroir will reveal itself in time. The understanding that some things can't be rushed or replicated—that's what this story is really about.

Elizabeth Chen, the fictional scientist at the centre of *Quantum Wine*, represents every researcher who's been dismissed for pursuing truth that seemed impossible. But she also represents the Hunter Valley winemakers who've insisted, against fashion and commercial pressure, that aged Semillon matters. That patience matters. That some things can't be rushed.

## A NOTE ON TRUTH

Everything in this novel is fiction except the wines, the terroir, and the people who shaped the Hunter Valley.

The Hunter Valley terroir described here—ancient alluvial soils, the Brokenback Range, the red earth of Pokolbin—is real. The wines are real: Tyrrell's Vat 1, Brokenwood's ILR Semillon, the way Hunter Semillon ages over decades into something profound. The wine professionals mentioned—Jancis Robinson, the Institute of Masters of Wine, the traditions of Berry Bros. & Rudd—are real.

The 1996 book signing at Bel Mondo in The Rocks, Sydney—where a Master of Wine encouraged a student to keep his passion alive—is real.

But quantum wine, as described in this novel, is speculative. I've tried to make the science plausible, drawing on real quantum biology research (quantum coherence in photosynthesis, quantum effects in bird navigation). But I don't claim it's proven. I claim only that it's *possible*. And that the possibility is worth exploring.

If this novel makes you want to taste Hunter Semillon—to open a twenty-year-old Tyrrell's Vat 1 or a thirty-year-old Brokenwood or any of the extraordinary aged Semillons that prove the Hunter Valley is one of the world's great white wine regions—then I've succeeded.

And if, when you taste that wine, you feel transported to the vineyard where it was made—to ancient alluvial soils where Semillon roots drive deep into sandy loams and clay, to the harvest morning when the grapes were picked, to the moment when a winemaker stood among those old vines and knew this vintage would be different—well, maybe quantum wine isn't fiction after all.

Maybe it's just wine, doing what wine has always done: preserving memory, connecting past to present, making the impossible feel real.


## ACKNOWLEDGMENTS

To Murray Tyrrell, who passed away the day I finished planting my vineyard and whose wines taught me that great Semillon is worth waiting for.

To Iain Riggs and the Brokenwood team, who showed me what integrity in winemaking looks like.

To Jancis Robinson MW, whose inscription in my copy of *Jancis*

*Robinson's Guide to Wine Grapes* at Bel Mondo in 1996 encouraged a career-changer to keep his passion alive, and whose rigour and honesty continue to set the standard for wine criticism.

To the Hunter Valley community—winemakers, vignerons, cellar door staff, wine writers—who've built one of the world's great wine regions through patience and stubbornness and refusal to chase fashion.

To The Vintry's guests over the years, who've shared bottles and stories and the kind of conversations that only happen when good wine and good company converge.

And to every wine professional who's ever opened a forty-year-old bottle and felt, just for a moment, that wine is more than chemistry. That it's memory. That it's time. That it's magic.

Maybe it's quantum wine.

Maybe it's just great Semillon doing what great Semillon does.

Either way, it's real.

Greg N Fincher
WINE WRITER AND EDUCATOR

The Vintry
Pokolbin, New South Wales, Australia
January, 2026

POKOLBIN, HUNTER VALLEY, NEW SOUTH WALES

JANUARY, 1987

THE WOMAN STOOD in the vineyard at dawn, holding a glass of last year's Semillon to the light.

The air already shimmered with heat. Cicadas were beginning their crescendo in the eucalyptus trees at the vineyard's edge. Summer in the valley—the season when grapes ripened and decisions were made that would echo for decades.

Within hours, the temperature would climb past thirty-five degrees.

The wine in her glass was young, not even a year in bottle. By all conventional wisdom, it should be tight, closed, acidic, a wine that needed years to develop, decades to show its true character.

She tasted it.

The vineyard disappeared.

She was in this vineyard. One year earlier. January 1986, harvest day. The heat more intense—forty-one degrees by noon. Her boots crunching on dry earth between the rows. The weight of secateurs in her hand, cutting clusters of Semillon, examining each bunch for ripeness. A magpie calling from the eucalyptus stand. Cicadas screaming. And her own voice, speaking aloud though she was alone: "This is it. This is the vintage that will prove them all wrong."

Not a memory. A reliving. Every detail perfect. Every sensation present.

She set down the glass. Her hands shook.

Fourth time this month. Seventh in the past year. Always the same vineyard, the same block, the same vines that defied everything she understood about wine chemistry.

She pulled out her notebook—number forty-three in a series stretching back to 1979. Date, time, temperature, wine details, sensory experience.

Precise. Scientific. Rational.

Impossible.

But how did you document the impossible?

Quantum coherence in biological systems was theoretical. Controversial. Most of her colleagues dismissed it as pseudoscience, the domain of mystics and frauds.

But she was a serious researcher. Elizabeth Chen. Forty-five years old. PhD in oenology from UC Davis. She'd come to Australia as a visiting researcher, collaborating with Marcus Webb. After losing her position in California—after the divorce, after her 1979 paper destroyed her career—she'd become what the academic world politely called "independent." What she called it was free.

And she'd discovered something that shouldn't exist.

Certain wines—rare wines, from specific terroirs under specific conditions—developed quantum-coherent molecular networks. Polyphenolic chains maintaining quantum states at room temperature. Storing information across time. Preserving sensory data across years. Decades. Centuries, potentially.

Wine that remembered.

Seven years she'd been tracking it. Forty-three notebooks.

Hundreds of chromatography results. Spectral analyses. Quantum signature measurements. The mechanism was there. Reproducible. Undeniable.

She couldn't publish it.

The moment she did, everything would change. Governments would classify it. Corporations would weaponise it. The wine would become interrogation tool, memory extraction device, weapon. A miracle turned into surveillance.

She would lose control of her life's work. Worse—she would betray it.

Better to wait. Document. Preserve. Let the wine itself carry the evidence forward, stored in glass and cork and time.

She looked out at the vineyard stretching before her in the morning light. Rows of Semillon vines spreading across the valley floor—forty years old, roots driven deep into ancient alluvial soils. Deep sandy loams layered over clay, built from millennia of Hunter River floods carrying minerals down from volcanic highlands. The kind of complex, free-draining earth that stressed vines just enough to concentrate flavour whilst providing the mineral matrix that made these wines... different.

The Brokenback Range rose beyond the vineyard's edge, blue-grey in the morning haze.

The grapes for this year's vintage were ripening now. Sugars climbing, acids balancing, the delicate chemistry of ripeness playing out in every berry on vines that drew their character from minerals washed down from ancient stone and settled here over geological time.

These vines had given her the 1979 vintage that first showed the phenomenon. The 1982 that confirmed it. The 1985 that removed all doubt.

And last year—1986—had produced perfection.

She'd been studying the soil itself lately. Not just the wine. The ground beneath these specific vines. The alluvial complexity—eroded volcanic material mixed with river sediments, quartz sand with piezoelectric properties, clay minerals that could hold electrical charge, iron oxides from upstream sources, trace rare earth elements concentrated over millennia. Not simple volcanic soils like those that produced great Shiraz on the upper slopes. Something more complex. A mineral matrix built from dozens of geological sources, mixed and deposited by floods, creating combinations that didn't exist anywhere else.

That was the key, she was beginning to understand. Not purity. Complexity. The quantum networks needed diverse mineralogy to stabilise. Homogenous soils—even rich volcanic ones—showed weaker effects. But these mixed alluvial matrices, with their unpredictable combinations of elements... they created something that could hold quantum coherence for decades.

The doubters could dismiss her. The funding committees could reject her. The journals could refuse her papers. She didn't need them anymore.

The 1986 was perfect. The quantum signatures were already there, already developing, already storing this moment—the vineyard, this heat, this morning when she stood alone with her impossible discovery.

In thirty-eight years, someone would taste this wine. They would experience exactly what she was experiencing now. They would access her memories, her moment, her certainty.

And they would know.

She thought about the others. The small network of researchers who'd seen what she'd seen, measured what she'd measured. Victoria in California, brilliant and cautious, already talking about walking away. Philippe in Bordeaux, still publishing despite the warnings. Marcus here in Australia, young and stubborn, refusing to believe they'd be silenced.

They would all make their choices. Stay or leave. Publish or hide. Fight or surrender.

She'd made hers.

Elizabeth Chen closed her notebook. Looked towards the horizon where the sun was climbing above the eucalyptus trees. The cicadas crescendoed. Somewhere in the vineyard, a magpie called—sharp, territorial, insistent.

She smiled.

The 1986 would prove them all wrong.

*PART 1*
*DISCOVERY*

# 1 / THE TASTING

The invitation had arrived six weeks earlier, cream-coloured card stock with embossed lettering: Mr James Wickham requests the pleasure of your company for a private tasting: Legends of Hunter Valley Semillon. Pall Mall, London. February 13, 2025. 7:00 PM. Twenty-four guests only.

Alex Hartley had nearly declined. Hunter Valley Semillon wasn't fashionable—most wine writers dismissed Australian whites as commercial pap compared to Burgundy or the Loire. But the vertical was extraordinary: Tyrrell's Vat 1 spanning nearly four decades, Lindeman's back to 1987, Brokenwood's flagship ILR Reserve Semillon named after the legendary Iain Riggs AM. Wickham had reportedly spent two years assembling it, and he was liquidating part of his cellar. This might be the only chance to taste these wines together.

Besides, she was trying to make a name for herself. At thirty-four, she was still "emerging"—a word that felt increasingly like "stuck." Her MW studies were progressing, her articles in Decanter were well-received, but she hadn't written anything that mattered yet. Nothing that would make Jancis take real notice.

# THURSDAY EVENING, 13 FEBRUARY 2025

## 6:55 PM

## LONDON

So here she was, climbing the steps of Wickham's Pall Mall town-house on a frigid February evening, her leather notebook tucked under her arm.

The tasting room was smaller than she'd expected—intimate, almost conspiratorial. Floor-to-ceiling windows overlooked Pall Mall, now dark except for streetlights gleaming on wet pavement. Twenty-four chairs arranged round a single long table, white tablecloth, six wine glasses at each setting in a single neat row.

Alex recognised a few faces: two Masters of Wine from the examination board, a sommelier from The Ledbury, a collector she'd interviewed once about Bordeaux futures. Everyone wore the careful neutrality of professionals trying not to seem too eager.

Wickham himself stood at the head of the table—early seventies, silver-haired, tailored suit. Australian expat, finance background, famously obsessive about provenance. The bottles were already arranged on a sideboard, labels facing out like soldiers on parade.

"Thank you all for coming," Wickham said, his voice carrying the flattened vowels of Sydney under decades of London polish. "What you're about to taste represents thirty years of collecting. Hunter Valley Semillon has been underappreciated for too long. Tonight, I hope to change a few minds."

Alex took her seat—middle of the table, left side. Good position for observing reactions without being too prominent. She uncapped her pen, dated the top of a fresh page: Thursday, 13 February 2025. Wickham Collection. Hunter Valley Semillon vertical.

A younger man—Wickham's assistant, probably—began pouring the first flight. 2018 Tyrrell's Vat 1, 2014 Brokenwood ILR Reserve,

2009 Lindeman's. The youngest wines in the lineup, though even these spanned nearly a decade of vintages.

Alex went through her ritual: appearance (pale gold, bright), nose (citrus, white flowers, struck match), palate (high acid, lean, mineral, long finish). She made notes, aware of the others doing the same. The room was quiet except for the scratch of pens and the occasional murmur of appreciation.

The wines were good. Very good. But not transcendent.

The second flight arrived. 2008 Tyrrell's, 2004 Brokenwood, 1998 Lindeman's. Fifteen to twenty-five years of age. This was where Hunter Semillon allegedly started to show its magic.

And it did. The 1998 Lindeman's had developed honeyed complexity, lanolin texture, a toasty character that seemed impossible for an unoaked wine. Alex found herself writing faster, trying to capture the paradox: How does this wine develop these flavours? No oak, no lees contact, just time and bottle.

The assistant moved quietly through the room, collecting glasses from the second flight. A brief pause—muted conversations, the scratch of pens completing notes—then fresh stemware appeared. The atmosphere shifted, anticipation building.

Across the table, a woman she didn't recognise—younger than Alex, Asian features, stylish in that effortless way sommeliers managed—caught her eye and smiled. They exchanged the small nod of mutual appreciation: Yes, this is why we do this.

The third flight. This was what everyone had come for.

1986 Tyrrell's Vat 1. 1987 Lindeman's. 1992 Brokenwood ILR Reserve.

Thirty to forty years in bottle. Wines that should, by conventional chemistry, be fading or dead. Instead, Wickham claimed, they were at their peak.

"The 1992 Brokenwood ILR Reserve—the first vintage of this wine," Wickham said. "Named after Iain Leslie Riggs - ILR - who joined Brokenwood in 1982 and transformed it from a weekend hobby into one of Australia's premier wineries. Riggs championed

Hunter Semillon when no one else would. Trained a generation of winemakers. Proved that Australian whites could age as magnificently as anything from France." Wickham's voice carried quiet reverence. "This wine is his legacy."

He gestured to the oldest bottle. "The 1986 Tyrrell's Vat 1 was harvested in January of that year—early, to preserve acidity. Picked in the cool of morning, before the Hunter heat could soften them. That decision, made nearly four decades ago, is why this wine has retained such extraordinary freshness."

The assistant moved behind Alex's chair and began with the 1986 Tyrrell's Vat 1, pouring carefully, reverently. The wine in Alex's glass was deep gold, almost amber. She lifted it, inhaled.

And stopped.

Something was wrong. Or not wrong, exactly. Different.

The aroma was extraordinary—honey, toast, beeswax, dried flowers, something like hay baking in summer sun. But underneath, or maybe alongside, or maybe through it, she perceived something else. Something that wasn't a smell.

A feeling of heat. Bright sun on bare arms. The sound of cicadas, distant and insistent.

Alex blinked, disoriented. She was in London, in February, in a climate-controlled room. There was no sun. No cicadas.

She looked round. No one else seemed affected. The MWs were making notes, the sommelier was holding her glass up to the light. Normal tasting behaviour.

Alex brought the glass to her lips, tasted.

The wine hit her palate—intense, complex, layer upon layer of flavour. Honey, yes. Toast and lanolin and something citric and mineral and impossibly long. But the moment she swallowed, something shifted.

She wasn't in the tasting room anymore.

She was standing in a vineyard—rows of Semillon vines stretching towards low hills, leaves green-gold in afternoon light. The soil beneath her—no, beneath *someone's* feet—was sandy loam, pale and fine, nothing like the red clay of Shiraz country. The air was hot, dry. She could feel it on her skin, the kind of summer heat that shimmered off pale earth and made the air thick. She could smell the dust and eucalyptus—sharp, medicinal, unmistakable. Cicadas thrummed in the heat, deafening and relentless. Somewhere, a magpie carolled its strange liquid warble—sharp, territorial.

She turned—no, someone turned—and saw a man in work clothes, weathered face, examining clusters of grapes. He was saying something, but the words were indistinct, like hearing a conversation through a wall.

Then a woman's voice, clear and close: "This is the vintage that will prove them all wrong."

The voice carried certainty, defiance, and beneath it all, bone-deep loneliness.

Alex gasped—the vineyard shattered like glass—and she was back in the tasting room, glass still in her hand, heart pounding.

The whole experience had lasted maybe ten seconds.

She set the glass down carefully, aware her hand was shaking.

What the hell was that?

She looked round again, trying to ground herself. The MWs were discussing acid structure. The collector was making notes about ageing potential. Everything normal.

Except—

The young woman across the table, the sommelier, was staring at her glass like it had bitten her. Her face had gone pale, her breathing quick and shallow. As Alex watched, the woman's eyes lifted and found hers.

They stared at each other across three glasses and two feet of white tablecloth.

The woman mouthed: *Did you—?*

Alex nodded slowly.

The woman looked like she might cry.

Wickham was talking, something about optimal ripeness, perfect acid balance. Alex heard the words but couldn't process them. Her mind was still in that vineyard, still feeling that Australian sun, still hearing that woman's voice: This is the vintage that will prove them all wrong.

She looked down at her notes. Her handwriting had devolved into jagged lines: honey toast mineral WHAT WAS THAT vineyard hot sun woman's voice who was—

She forced herself to breathe slowly. Professional. She was a professional. She picked up her pen and wrote, deliberately: 1986 Tyrrell's Vat 1—extraordinary development, honeyed complexity, impossibly fresh despite age.

Then, in smaller letters: Something else. Need to understand.

The tasting continued through the remaining flights, but Alex barely registered them. She went through the motions—swirl, sniff, taste, spit—but her attention kept returning to that glass of 1986 Tyrrell's Vat 1, sitting three-quarters full in front of her.

She didn't touch it again. Neither did the woman across the table.

When the tasting finally ended—nearly two hours after it began—the room filled with the noise of professionals being politely enthusiastic. Wickham was surrounded by people offering congratulations, asking about provenance, enquiring whether any bottles were for sale.

Alex stood, legs unsteady, and worked her way round the table towards the young sommelier.

Up close, she could see the woman was younger than she'd first appeared—late twenties, maybe. She wore a simple black dress and a name tag that read: Sophie Chen, Noble Rot.

"You felt it too," Sophie said quietly. Not a question.

"I don't know what I felt."

"A vineyard. Hot day. A woman's voice." Sophie's own voice was tight. "Saying something about proving people wrong."

Alex's skin prickled. "Yes. Exactly that."

"That's impossible."

"I know."

They stood there, two women who'd just experienced something impossible, surrounded by people discussing acidity levels and harvest dates.

Sophie glanced towards Wickham, still holding court. "We can't talk here. Do you have a card?"

Alex fumbled in her bag, found one. Sophie took it, slipped it into her clutch.

"I'll call you tomorrow," Sophie said. "I need to think about this. I need to—" She stopped, shook her head. "My grandmother spent forty years researching something like this. Everyone thought she was crazy."

"Your grandmother?"

But Sophie was already moving towards the exit, threading through the crowd with the practised grace of someone who knew how to leave a room without being noticed.

Alex stood alone, holding her wine-stained notebook, feeling the February cold seeping through the windows.

On the table in front of her, the glass of 1986 Tyrrell's Vat 1 sat undisturbed. In the overhead light, it glowed the colour of aged amber—beautiful, mysterious, and somehow aware.

Alex picked it up, intending to take it to the spittoon. Instead, she found herself staring into its depths, half-expecting to see that vineyard again, that impossible Australian sun.

"Remarkable wines, aren't they?"

She turned. Wickham had detached himself from his admirers and stood beside her, holding his own glass.

"Remarkable," Alex agreed, not trusting herself to say more.

"The 1986 Vat 1 in particular." Wickham swirled his glass, watching the wine coat the sides. "There's something about that vintage. Something I've never quite been able to explain. Every time I taste it, I feel..." He paused, searching for words. "Connected. To the place. To the people who made it. To everyone who's ever tasted it."

Alex's throat went dry. "Connected how?"

But Wickham just smiled, that distant smile of someone remembering something private. "You're Alex Hartley, aren't you? I've read your pieces in Decanter. You have a good palate. You pay attention to the wines no one else cares about."

"Thank you."

"Do you think Hunter Semillon deserves more recognition?"

"After tonight, absolutely."

"Good." Wickham raised his glass in a small salute. "Then I hope you'll write about this tasting. Tell people what you experienced."

The way he said experienced—not tasted, but experienced—made Alex's pulse quicken.

"Mr Wickham, did you feel anything unusual when you drank the 1986 Vat 1?"

He looked at her for a long moment, dark eyes unreadable. "What did you feel, Ms Hartley?"

She hesitated. This man was a respected collector, a pillar of the London wine scene. She was an emerging writer trying to build credibility. Saying she'd hallucinated a vineyard in Australia whilst drinking wine in London would make her sound unhinged.

"Something I can't quite explain," she said carefully.

Wickham's smile widened. "Then we have that in common. Here." He reached into his jacket pocket, produced a business card. Heavy stock, understated elegance. "If you decide to write about this, call me. I have some information that might interest you. About the provenance of these wines. Their history. What makes them... special."

Alex took the card: *James Wickham, Private Collections*.

"Thank you for inviting me," she said.

"Thank you for coming. And Ms Hartley? Be careful. Hunter Semillon has a way of... surprising people. Not everyone handles it well."

Before Alex could ask what he meant, he'd moved on to another guest, leaving her holding his card and her half-full glass of impossible wine.

Twenty minutes later, Alex stood on Pall Mall, cold air sharp in her lungs, trying to steady herself. Round her, other tasting guests dispersed into the night—shared cabs, Tube stations, discussions about where to get dinner.

She pulled out her phone, intending to call Emma, then hesitated. What would she even say? Hi love, I just hallucinated an Australian vineyard whilst drinking wine. Also, I might be having a psychotic break. Dinner at 10?

Instead, she opened her notes app and typed quickly before the details faded:

*1986 Tyrrell's Vat 1—experienced vivid hallucination or vision: Australian vineyard, hot day, intense summer heat shimmering off pale sandy earth, cicadas deafening and relentless, eucalyptus sharp and medicinal, magpie calling (sharp, territorial). Man examining grapes, woman's voice saying "this is the vintage that will prove them all wrong." Lasted approx. 10 seconds. Female taster across table (Sophie Chen, Noble Rot) experienced the same thing—SAME DETAILS. Wickham also hinted at something unusual about the wine.*

*This is not normal. This is not possible. But it happened.*

*Need to understand: What did I just experience?*

She stood there on the dark street, watching her breath fog in the cold air, holding her phone and Wickham's card and her notebook full of notes that wouldn't help her understand what she'd just experienced.

Somewhere in London, some of the tasting guests were probably already home—discussing the wines over dinner, making notes, going to bed thinking about acidity and ageing potential. Others remained.

But Alex knew, with absolute certainty, that at least one other person—Sophie Chen—was also standing somewhere, shaken and confused, trying to understand how wine could carry memories.

Or maybe trying to understand how wine could make you remember things that never happened to you.

Alex's phone buzzed. Unknown number. She answered.

"It's Sophie." The voice was tight, controlled. "Are you still near Pall Mall?"

"Yes."

"There's a pub. The Red Lion, just round the corner. Can you meet me there? Now?"

"Sophie, what—?"

"Please. I need to talk to someone who experienced it. And I need—" Her voice caught. "I need to tell you about my grandmother."

The line went dead.

Alex looked back at the townhouse. Through the windows, she could see people still mingling, Wickham still holding court, the bottles still arranged on the sideboard like soldiers.

Everything looked normal.

Everything was not normal.

She pulled her coat tighter and walked towards The Red Lion, towards Sophie Chen, towards an explanation she couldn't yet imagine.

Behind her, in the tasting room, twenty-four glasses of 1986 Tyrrell's Vat 1 sat on a white tablecloth, glowing amber in the light.

And in those glasses, in those molecules of wine forty years old, something quantum and impossible and alive waited to be understood.

# 2 / THE RED LION



10:00 PM

THE RED LION was the kind of pub that existed in every neighbourhood in London—dark wood, brass fixtures, the smell of old beer and fried food. A Thursday night crowd filled most of the tables: after-work drinkers nursing pints, a few couples sharing chips, someone's birthday party getting rowdy in the corner.

Alex found Sophie in a booth at the back, already halfway through a glass of white wine. She looked up when Alex approached, her expression somewhere between relieved and terrified.

"You came."

"Of course I came." Alex slid into the booth, set her bag down. "What the hell happened back there?"

Sophie glanced round the pub, lowered her voice. "What did you experience? With the 1986?"

"I was in a vineyard. Australian vineyard—I could tell from the heat, the light, the sounds. Eucalyptus trees. Cicadas. Someone examining grape clusters. And a voice saying 'This is the vintage that will prove them all wrong.'" Alex's hands were still shaking slightly. "It felt completely real. Like I was actually there."

Sophie's face went pale. "That's exactly what I experienced. Exactly. Same vineyard, same voice, same words."

They stared at each other.

"That's impossible," Alex said quietly.

"I know."

A server appeared. "What can I get you?"

"Gin and tonic," Alex said. "Double."

The server left. Sophie leaned forward, her voice barely above a whisper.

"My grandmother spent forty years researching... something like this. I never knew if she was brilliant or delusional." Sophie's hands shook as she reached for her wine. "Until tonight."

"Researching what, exactly?"

Sophie hesitated. "She called it quantum wine. I know how that sounds."

"It sounds insane."

"I know. But she was a serious scientist. Dr Elizabeth Chen. Oenologist, professor at UC Davis. Published, respected, tenured. Then in 1979 she published a paper that destroyed everything."

The server returned with Alex's drink. She waited until he left before responding.

"What kind of paper?"

"She found patterns. Certain old wines—aged in specific ways, from specific places—they developed... connections. Bottles stored in different cellars, different temperatures, different continents would develop identically. Not similarly. Identically. Like they were somehow linked." Sophie pulled out her phone, scrolled to a photo. "Here. This is from her 1979 paper."

Alex looked at the screen. Dense scientific notation, chemical formulae, margin notes in tight handwriting. The title read: "Anomalous Phenolic Correlation in Aged Semillon: Evidence for Non-Local Molecular Coherence."

"Non-local coherence," Alex said slowly. "That's quantum physics terminology."

"She thought wine could store information. Like a molecular memory. And under the right conditions, with the right... sensitivity... people could access it." Sophie's voice dropped. "Experience it. The way we did tonight."

Alex sat back, her mind racing. She wanted to reject it—quantum wine, stored consciousness, molecular memory. It violated everything she knew about chemistry, neuroscience, how reality worked.

But she'd felt Australian heat on her skin. Heard cicadas she'd never heard in real life. Stood in a vineyard seventeen thousand kilometres away. That had been real. Undeniable.

The question wasn't whether the experience had happened. The question was what it meant.

"I'm not saying I don't believe what we experienced," Alex said carefully. "I felt it. You felt it. We both know it was real. But quantum wine? Stored consciousness? That's..." She shook her head. "That's physics-rewriting, reality-bending territory. That requires extraordinary evidence."

"Which is exactly what my grandmother spent forty years trying to collect." Sophie's eyes filled with tears. "And was destroyed for it."

"What happened to her? After the paper?"

Sophie's voice went flat. "The reviewers didn't just dismiss her—they destroyed her. Called her a fraud. Said she'd fabricated data. One wrote that her paper was 'an embarrassment to UC Davis and a stain on oenology as a discipline.' They didn't critique her methodology—they attacked her personally. Questioned her sanity. Suggested she needed psychiatric help."

She wiped her eyes roughly. "She lost her tenure. Her colleagues stopped speaking to her. Overnight, she went from respected professor to pariah. She spent the next forty years teaching evening classes at community colleges to pay rent, whilst younger scientists built careers on work less rigorous than hers. She watched the wine world move on without her, knowing she was right, unable to prove it."

Alex felt the injustice of it viscerally. A brilliant researcher, meticulous and passionate, destroyed for documenting something real. Forty years of isolation and dismissal for telling an uncomfortable truth.

"Where is she now?"

"Dead. December 2022. Cancer." Sophie's voice cracked. "She left me everything. Her notes, her research, bottles she'd been studying for decades. Two years I've spent trying to understand it. Two years of wondering if she'd been right or if I was honouring a delusion."

She looked up at Alex, tears streaming. "And then tonight—tonight I stood in her vineyard. Heard her voice. Felt her certainty that this vintage would prove them all wrong. Tonight I knew. She was right. About all of it."

"The voice," Alex said quietly. "The woman's voice I heard in the vineyard. Was that her?"

Sophie nodded, unable to speak.

Alex took a long drink of gin. "Even accepting that we experienced something real—and I do, I felt it—that doesn't automatically mean your grandmother's quantum theory is correct. There could be other explanations we haven't considered yet."

"Then help me figure it out." Sophie leaned forward. "Tomorrow. Come to my flat. Look at her research. You're a wine professional, you understand chemistry, sensory analysis. Maybe you'll find flaws in her theory. Maybe you'll find alternative explanations. But at least look."

Alex thought about Jancis Robinson. About the Oxford Companion work. About the hundreds of tastings she'd attended, the reputation she'd built on being rational, evidence-based, rigorous.

This could destroy all of that. Quantum wine. Consciousness storage. She could end up exactly like Elizabeth Chen—dismissed, destroyed, her credibility demolished.

But she'd also learned to trust what she experienced. To pursue truth even when it was uncomfortable.

And she needed to know. Needed to understand what had happened tonight. What that voice had meant. Why she and Sophie —and possibly others—had accessed Elizabeth Chen's memory from four decades ago.

"All right," she said. "I'll look at her research. Tomorrow. But I'm not promising to believe it. I need to see the evidence, understand the methodology, evaluate it properly."

"That's all I'm asking."

They sat in silence for a moment, the pub noise washing over them. Someone laughed too loudly at the bar. The birthday party sang off-key. Normal Thursday night in London.

Except nothing was normal any more.

"Why did she stop publishing?" Alex asked. "After 1979. If she spent forty years researching this, why not keep trying to prove it?"

Sophie's expression darkened. "Her later notebooks are... different. Paranoid. Careful. She stopped dating entries, started using codes for names and places. And there are gaps—whole years missing. Like she destroyed certain sections."

"Why?"

"I think she discovered something that scared her. Something about the wine, or the people studying it, or what it could be used for. And she thought it was dangerous enough to spend forty years in silence rather than prove she was right."

A chill ran down Alex's spine. "Used for what?"

"She never wrote it down. Or if she did, she destroyed those pages." Sophie's hands trembled. "But whatever it was, she thought keeping silent was safer than being vindicated."

Alex thought about Wickham's warning. *Be careful. Hunter Semillon has a way of surprising people. Not everyone handles it well.*

"Wickham knew," Alex said. "At the tasting. He warned me. Said the wines had certain properties, that not everyone who experiences them handles it well. He knew about the quantum effect."

"Did he experience it himself?"

"I think so. He said every time he tasted the 1986, he felt connected to the place, to the people who made it. To something beyond the wine itself." Alex pulled out Wickham's business card, set it on the table between them. "He gave me this. Said if I wanted to write about the tasting, to call him. That he had information about the wines' provenance. Their history. What makes them special."

Sophie stared at the card. "We need to talk to him. Find out what he knows. What he's discovered about these wines."

"Carefully," Alex said. "If your grandmother was right about the danger—"

"We don't know who to trust. I know." Sophie pulled out her notebook, started writing. "But we can't do this alone. My grandmother tried that, and it destroyed her career. We need to understand what's happening. Who else might have experienced it tonight. What Wickham knows. What the danger actually is."

Alex's phone buzzed. Emma:

Getting worried. Everything okay?

She typed back:

Fine. Running late. Home soon. Promise.

"I need to tell my partner," Alex said. "Emma. She's an architect, very rational, very evidence-based. But she deserves to know what's happening."

"Maybe wait," Sophie said quietly. "Until we understand more. Until we know what we're dealing with. The fewer people who know right now, the safer we all are."

Alex wanted to argue. Emma deserved the truth. But what would she say? That wine could store consciousness? That she'd accessed a dead scientist's memories? Emma would think she'd lost her mind.

Or worse—Emma would believe her and become terrified for her safety.

"All right," she said reluctantly. "But only until we know more. Only until we can explain it properly."

"Tomorrow, nine o'clock. My flat—I'll text you the address." Sophie finished her wine. "I've got everything there. My grandmother's notebooks, her research, the bottles she was studying. We can go through it all systematically. Find the patterns she identified. Understand the mechanism."

Alex nodded, though part of her still wanted to reject all of this. To walk away, write her Decanter article, pretend tonight had never happened.

But she couldn't. She'd felt that vineyard. Heard that voice. Stood in Elizabeth Chen's moment of certainty.

That couldn't be undone. Couldn't be ignored.

"I should go," she said. "Emma's worried."

"Text me when you get home safe."

"You too."

They left together, stepping out into the cold February night. The street was quieter now, though voices still drifted from The Red Lion behind them. A few taxis passed, searching for late fares.

Normal London. Normal Thursday night.

Except nothing was normal any more.

Sophie headed towards the Tube. Alex walked towards the bus stop, her mind spinning with quantum mechanics and consciousness and impossible wines.

Her phone buzzed as she reached the corner. Unknown number.

She opened it.

> Ms Hartley. What you experienced tonight was real. Dr Chen warned me this would happen eventually. If you're investigating this phenomenon, you need to understand the danger. People have died protecting this research. Be very careful. —VM

Alex stopped walking.

VM. She didn't know anyone with those initials.

She stared at the message, ice spreading through her chest. How did this person have her number? How did they know about the tasting? About Dr Chen? About what Alex was planning to investigate?

Her number wasn't public. The tasting invitation had come through professional channels, but her mobile wasn't listed anywhere obvious.

Unless VM had access to Wickham's guest list.

Unless VM had been at the tasting.

Unless VM was watching right now.

She looked round the dark street. Empty. No one visible. At least no one she could see.

She took a screenshot of the message, then typed back:

> Who is this? How do you know about Dr Chen?

No response.

She waited five minutes, standing on the cold pavement, watching her phone screen. The street was silent except for distant traffic. A car passed slowly, windows tinted. Gone before she could see inside.

Nothing.

VM had gone silent.

Alex pocketed her phone and started walking faster. She needed to get home. Needed to tell Emma—no, she'd promised Sophie she'd wait. Needed to figure out what VM's warning meant. *People have died protecting this research.*

Past tense. People. Plural.

How many researchers had there been? How many had died?

The bus arrived. Alex climbed on, found a seat near the driver—safer, more visible—and tried to calm her breathing.

Her phone stayed silent. No more messages from VM. No new warnings.

But the earlier message burned in her mind: *People have died protecting this research. Be very careful.*

She pulled out Wickham's business card again. Studied it under the bus's fluorescent light.

*James Wickham, Private Collections*

The card of a man who'd warned her to be careful. Who'd known about quantum wine. Who might be the only person who could help her understand what was happening.

She'd call him tomorrow. After meeting with Sophie. After looking at Dr Chen's research. After she had more information about what she was really dealing with.

Tomorrow.

Alex tucked the card carefully into her wallet.

Outside the bus windows, London rolled past—normal streets, normal people, normal Thursday night.

Everything looked the same.

Everything had changed.

She thought about Elizabeth Chen, standing in a vineyard in 1986, speaking words into wine that would echo for forty years. Words of conviction and loneliness and certainty.

*This is the vintage that will prove them all wrong.*

Had she been right? Had the wine preserved her vindication?

Or had it preserved her warning?

Alex got off the bus at her stop, walked the remaining blocks to her flat. The street was empty, dark, quiet. She walked quickly, keys already in hand, hyper-aware of every shadow.

No one followed. No mysterious cars. No footsteps echoing behind her.

But she couldn't shake the feeling that tonight had crossed a threshold she couldn't uncross. That investigating quantum wine meant entering a world where researchers died, where warnings came from anonymous sources, where wine held more than flavour and memory.

Where wine held danger.

She climbed the stairs to her flat, unlocked the door, stepped inside to warmth and light and Emma's music playing in the kitchen.

Normal. Safe. Home.

But in her pocket, her phone held VM's warning. And in her bag, Wickham's card waited for tomorrow's call.

In her memory, Elizabeth Chen's voice echoed from forty years ago: *This is the vintage that will prove them all wrong.*

Tomorrow she'd start proving it.

Tomorrow she'd understand what she'd experienced.

Tomorrow she'd find out what Elizabeth Chen had died trying to protect.

If she survived that long.

—

## 3 / HOME



11:05 PM

EMMA WAS in the kitchen when Alex got home, barefoot in tracksuit bottoms and an old Cambridge rowing shirt, stirring something on the hob that smelt of garlic and tomatoes. Music played from the speaker on the worktop—something jazzy and instrumental that Emma liked when she was cooking. Normal. Comforting. A different world from the one Alex had just left.

"You're back," Emma said, not turning from the hob. "How was the tasting? Did you have dinner? I made pasta, there's plenty—"

She turned then, wooden spoon in hand, and stopped. "Christ, Alex. What happened?"

Alex set her bag down carefully, hung her coat on the hook by the door. Her hands were steadier than they'd been on the bus, but not by much.

"The tasting was..." She paused, searching for words. "Complicated."

Emma turned off the burner, set down the spoon. "Complicated how? You look like you've seen a ghost."

Close enough, Alex thought. "Can we sit? I need to tell you something, and it's going to sound completely mad."

Emma's expression shifted—concern mixed with wariness. Alex recognised that look. It was the look Emma got when she thought Alex was about to tell her something she didn't want to hear. Like when Alex had mentioned applying for the MW programme. Or when she'd proposed writing a book about underappreciated wine regions. Ideas that seemed expensive, time-consuming, obsessive.

They sat at the small kitchen table—IKEA, bought when they'd first moved in together six years ago. Emma folded her hands, waiting. Patient. An architect's calm, learnt from dealing with difficult clients.

"One of the wines tonight—1986 Hunter Valley Semillon—when I drank it, I had a... I don't know what to call it. A vision? A hallucination? I wasn't in the tasting room anymore. I was in a vineyard in Australia. I could feel the heat, hear the sounds, smell the eucalyptus. And there was a woman's voice, very clear, saying 'This is the vintage that will prove them all wrong.'"

Emma was very still. "You hallucinated whilst wine tasting."

"That's what I thought at first. But another taster—a sommelier named Sophie—experienced exactly the same thing. Same vineyard, same voice, same words. We compared notes afterwards. It wasn't a hallucination, Em. Or if it was, we both had the identical hallucination at the identical moment."

"That's not possible."

"I know it sounds impossible."

Emma leant back in her chair, processing. Alex could see her architect's brain working, looking for structural explanations. "Could the wine have been drugged? Contaminated with something?"

"Twenty-four people tasted it. Only two of us—that we know of —experienced the effect. If it was contamination, wouldn't everyone have reacted?"

"Not necessarily. People metabolise things differently. You might have been more susceptible." Emma was in problem-solving mode now. "Or maybe you didn't eat enough before the tasting. Low blood sugar, dehydration, stress—"

"I ate. I was hydrated. I've been to hundreds of tastings, Em. This was different."

"Different how?"

Alex struggled to articulate it. "It was too specific. Too real. I could feel the sun on my skin—Australian sun, that particular quality of light and heat. I could hear a magpie. I've never heard a magpie in real life, but I knew that's what it was. The call was unmistakable. And that voice... it wasn't my voice. It wasn't my thought. It was someone else's voice, inside my head, saying words I've never thought."

Emma was quiet for a long moment. When she spoke, her voice was carefully controlled. "You're scaring me."

"I'm scared too."

"Then let's be rational about this. You experienced something unusual. Could be neurological—have you had any headaches lately? Vision changes? Dizziness?" Emma reached across the table, took Alex's hand. "Maybe we should book you a GP appointment. Get you checked out properly."

Alex wanted to accept that explanation. Wanted it to be something medical, something fixable with tests and prescriptions. But she'd seen Sophie's face across that table. Sophie had experienced the same thing. The exact same thing.

"Sophie's grandmother spent forty years researching this phenomenon," Alex said. "Dr Elizabeth Chen. She was an oenologist at UC Davis. She published a paper in 1979 about wines that aged in impossible ways, bottles that seemed to share information across distances. She thought it was quantum entanglement. She died in 2022—cancer. She left all her research to Sophie."

Emma closed her eyes. "Quantum entanglement. In wine."

"Quantum biology is real, Em. Photosynthesis uses quantum

coherence. Birds navigate using quantum effects in their eyes. It's not pseudoscience—it's established physics."

"I know." Emma opened her eyes. "I've read about it. Quantum effects in biological systems. But Alex, that's photosynthesis. That's bird navigation. Controlled, evolved processes that took millions of years to develop. Not fermented grapes sitting in a bottle."

"Why not? Wine is incredibly complex organic chemistry. Thousands of compounds interacting in a sealed environment, protected from light, aged in darkness for decades. If quantum effects can persist in a bird's eye, why not in wine?"

"Because..." Emma stopped, searching for the argument. "Because it sounds insane. Because if wine could store memories or consciousness or whatever you're suggesting, someone would have discovered it before now. Properly. With scientific equipment and peer review, not some dismissed researcher's fringe theory."

"Dr Chen tried. She published her findings. She was destroyed for it. Career ruined, reputation demolished. She spent the next forty years researching it privately because no one would listen."

"Or because she was wrong." Emma pulled her hand back. "Alex, I love you. You know that. And I know how passionate you are about wine, how much it matters to you. But what you're describing— memories stored in wine, quantum entanglement—this isn't you. You're rigorous. Evidence-based. You don't jump to conclusions based on one strange experience."

"I'm not jumping to conclusions. I'm trying to understand what I experienced."

"By accepting some dead researcher's fringe theories?" Emma's voice rose slightly. "By assuming that the impossible explanation is the correct one?"

"I'm not assuming anything. I'm investigating. Sophie has her grandmother's research—forty years of documentation. I'm going to look at it. See what patterns she found, what evidence she collected. Then I'll decide whether it's credible."

Emma stood abruptly, went to the worktop, poured herself a glass of water. Drank it slowly, her back to Alex. When she turned round, her expression was carefully neutral.

"Do you hear yourself?" Emma asked quietly. "A woman you just met tonight tells you her grandmother—who was discredited and dismissed—spent forty years researching quantum wine. And you're ready to investigate it based on one weird experience?"

"Two people had the same experience. That's not coincidence, Em. That's data."

"That's two people who might have had similar reactions to something in the wine, or the room, or the stress of a high-level professional tasting. Similar, not identical. You're filling in the gaps with each other's descriptions."

"We compared notes before we could influence each other. Same vineyard. Same voice. Same exact words."

"You think you did. But memory is unreliable, especially under stress. You want your experiences to match because it validates what you felt. So your brains are making them match."

Alex felt frustration rising. "You weren't there. You didn't experience it."

"Exactly. I wasn't there. So I can be objective about this." Emma set down her water glass. "And objectively, Alex, what you're describing sounds like a shared delusion, or a stress reaction, or something neurological that you both need to get checked out. Not quantum wine."

"I know how it sounds."

"Do you? Because it sounds like you're about to throw away your credibility chasing something that will make you look exactly like Dr Chen—dismissed and destroyed."

The words hung between them, sharp and cutting.

"Is that what worries you?" Alex asked slowly. "That I'll damage my career? That I'll embarrass you?"

Emma winced. "That's not fair."

"Isn't it? You've always been uncomfortable with how much I care about wine. How much time I spend on it, how seriously I take it. You smile and nod when I talk about articles or tastings, but I can see you thinking it's frivolous. A nice hobby, but not a real career. Not like architecture."

"That's not true."

"Then why do you remind me how expensive the MW programme is every time I mention it? Why do you ask if my articles pay enough to justify the time? Why do you look relieved when I say I'm not going to a tasting because it would mean a late night?"

Emma's face went pale. "Because I worry about you. Because I see how stressed you are, how much pressure you put on yourself. Because I want you to be happy, not exhausted and anxious and obsessed with proving yourself."

"I'm not obsessed with proving myself."

"Aren't you? You're thirty-four and still calling yourself 'emerging.' You work twice as hard as other wine writers and get half the recognition. You take on projects that don't pay well because you think they'll build your reputation. And now—" Emma stopped, took a breath. "And now you've had one strange experience at a tasting, and instead of being cautious, instead of questioning it, you're ready to chase it down because maybe, finally, this will be the thing that makes you matter."

Alex felt like she'd been slapped. "That's what you think? That I'm doing this to feel important?"

"I think you're brilliant and driven and you desperately want Jancis Robinson and the MW board and everyone else in the wine world to see what I see. And I think that makes you vulnerable to latching onto something extraordinary—something that would make you special if you could prove it."

"You think I'm delusional."

"I think you're under enormous pressure and you had a strange experience and now you're making it mean more than it does."

Emma's voice cracked. "And I'm terrified you're going to destroy yourself chasing it."

Alex stood slowly. "I need to go to bed. I'm exhausted."

"Alex, please—"

"I heard what you said. I heard all of it." Alex walked towards the hallway, then stopped. "For what it's worth, I'm not doing this to feel important. I'm doing it because something impossible happened tonight, and I need to understand it. Whether you believe me or not."

She went to the bedroom, closed the door quietly. Not a slam, but close enough.

The bedroom was dark except for streetlight filtering through the curtains. Alex sat on the edge of the bed, still in her tasting clothes, and pulled out her phone.

A text from Sophie, sent twenty minutes ago:

> Did you tell your partner?

Alex:

> Tried. She thinks I'm stressed and making it mean more than it does.

Sophie:

> Mine suggested I take some time off. Said I've been "obsessing" over my grandmother's research.

Alex:

> Emma thinks I'm chasing this to feel important. Like I'm latching onto something extraordinary to validate myself.

Sophie:

> Are we?

Alex stared at the question. Was she? Was this about proving something—to Jancis, to the MW board, to Emma, to herself?

No. She'd felt that Australian sun. Heard that voice. Stood in that vineyard. It had been real.

Alex:

> We both experienced the same thing. That's not validation-seeking. That's reality.

Sophie:

> My grandmother died thinking everyone believed she was crazy. I won't let that be her legacy. Tomorrow, 9 AM, my flat. We'll go through her research properly. Find the proof.

Alex:

> Tomorrow.

She set the phone on the bedside table, lay back on the bed fully clothed. Stared at the ceiling.

In the kitchen, she could hear Emma moving about—the clink of dishes, water running, the flat settling into night sounds.

A year ago, they'd talked about getting married. Buying a flat instead of renting. Maybe getting a dog. Normal relationship progression, normal life plans.

Now Alex was lying alone in the dark, thinking about quantum wine and dismissed researchers, whilst Emma cleaned up dinner Alex hadn't eaten.

The gap between them felt wider than it ever had.

Alex closed her eyes, tried to settle her breathing. Tomorrow she'd see Dr Chen's research. Tomorrow she'd understand what had happened tonight. Tomorrow she'd figure out how to explain it in a way that Emma—and everyone else—might believe.

Tomorrow.

But sleep didn't come easily. Her mind spun with vineyards and voices and Emma's words: *You're making it mean more than it does.*

Was she?

Outside the bedroom, she heard Emma moving about. A door closing. The sofa creaking. Emma wasn't coming to bed.

Eventually, exhaustion won. Alex fell into restless sleep, still fully dressed, her dreams full of Australian vineyards and voices that weren't her own.


## FRIDAY MORNING, 14 FEBRUARY 2025

### 7:15 AM

Alex's phone woke her—not the alarm, but the insistent buzz of notifications piling up. She fumbled for it, eyes gritty with sleep, head aching from stress and too little rest.

The bedroom was grey with early morning light. Emma's side of the bed was empty, covers pulled up neatly. She'd slept on the sofa, then.

Alex checked the time: 7:15 AM. Then she saw the notifications.

Three messages from Sophie:

> Alex. Turn on the news.

> Wickham is dead.

> Call me when you wake up. This changes everything.

Alex's chest tightened. She sat up, suddenly completely awake. Opened the BBC News app with shaking hands.

The headline hit her like cold water:

### SUSPICIOUS DEATH: Wine Collector Found Dead in Pall Mall Home

*Police are investigating the death of James Wickham, 72, whose body was discovered early Friday morning at his Pall Mall residence. Authorities are treating the death as suspicious. Mr Wickham, a prominent figure in London wine collecting circles, had hosted a private tasting Thursday evening. The Met is appealing for anyone who attended the event or has relevant information to come forward.*

*Detective Inspector Karen Morrison is leading the investigation.*

Alex read it twice. Then a third time, as if the words might change.

Wickham. Dead.

The man who'd warned her to be careful just hours ago. The man who'd given her his business card, promised to share information about the wines, about what made them special. The man who'd stood in that tasting room, alive and enthusiastic, talking about Hunter Semillon with quiet reverence.

Dead. Suspicious death.

Her hands were shaking so badly she nearly dropped the phone.

She thought about Wickham's last words: Be careful. Hunter Semillon has a way of surprising people. *Not everyone handles it well.*

Had he known? Had he sensed something?

Her phone buzzed. Another message. Unknown number.

VM.

> I tried to warn you. Wickham knew too
> much and refused to stay quiet. You're in
> danger now too. The wines you
> experienced are being hunted. Delete this
> message. —VM

Alex stared at the screen, ice spreading through her chest.

VM had warned Thursday night that Wickham might be in

danger. Now he was dead. Which meant either VM had tried to save him and failed—

Or VM had killed him.

She screenshot the message, then deleted it. Evidence. But evidence of what? Of a warning? Or a confession?

She typed back with shaking fingers:

> Who are you? How did you know about Wickham?

The response came within seconds:

> Elizabeth Chen was my colleague before her career was destroyed. I've been tracking quantum wine research for 45 years. There are people who will kill to suppress it—you've just seen proof. Wickham collected quantum-active wines and planned to reveal them publicly. Now he's dead. You and Sophie Chen experienced the effect. That makes you witnesses. And witnesses are being eliminated. I can help you survive this, but you need to trust me.

Alex's breath caught.

> Why should I trust you?

> Because I'm the only one who knows what you're facing. And because if I wanted you dead, you'd already be dead. Check your email. I'm sending you something that will prove I knew Elizabeth Chen. Don't share it with anyone. Not even Sophie. Not yet.

The messages stopped. Alex waited, heart pounding, but VM had gone silent.

She opened her email. One new message, no subject line, from an anonymous ProtonMail address.

Inside: a scanned photograph.

Two women in a vineyard, mid-1970s by the clothing and photo quality. One was clearly Dr Elizabeth Chen—younger, maybe thirty, dark hair pulled back, wearing practical field clothes. She was smiling at the camera, holding a clipboard.

The other woman was white, perhaps a few years younger, with dark hair and sharp, intelligent eyes. She stood slightly apart from Dr Chen, not smiling, her expression serious and focused.

On the back of the photo, handwritten: *Napa Valley, August 1976. E.C. and V.M. First vintage trials.*

V.M.

Victoria? Veronica? Valerie?

Alex stared at the photo. This was proof VM had known Dr Chen. Proof they'd worked together before the 1979 paper that destroyed her career.

But proof of what else? That VM was trustworthy? Or that VM had been there from the beginning, had seen Dr Chen's research, and had reasons of her own to want it suppressed?

Alex's phone buzzed. Sophie calling.

"You saw," Sophie said without preamble. Her voice was tight, controlled, on the edge of panic.

"I saw."

"This isn't coincidence, Alex. We experience quantum wine for the first time in our lives, and hours later the host is dead under suspicious circumstances? That's not random. That's connected."

"We don't know it's connected—"

"Of course it's connected. Someone doesn't want quantum wine to become known. Wickham collected it, understood it, maybe planned to reveal it publicly. So they killed him."

Alex's mind raced. "That's a leap, Sophie. People die. Heart attacks, accidents—"

"The news says *suspicious*. That means the police think someone killed him. Which means everyone at that tasting might be in danger. Everyone who experienced the quantum effect."

"You and me."

"At minimum." Sophie's voice dropped to a whisper. "But there might be others. We don't know who else felt it, who else Wickham might have told about it."

Alex thought about the twenty-four people in that room. Twenty-two others who might have experienced what she and Sophie had. Twenty-two potential witnesses.

Twenty-two potential targets.

"We need to meet," Alex said. "Today. Now. We need to go through your grandmother's research, figure out what Wickham knew, what he might have been planning."

"My flat. 127 Dalston Lane, Flat 4B. How soon can you get here?"

"Give me an hour. I need to—" Alex stopped. She needed to deal with Emma. To tell her about Wickham's death. To... what? Apologise? Explain? Prove she'd been right to investigate?

No. She needed to make sure Emma was safe.

"An hour," Alex said. "I'll be there by nine."

"Alex?" Sophie's voice was small. "I'm scared."

"Me too."

The line went dead.

Alex sat on the edge of the bed, phone in hand, trying to steady her breathing. Yesterday morning she'd been a wine writer working on an article about Portuguese whites. Now a man was dead, she was receiving cryptic warnings from someone who might be an ally or a threat, and she was about to chase down research that had destroyed Dr Chen's career.

She found Emma in the kitchen, already dressed for work in tailored trousers and a grey jumper, hands wrapped round a mug of tea. Her eyes were red-rimmed, shadowed with exhaustion. She looked up when Alex entered, and something passed between them— recognition of damage done, neither knowing how to repair it.

"You saw the news," Emma said. Not a question.

"Yes."

"The man who hosted the tasting. Dead. Suspicious circumstances." Emma's voice was carefully flat. "Hours after you left his house."

"I know."

"The police will want to interview you. Everyone who was there."

"I know."

Emma set down her mug. Her hands were shaking slightly. "And you're still planning to meet Sophie. To chase this quantum wine theory."

It wasn't a question, but Alex answered anyway. "I have to."

"No." Emma's voice cracked. "No, you don't. You can call the police right now, tell them everything you know, let them investigate. You can stay out of it, stay safe."

"And tell them what? That wine stored a dead scientist's consciousness?" Alex shook her head. "They'll think I'm insane."

"Better unreliable than dead!"

The words hung in the air between them.

"A man is dead, Alex." Emma stood abruptly, began pacing. "Someone killed him. Someone dangerous enough to murder a respected collector in his own home. And you want to investigate? To make yourself a target?"

"I need to understand what happened before the police interview me. Otherwise I'm walking blind, and that's dangerous for different reasons."

"And when they ask why I didn't mention it immediately? When they ask why I met with Sophie at a pub hours after the tasting to discuss it? When they realise I've been withholding information?" Alex's voice was steady. "I become a suspect, Em. Or at minimum, an unreliable witness whose testimony they'll dismiss."

Emma's face went pale. "You've already thought this through. You've already decided to investigate rather than cooperate."

"And what about me?" Emma's voice broke. "What about us? Don't I deserve a partner who doesn't run headfirst into danger?"

Alex crossed the room, reached for Emma's hands, but Emma pulled away.

"I love you," Alex said quietly. "But I can't walk away from this."

Emma picked up her laptop bag, her phone, her keys. "I have to go to work. I can't—I can't do this right now."

"Em—"

"No. I can't watch you choose this over your own safety. Over us." Emma walked to the door, paused with her hand on the knob. "The police will call. When they do, tell them the truth. All of it. Including the quantum experience. Let them think you're crazy if that's what it takes. At least you'll be alive."

"I'll think about it."

"No, you won't. You've already decided." Emma opened the door, then turned back one last time. Her eyes were wet. "I love you, Alex. But I can't love you into staying safe. You have to want that for yourself. And right now, I don't think you do."

The door closed softly behind her.

Alex stood alone in the kitchen, listening to Emma's footsteps recede down the hallway, the outer door of the building closing with a distant thud.

Six years together. Six years of building a life, making plans, talking about marriage and flats and dogs.

And now this.

Alex looked at her phone. 7:45 AM. She needed to shower, get dressed, get to Dalston by nine.

She needed to understand what had got Wickham killed before it got her killed too.

But first, she pulled out her laptop, opened a new document, and began typing everything she could remember about Thursday night. The tasting. The wines. The experience. Wickham's warning. Sophie's grandmother's research. VM's messages.

Everything.

If something happened to her, Emma would find this. The police would find this. Someone would know what she'd been investigating, what she'd discovered.

Evidence. Insurance. Legacy.

Twenty minutes later, she saved the document to the cloud, emailed a copy to herself, and to Sophie.

Then she showered, dressed, and walked out into the cold February morning, towards Dalston, towards Dr Elizabeth Chen's forty years of research, towards answers that might get her killed.

Behind her, the flat was empty and silent.

Emma was gone.

# 4 / THE RESEARCH



9:05 AM

127 Dalston Lane was a converted warehouse building—red brick, industrial windows, the kind of trendy renovation that cost more than it looked like it should. Sophie buzzed Alex in from Flat 4B on the third floor.

Sophie answered the door in jeans and an oversized jumper, hair pulled back, no makeup. She looked like she'd slept as badly as Alex had. Her eyes were red-rimmed, her face pale.

"Come in," she said. "Coffee's on. You look like you need it."

The flat was small but beautifully appointed—exposed brick, high ceilings, morning light streaming through tall windows. A small kitchen opened onto a living area dominated by a large dining table.

The table was covered in notebooks, papers, and wine bottles.

Elizabeth Chen's research.

Alex stopped in the doorway, staring. There were dozens of notebooks—leather-bound, spiral-bound, composition books—arranged in rough chronological order. Loose papers covered in handwritten notes, chemical formulas, spectral analyses. And bottles. At least twenty bottles of wine, some clearly very old, labels faded and stained.

"This is everything?" Alex asked.

"Everything she left me." Sophie handed Alex a mug of coffee—black, strong, exactly what she needed. "Forty-three notebooks spanning 1976 to 2022. Research papers she never published. Wine samples she'd been studying. Her entire life's work, dismissed and hidden."

Alex set down her bag, approached the table slowly. The notebooks closest to her were dated 2018-2022—the final years of Dr Chen's life. The handwriting was shakier than in earlier volumes, but still precise, still meticulous.

"Where do we start?" Alex asked.

"With the 1986." Sophie picked up a particular notebook, leather-bound, pages yellowed with age. "My grandmother was in the Hunter Valley in January 1987, nine months after the vintage. She tasted the 1986 Tyrrell's Vat 1 and experienced the quantum effect for the first time in her career. This is her documentation of that experience."

She opened the notebook to a marked page. Alex leaned close, studying the handwriting she'd seen in the photo Sophie had shown her at the pub—precise, scientific, dense with notation.

*January 15, 1987. Pokolbin, Hunter Valley. Temperature 22°C at time of tasting. Humidity 45%. Wind from NW.*

*Wine: 1986 Semillon, Tyrrell's Vat 1. 10 months in bottle. Tasted alone in vineyard at 6.15 AM local time.*

*Fourth quantum experience this month. Seventh documented instance in the past year. Coherence duration: approximately 12 seconds. Full sensory immersion: vineyard location (specific rows visible, soil type identifiable as sandy loam characteristic of Semillon sites), temperature (estimated 40+ degrees during harvest), time of day (afternoon sun angle suggesting 2-3 PM), presence of other indi-*

*viduals (one male, examining grape clusters—possibly Murray Tyrrell or vineyard manager).*

*Audio component included my own voice, speaking aloud though I was alone during both the harvest moment and the tasting: "This is the vintage that will prove them all wrong."*

*Critical observation: The wine is not merely recording sensory data. It is storing my consciousness—my certainty about this research, my isolation, my determination to prove the effect is real. The phenomenon is not passive playback. It is preserving the emotional and cognitive state at the moment of encoding.*

*Implications: If wine can store consciousness, the applications are—*

The entry stopped there. Below it, in different ink, dated weeks later:

*Cannot publish this. Cannot risk it. The implications are too dangerous. Must document privately. Must protect the research until I understand what I've discovered.*

Alex read it twice, her skin prickling. "That's exactly what I experienced. Her voice, her words, her conviction. Even the loneliness—I felt that too. She was alone in that vineyard."

"She was alone for most of her career after 1979," Sophie said quietly. "No colleagues, no collaborators, no one who believed her. She did this work in isolation for forty years because no one else would touch it."

"Why that particular moment?" Alex asked. "Why did the wine capture her speaking that sentence?"

"She has theories. Look." Sophie flipped forward several pages to a section titled *Encoding Conditions—Hypotheses.*

Alex read:

*Hypothesis 1: Quantum encoding requires the presence of the consciousness that will be stored at the moment of critical chemical transition. In the 1986 vintage, I was present during harvest and spoke the encoded phrase aloud. The wine was beginning its primary fermentation—the moment when the chemical structure is most dynamic, most susceptible to quantum coherence.*

*Hypothesis 2: Emotional intensity amplifies encoding. My certainty about the research, my determination to prove it, my isolation—these emotional states were intense at that moment. The wine captured not just the words but the feeling behind them.*

*Hypothesis 3: Not all wines can store consciousness. Specific conditions required:*

*Old vine material (50+ years preferred)*
*Specific soil types (ancient alluvial, limestone, volcanic)*
*Minimal intervention winemaking (no additives that disrupt molecular coherence)*
*Sealed environment (bottle, cork, darkness)*
*Extended ageing (10+ years for coherence to stabilise)*

*Working theory: Wine that meets these conditions develops quantum-coherent phenolic networks. These networks can become entangled with the consciousness of individuals present during critical moments (harvest, fermentation, bottling, tasting). The information is stored in the molecular structure and can be retrieved by individuals with sufficient sensory sensitivity.*

Alex looked up. "This is rigorous science. She's documenting conditions, testing hypotheses, building a theory from observations. This isn't pseudoscience, Sophie. This is methodical research."

"I know. But try explaining quantum-coherent phenolic networks to wine critics who think she was delusional." Sophie's voice was bitter. "She couldn't prove the mechanism. She didn't have access to quantum measurement equipment. All she had were her experiences and the patterns she observed."

"What patterns?" Alex asked. "You said she identified which wines consistently show the effect."

Sophie pulled out another notebook, this one from the mid-1990s. "She spent fifteen years documenting quantum-active wines. Specific vineyards, specific vintages, specific conditions." She opened to a page titled *Confirmed Quantum-Active Sources*.

Alex leaned close:

*Hunter Valley, Australia:*
    *Tyrrell's Vat 1 Semillon (1966, 1973, 1986, 1991, 1998)*
    *Brokenwood ILR Reserve Semillon (1992, 1996, 2001)*
    *Mount Pleasant Lovedale Semillon (1981, 1989)*

*Bordeaux, France:*
    *Château Haut-Brion (1961, 1982, 1989)*
    *Château Margaux (1953, 1983, 1990)*
    *Château Palmer (1961, 1983)*

*Barolo, Italy:*
    *Giacomo Conterno Monfortino (1971, 1978, 1985)*
    *Bruno Giacosa Collina Rionda (1982, 1989, 1996)*

*Mosel, Germany:*
    *Egon Müller Scharzhofberger (1976, 1983, 1990)*

*Central Otago, New Zealand:*
    *Felton Road Block 3 Pinot Noir (2006, 2009, 2013)*

*Common characteristics across all sites:*
    *Vines 50-100+ years old*
    *Specific soil geology (limestone, schist, ancient alluvial)*
    *Traditional winemaking (minimal intervention)*

*Documented winemaker presence during harvest/fermentation*
*Long bottle ageing before effect manifests (minimum 10 years)*

Alex stared at the list. These were some of the most legendary wines in the world. First-growth Bordeaux. Historic Barolo. Top-tier German Riesling. And Hunter Valley Semillon—dismissed by most critics as regional curiosities, but capable of ageing magnificently.

"This is extraordinary," Alex said. "She's documented a pattern across completely different regions, grape varieties, winemaking traditions. The only common factors are vine age, soil type, and ageing potential."

"And something else." Sophie flipped to the next page. "Look at the dates. The effect only appears in exceptional vintages. Years when conditions were perfect—not too hot, not too cold, proper ripening, optimal harvest timing. The wines that age into legendary status."

Alex studied the list again. 1961 Bordeaux—one of the greatest vintages of the 20th century. 1985 Barolo—legendary. 1986 Hunter Valley—the vintage that defined what aged Semillon could become.

"She's saying that quantum encoding only happens when everything aligns perfectly," Alex said slowly. "Old vines, right soil, perfect vintage, minimal intervention, passionate winemaker present during the critical moments. It's not just chemistry. It's... art and science and chance all converging."

"My grandmother called it 'terroir of consciousness,'" Sophie said. "The idea that great wine doesn't just express place—it expresses the people who made it. Their passion, their knowledge, their presence at the critical moment. And under rare conditions, that consciousness gets preserved in the wine itself."

Alex felt something shift in her understanding. This wasn't about technology or weaponisation or intelligence applications. This was about wine at its most profound—the idea that a bottle could contain not just the grape and the soil and the vintage, but the winemaker's soul.

"That's beautiful," Alex said quietly.

"It's also dangerous." Sophie pulled out a later notebook, this one from 2018. "Look at this."

The handwriting was shakier now, Dr Chen in her final years. The entry was dated March 2018:

*They're watching again. Same car, different licence plate. Third time this month. Don't know who sent them. Government? Corporate? Someone who knows about the research and wants it suppressed.*

*Destroyed the following materials today:*
    *Field notes from Bordeaux 2001-2005*
    *Spectral analysis data from Barolo project*
    *Contact information for other researchers*
    *Draft manuscript for revised paper*

*Cannot risk this information falling into the wrong hands. Applications too dangerous:*
    *Memory extraction (intelligence agencies)*
    *Consciousness transfer (immortality seekers)*
    *False memory implantation (legal applications, warfare)*
    *Corporate espionage (wine fraud at industrial scale)*

*If they understand what I've discovered, they'll either suppress it completely or weaponise it. Either outcome destroys the beauty of what wine can be.*

*Sophie will inherit this research. She must be careful. She must understand the danger. She must—*

The entry stopped mid-sentence.

Alex looked up at Sophie. "She knew someone was watching her. Tracking her research."

"For years," Sophie said. "The later notebooks are full of paranoia. Or what I thought was paranoia. Now..." She gestured at her phone, where the BBC News article about Wickham's death was still open. "Now I think she was right to be afraid."

"VM," Alex said. "The messages I've been getting. Someone who claims they knew your grandmother, who says they've been tracking quantum wine research for decades. They warned me about Wickham. Now he's dead."

Sophie's face went pale. "Show me."

Alex pulled out her phone, showed Sophie the messages from VM. Then the photograph—Dr Elizabeth Chen and the other woman in Napa Valley, August 1976.

Sophie stared at the photo. "I've never seen this. My grandmother never mentioned working with anyone in the seventies. She told me she'd been alone from the beginning."

"Maybe she was protecting whoever this is," Alex said. "If VM was her colleague, if they worked together on early research, maybe your grandmother kept VM's name out of it to protect them from the same career destruction."

"Or VM betrayed her," Sophie said. "Worked with her, saw the potential, then had her discredited to keep the research for themselves."

Alex hadn't considered that. "You think VM destroyed your grandmother's career?"

"Someone orchestrated it—that much is obvious. Her 1979 paper was professionally demolished. Not just criticised—destroyed. The reviews were vicious, personal, coordinated." Sophie's hands were shaking. "What if it was VM? What if they've been suppressing this research for forty years, killing anyone who gets close to revealing it?"

"Or," Alex said carefully, "VM is exactly what they claim—someone who's been protecting the research, tracking it, trying to keep it from being weaponised or destroyed. Someone who tried to warn Wickham and failed."

They stared at each other across forty years of research.

"We need to decide," Sophie said. "Do we trust VM? Do we meet with them?"

"When does VM want to meet?"

"Tomorrow. Saturday, noon. Postman's Park."

Alex thought about Emma's words: *Tell the police everything. Let them investigate. Stay safe.*

But the police didn't know quantum wine existed. How could they investigate Wickham's death without understanding what he'd been protecting?

"I think we meet VM," Alex said. "Carefully. In a public place, during daylight. But we meet them. Because right now they're the only person who might know who killed Wickham and why."

Sophie nodded slowly. "Together. We both go."

"Together."

Alex's phone rang. Unknown number. She answered.

"Ms Hartley? This is Detective Inspector Karen Morrison, Metropolitan Police. I'm investigating the death of James Wickham. I understand you attended an event at his residence Thursday evening."

Alex's mouth went dry. "Yes. A wine tasting."

"I'd like to speak with you about that. Would you be able to come to Charing Cross Police Station this afternoon? Say, three o'clock?"

Not a request. A politely phrased summons.

"Yes, of course. Three o'clock."

"Thank you, Ms Hartley. We'll see you then."

The line went dead.

Sophie was watching her. "Police?"

"They want to interview me. This afternoon at three."

"They called me earlier. I'm going in at one." Sophie set down the notebook. "We need to decide what to tell them. If we mention the quantum experience, they'll think we're insane. If we don't, and they find out later we withheld information—"

"We become suspects," Alex finished.

They looked at each other across Elizabeth Chen's forty years of research. The notebooks, the wine bottles, the evidence of something impossible and real.

"We tell them about the tasting," Alex said slowly. "About the wines we tasted, about Wickham's enthusiasm for Hunter Semillon. We tell them he warned me to be careful—that's true, I can quote him exactly. We tell them it was an extraordinary experience, that the wines were remarkable."

"But not the quantum effect," Sophie said.

"Not yet. Not until we understand what we're dealing with. Not until we know who killed Wickham and why."

"That's lying by omission."

"That's staying alive." Alex picked up one of the notebooks, felt the weight of Dr Chen's forty years of work. "Your grandmother spent four decades documenting this, hiding it, protecting it because she knew how dangerous it could be. She died before she could vindicate herself. We're not going to let that happen to us."

Sophie's expression hardened. "What about VM? Do we mention them?"

Alex thought about the messages, the warnings, the photograph. "No. VM told me to come alone to the meeting. That suggests they're afraid of exposure, afraid of being tracked. If we tell the police about VM, we might lose our only source of information about who's suppressing this research."

"Or we might be protecting my grandmother's murderer," Sophie said quietly.

The words hung between them.

"You think VM killed your grandmother?" Alex asked.

"I think someone did." Sophie's voice was flat. "Not directly—it was cancer. But she was under surveillance, constantly stressed, destroying her own research to keep it from falling into the wrong hands. That kind of fear, that kind of constant pressure—it takes a physical toll. Maybe she would have lived longer if she wasn't being hunted."

Alex didn't have an answer for that.

Sophie checked her phone. "I need to get ready for my interview. And you should too." She started gathering the notebooks carefully, putting them back in order on the table. "Be careful what you tell Morrison. She's good at her job—she'll be looking for inconsistencies, things we're not saying."

"You too." Alex stood, pulled on her coat. "After the interviews, we need to decide about VM. Saturday, noon. That's less than twenty-four hours away."

"Come back tomorrow morning? Early—say nine? We can plan the Postman's Park approach together, decide if we're actually going through with it."

"Nine. I'll be here." Alex paused at the door. "Sophie? Your grandmother's research—it's extraordinary. She documented something real. Whatever happens with Morrison, with VM, with all of this—her work matters. We're going to make sure people know that."

Sophie's eyes filled with tears. "Thank you."

Alex left Sophie's flat and stepped out into cold February afternoon. The winter sun was already low, casting long shadows across Dalston Lane. Normal people going about normal Friday activities— shopping, meeting friends, heading home from work.

Alex was walking towards a police interview about a murder, carrying knowledge of quantum wine that might get her killed, about to lie by omission to a detective investigating a death she didn't understand.

She pulled out her phone, checked the time. 1:45 PM. Just over an hour until her interview with Morrison.

She needed to prepare. To organise her thoughts. To decide exactly what she'd say and, more importantly, what she wouldn't.

The Tube journey gave her time to think. What she'd tell Morrison: the tasting, the wines, Wickham's warning. What she wouldn't mention: the quantum experience, Dr Chen's research, VM's messages. Truth mixed with omission. Facts arranged to obscure the impossible.

Her phone buzzed. Emma:

Thinking about you. Be careful.

Alex:

I will. Love you.

She changed at King's Cross, walked from Charing Cross station to the police station.

At 2:45 PM, Alex stood outside Charing Cross Police Station, cold February wind cutting through her coat. She'd rehearsed her statement, organised her thoughts, prepared for Morrison's questions.

She pulled out her phone one last time, texted Emma:

At police station. Going in now. I'll be careful.

No response. Emma was probably in meetings.

Alex pocketed her phone, took a deep breath, and climbed the steps.

Detective Inspector Morrison was waiting.

## 5 / STATEMENTS



FRIDAY, 14 FEBRUARY 2025

3:00 PM

CHARING CROSS POLICE Station was just off the Strand. Alex arrived at three minutes to three, climbed the steps, passed through security, and gave her name to the desk sergeant.

"Have a seat, Ms Hartley. Detective Inspector Morrison will be with you shortly."

The waiting area had that institutional quality all police stations shared: hard chairs, health and safety posters, a noticeboard covered in community alerts. A young woman sat in the corner, hunched over her phone. An older man flipped through a well-worn magazine. Normal people dealing with normal problems.

Alex checked her phone. VM's messages from this morning were still there, screenshot and stored. Evidence, though of what, she wasn't sure yet.

Sophie had already been through this—her interview was at one. By now she'd be back at work, preparing for the Valentine's Day rush.

Alex hoped she'd managed to deflect Morrison's questions about the quantum experience.

"Ms Hartley?"

Alex looked up. A woman in her mid-forties stood in the doorway —dark hair pulled back, wearing a grey suit that had seen better days. Tired eyes that suggested too many cases and not enough sleep.

"I'm Detective Inspector Karen Morrison. Thank you for coming in. This way, please."

Alex followed her down a corridor, past interview rooms with closed doors, into a small room with a table, four chairs, and a recording device. Everything beige and functional.

"Please, sit." Morrison gestured to the chair opposite her own.

"Can I get you tea? Coffee?"

"I'm fine, thank you."

Morrison sat, opened a manila folder, extracted a pen. "Right. I'm going to record this interview for accuracy. You're here voluntarily, providing a witness statement. You're not under caution and you're free to leave at any time. Is that clear?"

"Yes."

Morrison pressed record on the device. "Interview with Alexandra Hartley, Friday fourteenth February 2025, 15:02 hours. Present: DI Karen Morrison and Ms Hartley. Ms Hartley, please state your full name, address, and occupation."

"Alexandra Jane Hartley. Flat 3, 42 Cloudesley Road, Islington, N1. Wine writer and Master of Wine candidate."

"Ms Hartley, you attended a private wine tasting at Mr Wickham's Pall Mall residence on Thursday evening. Can you tell me about that?"

Alex took a breath. Stick to facts. Professional. Nothing about quantum wine.

"I received an invitation about six weeks ago from James Wickham. I'd never met him before, but he knew my work—I write for Decanter magazine. The tasting was a vertical of Hunter Valley Semillon, quite rare. Twenty-four guests, invitation only."

"What time did you arrive?"

"Just before seven. The tasting started at seven."

"And Mr Wickham—how did he seem?"

"Fine. Normal. He was enthusiastic about the wines, gave some background on the vintages. He seemed..." Alex paused, choosing her words carefully. "He seemed proud of the collection he'd assembled."

"Did he mention feeling unwell at any point? Complain of chest pain, dizziness, anything unusual?"

"No. Nothing like that."

Morrison made a note. "How well do you know the other guests?"

"Not well. I recognised a few faces from industry events—other wine professionals—but we're not friends."

"Did you speak with anyone in particular?"

Here it was. The moment where omission became deliberate.

"Briefly with some of the other guests. Professional chat about the wines, that sort of thing. Everyone was there for the Semillon."

"Anyone stand out? Anyone who seemed particularly interested in Mr Wickham, or behaved unusually?"

Alex thought about Sophie, about their locked eyes across the table when the quantum experience hit. About Sophie mouthing *Did you—?* and Alex nodding.

That had been unusual. That had stood out.

But explaining it meant explaining quantum wine. Which meant sounding delusional.

"Not really," Alex said. "Everyone was focused on the tasting. It's quite rare to taste wines like that—some of them were decades old."

Morrison consulted her notes. "The tasting ended around nine PM?"

"Just after, yes. Maybe quarter past nine."

"And then what did you do?"

"I left. Walked towards the main road and caught the bus home."

"Did you see Mr Wickham before you left?"

"Yes. He approached me near the end, asked if I'd enjoyed the wines. We spoke briefly—maybe two or three minutes. He gave me his business card, said he had information about the wines' provenance if I wanted to write about the tasting."

"Did he seem concerned about anything? Worried? Frightened?"

Alex thought about Wickham's warning: Be careful. Hunter Semillon has a way of surprising people. Not everyone handles it well.

"He seemed..." She chose her words carefully. "Thoughtful. A bit cryptic, maybe. But not frightened."

"Cryptic how?"

"He said the wines had a way of surprising people. That not everyone handles them well. I assumed he meant emotionally—some people get quite moved by great wine. It's not uncommon."

Morrison's pen paused. "Did you handle them well?"

The question hung in the air. Alex felt her pulse quicken.

"I thought they were extraordinary. Some of the best expressions of Hunter Semillon I've ever tasted."

"But did anything unusual happen whilst you were tasting? Anything out of the ordinary?"

Christ. Did Morrison know something? Had one of the other guests mentioned it?

"Wine tasting can be quite intense," Alex said slowly. "When you're really concentrating, trying to identify specific flavours, aromas, characteristics... sometimes you can get quite absorbed in it. But nothing I'd call unusual."

Morrison held her gaze for a long moment. "Ms Hartley, Mr Wickham died under suspicious circumstances. I need you to be completely honest with me. If something unusual happened at that tasting—anything at all—I need to know about it."

She consulted her notes. "Several other guests mentioned feeling... disoriented. Light-headed. One said the wines seemed 'unusually affecting.' But no one could quite articulate what they meant. Can you?"

Alex felt the weight of the lie by omission. But what could she say? I hallucinated a vineyard in Australia and shared a consciousness experience with another taster, and I think it's because the wine stored quantum-encoded memories from forty years ago?

"I experienced what I always experience when I taste great wine," Alex said. "Connection to the place it came from. A sense of the people who made it. That's what makes wine special—it tells stories. But nothing beyond that."

Morrison studied her for another moment, then made a note.

"Did anyone contact you after the tasting? Before news of Mr Wickham's death became public?"

Sophie. Sophie had rung her at The Red Lion, they'd met at the pub, they'd discussed the quantum experience.

But if Alex admitted that, Morrison would ask why. What had been so urgent that Sophie needed to meet immediately? What had they discussed?

"I received a phone call," Alex said carefully. "From another guest at the tasting. Sophie Chen. She's a sommelier at Noble Rot."

"What time was this call?"

"Around half past nine, maybe quarter to ten."

"What did you discuss?"

"The wines. She was interested in my thoughts on the Semillon, whether I thought it deserved more recognition in the wine press."

The lie came easier than Alex expected. It was close enough to truth—they had discussed the wines. Just not in the way Morrison would assume.

"And did you meet her?"

No point denying it. If Morrison was thorough—and she seemed thorough—she'd check CCTV, phone records, everything.

"Yes. We met at a pub near Pall Mall. The Red Lion. Just for a drink and a chat about the wines."

"What time was this?"

"Ten o'clock, maybe a bit after."

"And how long did you stay?"

"Half an hour? Forty minutes? I got home around eleven."

Morrison made detailed notes. "So you and Ms Chen discussed the wines. Anything else?"

"Industry gossip. Where we worked, what we were working on. The sort of things wine professionals talk about."

Morrison made a note. "Ms Hartley, one more question. In your professional opinion, was there anything unusual about the wines you tasted last night?"

There it was again. That word: unusual.

"They were exceptionally well-preserved for their age," Alex said. "Hunter Semillon can age for decades, but these were particularly impressive. The 1986 Tyrrell's Vat 1 especially—it should have been declining by now, but it was vibrant, alive. Almost impossibly fresh."

"Impossibly?"

"Figure of speech. Just very, very good."

Morrison studied her. "You write about wine professionally. Have you ever written about wines that produce unusual effects on tasters?"

Alex's mouth went dry. "Unusual effects?"

"Hallucinations. Altered states. That sort of thing."

So Morrison did know something. Someone must have mentioned it. One of the other tasters, maybe. Or had Sophie said something?

"Wine doesn't produce hallucinations," Alex said carefully. "Unless it's contaminated with something, which would be immediately obvious. High alcohol content can affect people, especially if they're not eating properly during a tasting. But these wines were all quite low alcohol—Semillon typically is."

"So nothing like that happened to you?"

"No."

The lie felt heavier this time. More deliberate. More dangerous.

Morrison held her gaze for what felt like a full minute, then nodded. "All right. Is there anything else you think I should know?

Anything you saw, heard, experienced that might be relevant to Mr Wickham's death?"

"No. Nothing."

"If you remember anything later, no matter how insignificant it seems, please call me." Morrison pulled out a business card, slid it across the table. "We're treating this as a suspicious death. That means someone may have harmed Mr Wickham. If you know anything—anything at all—that could help us find out who, I need you to tell me."

Alex took the card. "I understand."

Morrison stopped the recording. "15:34 hours, interview concluded. Thank you for your time, Ms Hartley. You're free to go."

Alex stood, legs slightly unsteady. "Detective Inspector, can I ask —how did he die? Mr Wickham?"

Morrison's expression gave nothing away. "I can't discuss specific details of an ongoing investigation. But I will say this: we're treating Mr Wickham's death as suspicious. That means someone may have harmed him. And if you were there that evening, if you experienced something unusual, you might be in danger too."

The words sent ice through Alex's veins. "Danger from who?"

"That's what I'm trying to find out. Be careful, Ms Hartley. And if anyone contacts you about the tasting, about the wines, about anything related to Thursday night—you call me immediately. Understood?"

"Understood."

Alex emerged from the police station into weak February sunlight. Her hands were trembling slightly—adrenaline, or guilt about the lies, or fear about Morrison's warning.

You might be in danger too.

She pulled out her phone, rang Sophie.

"How did it go?" Sophie answered immediately.

"She asked about unusual experiences. About whether anything strange happened during the tasting."

"She asked me that too. I said no. Told her I had some intense flavour experiences but nothing beyond normal wine tasting."

"Same. I didn't mention the quantum experience."

"Neither did I. But Alex, she knows something. Someone must have told her."

"Or she's fishing. Trying to see if we'll admit to something."

"Did you tell her we met at the pub?"

"I had to. If she checks CCTV or phone records, she'd find out anyway. I said we discussed the wines, exchanged professional gossip. Nothing about your grandmother's research."

Sophie was quiet for a moment. "She told me I might be in danger. That whoever killed Wickham might target other guests at the tasting."

"She told me the same thing."

"Which means she thinks it's connected to something that happened at the tasting. To the wines, maybe. Or to what we experienced."

Alex looked round the street, suddenly hyperaware of people passing. Any of them could be watching. Any of them could be VM.

"We need to finalise our plan for tomorrow," Alex said. "VM wants to meet at noon. Postman's Park."

"I know. I got the messages you forwarded." Sophie's voice was tight. "Listen, I'm working tonight—Valentine's Day, we're fully booked, two sittings. I'll be exhausted. Can we talk early tomorrow morning instead? Meet at yours, say nine AM, plan everything before the noon meeting?"

Alex felt a flash of relief. Emma wouldn't have to deal with Sophie tonight. They could have Valentine's evening alone—though given their fight this morning, that might not be a good thing.

"That works better," Alex said. "Nine tomorrow. We'll figure out the VM approach then."

"Good. And Alex? Morrison asked if I'd received any strange messages or contacts since the tasting. I said no."

"Same. I didn't mention VM."

"Should we have?"

"I don't know. If we tell the police about VM, they'll ask what VM knows. Which means explaining the quantum experience. Which means—"

"Which means we sound like lunatics and possibly become suspects ourselves."

"Exactly."

They were silent for a moment, both processing the impossible situation they were in.

"Tomorrow morning," Sophie said. "We decide what to do about VM. Together."

"Tomorrow. Be careful tonight."

"You too. Happy Valentine's Day," Sophie added with bitter irony.

Alex ended the call, started walking towards the Tube. Her phone buzzed immediately.

Unknown number. VM again.

> Ms Hartley. Lying to the police is unwise. I know what you experienced. I know about the wine. We need to talk before someone else gets hurt. Tomorrow, noon, Postman's Park. Come alone. —VM

Alex stopped dead in the middle of the pavement. Someone jostled past her, muttering.

VM knew she'd lied to Morrison. Which meant either VM had inside information—someone at the police station, or access to surveillance—or VM was making an educated guess based on how these interviews typically went.

Either way, VM was watching. Closely.

But the message was more specific now. Before someone else gets hurt.

Was that a threat? Or a warning?

Alex took a screenshot, then typed a reply:

Who are you?

The response came within seconds:

Someone who understands quantum wine.
Someone who can help you. Tomorrow,
noon. Don't tell anyone.

Alex stared at the message. Every instinct screamed danger. Meeting an unknown person in a secluded location to discuss an impossible phenomenon related to a suspicious death was objectively stupid.

But VM knew something. And right now, VM knew more than Alex did.

She typed:

How do I know you're not dangerous?

VM:

You don't. But I'm not the one you should
be afraid of. The people who killed
Wickham are looking for quantum-active
wines. If they find out you experienced the
effect, you're a threat to them. I can help
protect you. Tomorrow, noon.

Alex's finger hovered over the delete button. Then she typed:

Why should I trust you?

VM:

Because I'm the only one who can explain
what you experienced. The police can't help
you. They don't understand quantum wine.
But I do. And I know who's hunting it.

Alex stared at the message. VM was right—Morrison had no framework for understanding the quantum effect. But that didn't mean VM was safe.

Alex typed:

> I'll think about it.

VM:

> Don't think too long. Wickham hesitated. Now he's dead. Tomorrow, noon, Postman's Park. Don't make me wait.

## FRIDAY AFTERNOON, 14 FEBRUARY 2025

### 4:15 PM

The messages stopped. Alex stood on the pavement, commuters flowing round her, trying to process.

Someone who'd known Elizabeth Chen. Someone who believed in quantum wine. Someone who knew about Wickham's death, knew Alex had lied to police, knew about the quantum experience.

Someone who might be able to help.

Or someone who might be the killer.

Alex started walking again, faster now. She needed to get home. Needed to talk to Emma. Needed to decide whether tomorrow's meeting was the answer they needed or a trap she wouldn't escape.

Emma was home when Alex arrived, sitting at the kitchen table with architectural drawings spread out, a pencil behind her ear. She looked up when Alex came in, her expression carefully neutral.

"How did it go?"

"Fine. Standard witness statement. I told them about the tasting, about Wickham, about when I left."

"Did they ask if anything unusual happened?"

Alex hung up her coat, buying time. "They asked if Wickham seemed worried or unwell. He didn't. They asked if anyone behaved strangely. No one did. Straightforward stuff."

Emma set down her pencil. "Alex, you're a terrible liar. What aren't you telling me?"

"I'm not lying."

"You're telling half-truths. And that's the same as lying." Emma stood, crossed to the kitchen, filled the kettle. "Morrison asked about unusual experiences, didn't she? And you didn't tell her about the quantum thing."

"How did you—"

"Because I know you. And because it's the obvious question to ask if someone died suspiciously at a wine tasting. Did the wine do something unusual? Did anyone react strangely?" Emma switched on the kettle. "And you lied to a police officer about it."

"I didn't lie. I just didn't volunteer information that would make me sound insane."

"Alex, a man is dead. If what you experienced is connected to his death—"

"It's not."

"How do you know?"

"Because quantum wine isn't dangerous. It's just... wine. With unusual properties. No one kills someone over wine."

"People kill over rare art. Over expensive jewellery. Over anything that's valuable enough." Emma pulled mugs from the cupboard. "If quantum wine is real, if it's as valuable as you and Sophie think, then yes, someone might kill for it."

Alex sat heavily at the table, pushing Emma's architectural drawings aside. "VM messaged again. After the police interview. They know I lied to Morrison. They want to meet tomorrow at noon."

Emma froze. "Please tell me you're not considering it."

"They warned me Thursday night that Wickham needed to be more careful—before he died. Now they're saying I'm a threat, that the people who killed Wickham might come after me too, and they might be the only person who can help."

"Or they killed Wickham and are trying to lure you into a trap." Emma's voice shook. "Alex, this is insane. You need to go back to Morrison and tell her everything. The quantum experience, the VM messages, all of it."

"And sound like a lunatic? She already thinks I'm hiding something."

"Because you are!" Emma's voice rose. "You're hiding that you had a shared hallucination with another taster, that you've been investigating quantum wine theories from a dead researcher, that some mysterious person has been texting you about it and warned you about Wickham before he died. Do you understand how that sounds?"

"I know how it sounds."

"Then why are you doing this?"

"Because someone needs to." Alex looked up at Emma. "Elizabeth Chen spent forty years documenting something real. Wickham collected those wines, understood them, and now he's dead. If I don't follow this through, if I don't prove what's happening, then Chen died dismissed, Wickham died for nothing, and whoever's killing over quantum wine gets away with it."

"That's not your responsibility. That's the police's job."

"The police don't believe in quantum wine. They don't even know it exists. How can they investigate something they don't understand?"

Emma poured boiling water into the mugs, her movements sharp with frustration. "So you're going to solve it? You're going to catch a murderer because you drank some wine that made you hallucinate?"

"I'm going to understand what happened. That's all. Just understand it."

"And then what? You prove quantum wine exists, you write an article, you get your name in the papers? Is that what this is about?"

The words stung because they were partly true. But it was more than recognition.

"It's about truth," Alex said quietly. "Chen was right. Wickham knew she was right. And they both paid for it—one with her career, one with his life. If I walk away now, I'm saying their truth doesn't matter. I'm saying wine is just wine, and anyone who claims otherwise is crazy."

Emma set a mug of tea in front of Alex. "I know you believe that. But believing doesn't make it safe. Meeting VM tomorrow could get you killed."

"Or it could give me answers."

"Is that worth dying for?"

Alex thought about that. About Elizabeth Chen's notebooks, forty years of lonely observations. About Wickham's warning: Be careful. About that voice in the vineyard, preserved for four decades, waiting to be heard.

"I don't know," she said honestly. "I know that terrifies you. I know this isn't fair. But I can't walk away. Not yet."

Emma's eyes filled with tears. "I know you can't. That's what scares me." She reached across the table, took Alex's hand. "Then I'm coming with you tomorrow. To Postman's Park. You're not meeting a potential murderer alone."

"VM said to come alone."

"And you're going to follow instructions from someone who might have killed Wickham? No. Absolutely not. I'm coming, or you're not going."

Alex wanted to argue. Wanted to say she could handle it, that she'd be careful, that Emma's presence would just complicate things.

But she was also terrified. And the idea of having Emma there, solid and rational and protective, was more comforting than she wanted to admit.

"Okay," Alex said. "But we need to be strategic. VM said to come alone—if they see you, they might not show. Or worse, they might panic and do something dangerous."

"So what's the plan?"

"Sophie and I are meeting here tomorrow morning. Nine AM. She's working tonight—Valentine's Day service at Noble Rot, two full sittings—but she'll be here tomorrow. We'll plan everything together, then the three of us go to Postman's Park. But you and Sophie stay back, hidden. I approach VM alone whilst you watch from a distance. If something goes wrong—"

"I call the police. I know." Emma reached across the table, took Alex's hand. "I don't like it. But I understand it."

Emma squeezed her hand. "I know this morning was awful. I know I said terrible things about your work. But Alex, I meant what I said too—wine isn't worth dying for. Come home tomorrow. Alive. That's all I ask."

"I will. I promise."

They sat in silence for a moment, hands clasped, the kitchen warm round them.

"Happy Valentine's Day," Emma said with a weak smile.

"Happy Valentine's Day," Alex echoed. "Sorry it's not more romantic."

"We can do romantic when you're not being hunted by quantum wine enthusiasts." Emma stood. "I'm going to order takeaway. Thai? And we're going to watch something mindless on Netflix and pretend for a few hours that our lives are normal."

"That sounds perfect."

But as Emma pulled out her phone to order food, Alex couldn't shake the feeling that normal was gone forever. That tomorrow at Postman's Park, something would happen that would change everything again.

For better or worse, she'd know the truth about VM. About quantum wine. About who killed Wickham.

She just hoped she'd survive learning it.

▭

# 6 / POSTMAN'S PARK

SATURDAY, 15 FEBRUARY 2025

7:15 AM

Alex woke to Emma watching her in the grey dawn. Rain tapped the window like nervous fingers. The bedside clock read 7:15.

"I keep imagining it," Emma said quietly. "All the ways this could go wrong."

Alex's stomach tightened. She'd been imagining it too—VM not showing, or showing with others, or the police arriving, or worse. "We don't have to go."

"Yes, we do." Emma's hand found hers under the duvet, squeezed hard. "I just wish we didn't."

They lay there in silence, rain drumming, London waking beyond their window. Alex wanted to say something reassuring, something certain. But certainty had evaporated the moment she'd tasted that 1986 Tyrrell's and felt another woman's consciousness flood through her own.

Emma sat up first, pushed her hair back. "Coffee. We need coffee."

They made it in silence, the kitchen filling with warmth and the smell of dark roast. Emma buttered toast neither of them would finish. Alex scrolled through news on her phone—nothing new about Wickham. Just the same story from yesterday: *Suspicious death, investigation ongoing.*

"Promise me something," Emma said. "If VM asks you to go anywhere else—a second location, anywhere that's not that public park in daylight—you say no. You walk away."

"I promise."

"And if they try to give you anything to drink or eat—"

"I won't take it." Alex set down her phone, crossed the kitchen, wrapped her arms round Emma. She felt Emma's heart beating fast against her own. "I'm terrified too."

Emma held her for a long moment. Then, against Alex's shoulder: "I know. That's what I love about you. And what terrifies me about you."


## 9:00 AM

Sophie arrived looking like she'd slept as badly as they had. Dark jeans, black jumper, hair pulled back severely. She carried a rucksack that she set on the sofa with the careful weight of someone handling ammunition.

"Sophie, this is Emma," Alex said. "Emma—Sophie Chen."

They shook hands briefly, sizing each other up. Two women who'd heard about each other but never met, now bound together by impossible wine and a dead man.

"Supplies," Sophie said, turning to the rucksack. "Water. Protein bars. First aid kit. Power bank. And this—" She pulled out a small canister.

Emma raised an eyebrow. "Is that pepper spray? It's illegal here."

"Rape alarm. But in a panic, most people can't tell the difference." Sophie set it on the table. The red canister looked absurdly cheerful against the wood grain. "I spent half the night thinking about my grandmother. About how she must have felt—alone with truth no one believed. And I thought, what if there were others? What if they kept quiet because they were afraid?"

"Afraid of what happened to Wickham," Alex said.

The words hung there. Rain drummed against the windows.

They spent the next hour planning. Sophie sketched scenarios: what if VM was armed, what if they tried to take Alex somewhere else, what if multiple people showed up. Emma pulled up Postman's Park on her phone, studied the layout, identified exits and sight lines.

Alex felt absurd—like characters in a spy novel. Except Wickham was actually dead. VM had actually warned them. And somewhere in London, people who'd spent forty years suppressing quantum wine research were doing... what? Watching? Waiting? Planning?

At 10:30, they took the Tube. Northern Line to Bank, then walked through the City's Saturday quiet. The financial district was nearly deserted—office workers replaced by a handful of tourists photographing Wren churches.


## 11:25 AM

Postman's Park hid behind an office block and church, the kind of place you'd pass a hundred times without noticing. Fifty metres of damp grass surrounded by bare trees, their branches black against grey sky. The memorial wall dominated the western side—Victorian tiles protected under a wooden shelter, commemorating ordinary Londoners who'd died saving others.

*Sarah Smith, pantomime artiste, died of terrible injuries received when attempting to extinguish the flames which had enveloped her companion.*

*Alice Ayres, daughter of a bricklayer's labourer, who by intrepid conduct saved three children from a burning house in Union Street, Borough, at the cost of her own young life.*

The rain had stopped but water still beaded on benches. Alex's breath misted in the cold air.

Scattered visitors dotted the space: an elderly man reading a newspaper on a damp bench, a young couple sharing earbuds, someone sketching the memorial tiles. Normal Saturday morning in London. Except one of these people might be VM. Or watching for VM. Or watching Alex.

"Too exposed," Emma murmured. "I thought it would be more secluded."

"Public is safer," Sophie said. But her eyes kept scanning the park's edges.

They positioned themselves carefully: Alex on a bench facing the memorial, trying to look casual. Emma near the entrance with a paperback thriller she wasn't reading. Sophie by the far exit, scrolling her phone, positioned to see everything.

Alex checked the time: 11:48. Twelve minutes.

She wore her navy wool coat—smart enough for a professional meeting, warm enough for February. Her notebook sat in her bag though she wasn't sure why she'd brought it. Habit, maybe. The journalist's instinct to document everything. To make it real by writing it down.

11:52.

A pigeon landed near her feet, pecked at nothing, flew away.

11:56.

Her phone felt heavy in her pocket. She resisted checking it again.

Noon.

Her phone buzzed.

**Look up.**

Alex did. Across the park by the memorial wall stood a woman. Late seventies, maybe early eighties. Silver hair cut short, face weathered but strong. Waxed jacket the colour of moss, sturdy walking shoes. She wasn't looking at Alex. She was reading the memorial tiles like any tourist.

But there was something in the way she held herself—alert, watchful, completely aware of her surroundings despite appearing absorbed in Victorian heroism.

Another text:

> Walk towards the memorial. Slowly. Alone.
> Your friends stay where they are or I leave.

Alex glanced at Emma, gave a small nod. Emma's hand tightened on her book but she didn't move.

Alex stood. Her legs felt unsteady. She crossed the lawn, wet grass dampening her shoes. Thirty feet. Twenty. Ten.

The woman didn't turn. Just kept reading tiles, hands deep in jacket pockets.

"Ms Hartley." The voice was cultured, educated, with something American underneath the British vowels. "Thank you for coming. Though I see you didn't follow instructions about coming alone."

"Would you have?" Alex asked. "If someone you didn't know asked you to meet alone after a suspicious death?"

The woman's lips twitched. Almost a smile. "No. I suppose not." She finally turned.

Alex got her first clear look: strong features, intelligent eyes behind wire-rimmed glasses, lines etched deep around her mouth. The kind of face suggesting a lifetime of thinking, questioning, refusing easy answers. A lifetime of carrying secrets.

"Who are you?" Alex asked.

"Dr Victoria Mills. Though I use my maiden name professionally now—Victoria Marsh. VM." The almost-smile returned. "I wondered if you'd work that out."

Victoria Mills. V.M.

The initials from the photograph. The mysterious texter who'd warned her about Wickham, who'd known about the quantum experience, who'd been sending cryptic messages for days.

How had she missed it?

"Victoria Marsh," Alex said, the pieces rearranging themselves. The name felt familiar, like something glimpsed in footnotes and forgotten. "Should I know you?"

"Probably not. I've kept quiet for forty years. After what happened to Elizabeth, most of us learned to hide." Victoria glanced towards Emma and Sophie—checking, assessing. "Your friends are nervous. Tell them I'm not armed or dangerous. Though I would prefer privacy for this conversation."

Alex pulled out her phone, texted Emma:

> Victoria Mills/Marsh. Says she knew Sophie's grandmother. Seems okay but stay alert.

Emma's reply came immediately:

> Watching. Anything suspicious, we're coming over.

"Your partner?" Victoria asked.

"How did you—"

"The way you looked at her when you arrived. The way she positioned herself between you and the entrance." Victoria's expression softened. "That's not a friend. That's someone who loves you enough to be terrified for you."

The observation was so precise, so kind, that Alex felt something loosen in her chest.

"Hold onto that," Victoria said quietly. "People who love you despite your obsessions are rare. I know."

"You said you knew Elizabeth Chen," Alex said, pulling herself back to business. "Prove it."

Victoria reached into her jacket slowly—clearly aware of Emma and Sophie watching—and pulled out a faded photograph protected in a plastic sleeve. She handed it to Alex.

Five young people in a laboratory. Early 1970s judging by the clothes and hair. Three women, two men, all in their twenties or early thirties, all smiling at the camera. Someone had written on the back in fountain pen: *UC Davis & Beyond - 1971.*

Alex recognised Elizabeth Chen immediately—young, vibrant, wearing a lab coat and holding a wine glass up to the light. Next to her stood a younger Victoria Mills, dark hair instead of silver, also in a lab coat. A young man with an Australian tan and an easy grin. Another man, darker, French perhaps. And a younger man, well-dressed, holding a bottle like it was precious, like it mattered more than anything.

"I was twenty-four when I met Elizabeth," Victoria said quietly. She reached out, touched the photograph in Alex's hands. "UC Davis, 1971. I was just starting my PhD, thought I knew everything. She was this brilliant post-doc who asked the simplest questions that unraveled everything we thought we understood about wine chemistry."

Her finger moved across the photo. "By '73, Marcus Webb had found us—the Australian there. He'd been seeing impossible correlations in aged Semillon, thought he was going mad until he read Elizabeth's early papers. Then Philippe in Bordeaux started writing. We realised we were all seeing the same thing. Wines ageing identically in different cellars. Patterns that shouldn't exist. Quantum effects in fermented grapes."

Victoria's finger stopped on the youngest man. "James found us in '76. He was twenty-three, rich from family money, obsessed with wine in that way people get obsessed when they finally find meaning. He read Elizabeth's work and recognised something important. He became our patron. Connected us across continents. Funded research trips. Made everything possible."

She looked up from the photo, met Alex's eyes. "He was the heart of it. The one who believed we could prove it, change the world. And now he's dead because he refused to stay quiet."

"What happened?" Alex asked. "After you discovered quantum wine?"

Victoria gestured to a bench away from the memorial, away from the other visitors. "This is a long story. Shall we sit?"

They sat. Two women separated by two generations, connected by wine that defied physics.

Victoria was silent for a moment, staring at the bare trees. Then: "We called ourselves the Quantum Network. Grandiose name for five researchers who thought we'd discovered something impossible. We spent years documenting it—comparing notes, running experiments, building the theoretical framework. Elizabeth was the one who proposed quantum coherence as the mechanism. She was always the brilliant one."

"When did she publish?"

"1979. We thought it would make her famous. We thought the data was undeniable." Victoria's mouth twisted. "It was torn apart. Reviewers called it pseudoscience, fraud, incompetent methodology. They destroyed her career. Post-doc position gone. Grants withdrawn. Other universities wouldn't touch her. She spent the next forty years documenting quantum wine alone, dismissed by everyone."

"But the data was real."

"The data was real." Victoria removed her glasses, rubbed her eyes. Without them she looked older, more fragile. "Which is exactly why certain people took notice. The wrong kind of people."

"Intelligence agencies?"

"I never knew exactly who." She put her glasses back on, focused on Alex. "In 1981, I was approached. A man in a good suit with government credentials. Said my research had 'interesting applications.' Offered me funding—unlimited budget, state-of-the-art facilities. All I had to do was continue researching quantum wine. Privately. Without publishing."

"You said yes."

"I was thirty-four. Ambitious. Stupid." Victoria's voice went flat. "I said yes."

"For how long?"

"Fifteen years. 1980 to 1995. Private lab in California funded through university contracts with classified attachments. DOD connections I wasn't supposed to notice. One directive: understand quantum wine well enough to control it. To use it."

Alex felt cold despite her coat. "Use it how?"

Victoria's hands gripped the bench, knuckles going white. "They wanted me to extract memories. Plant false ones. Make people believe they'd witnessed crimes they hadn't. Experienced abuse that never happened." She turned to look at Alex. "Imagine a witness drinking wine at a diplomatic dinner, then suddenly 'remembering' secret conversations that never occurred. Imagine creating confessions from nothing. Perfect legal evidence, completely fabricated."

"Christ."

"That's what fifteen years of my life produced. Tools to destroy innocent people." Victoria's voice shook. "I learned to identify quantum-active wines with ninety-percent accuracy. Learned which terroirs consistently produce them—Hunter Valley, Bordeaux, Barolo, specific sites with ancient soils and high transition metals. Learned the basics of emotional transfer through phenolic networks. But targeted memory extraction? Thank God I never solved that. The human brain is too complex. I couldn't crack it."

"What happened in 1995?"

Victoria was quiet for a long moment. When she spoke, her voice was flat. "A demonstration. March 1995. They brought someone to my lab—a 'subject,' they called him. Former intelligence analyst who'd witnessed something classified. Something they needed him to forget, or better yet, remember differently."

She removed her glasses, rubbed her eyes. "My supervisor had me prepare quantum wine. Stress-harvest grapes, high cortisol markers, fermented under controlled anxiety conditions. We made the subject drink it whilst they showed him fabricated documents, played recordings, built a false memory structure around something that never happened."

Victoria's hands were shaking. "Three hours later, he confessed.

Gave detailed testimony about events he'd never witnessed. Completely convinced. Perfect recall of things that never occurred. And my supervisor turned to me and said: 'Victoria, you've just revolutionised interrogation. Imagine what we can do with this—courtrooms, diplomatic negotiations, congressional hearings.'"

She put her glasses back on, but her eyes were wet. "I walked into my lab the next morning and saw fifteen years of work—boxes of notes, spectroscopy data, chemical analyses—and understood they were going to use it to destroy people. Not criminals. Not terrorists. Anyone. Witnesses. Journalists. Political opponents. Anyone who knew inconvenient truths."

She looked at Alex. "So I destroyed it. Burned the lab notes. Wiped the computers. Erased everything. I kept only personal copies —insurance against them coming after me. Then I changed my name, moved to England, disappeared. I thought it was over. I thought they'd move on to other projects."

"But they didn't."

"They never stopped. They've been hunting quantum-active wines for thirty years, trying to understand what I wouldn't give them. Trying to complete the weaponisation." Victoria glanced around the park—checking, Alex realised. Checking for watchers. "And now they've started killing anyone who gets close to proving quantum wine publicly. Because public knowledge destroys their monopoly. Makes it impossible to weaponise in secret."

"Wickham."

"James never stopped researching. Never stopped believing. He kept quiet about it, collected quantum wines privately, waited for the right moment." Victoria's voice caught. "That tasting Thursday night —he'd finally assembled enough quantum-active wines in one place to prove the phenomenon beyond doubt. He invited people with scientific backgrounds, people who might experience the effect and understand what it meant. He was trying to force the truth into the open."

"And they killed him for it."

"Yes."

The word hung between them. Across the park, Emma shifted position, still watching. A pigeon landed near the memorial, pecked at nothing.

"Ms Hartley—Alex—you and Sophie Chen experienced quantum entanglement Thursday night," Victoria said. "That makes you witnesses. More than that, it makes you proof. If you can describe exactly what you experienced, if you can testify that you accessed Elizabeth Chen's memories from 1986—"

"It proves quantum wine exists."

"Yes. And that makes you extraordinarily dangerous to people who've spent forty years trying to keep this secret." Victoria pulled something from her pocket. Small, black, ordinary-looking. A USB drive. She held it between them.

"This contains everything I learned in fifteen years of classified research. Every formula. Every protocol. Every discovery they wanted kept secret." She didn't offer it yet, just held it there. "I destroyed my lab notes when I walked away in 1995. Burned them, wiped the computers, erased everything. But I kept personal copies. Insurance against them coming after me. This drive and one other hidden copy are all that remain of that work."

Alex stared at the small black rectangle. It looked so ordinary. Like something you'd use to transfer holiday photos or backup files. Not like forty years of suppressed science. Not like something people had died to protect.

"Why give this to me?"

"Because you experienced quantum wine. Because you're a writer with a platform. Because you're stubborn enough to pursue truth even when it's dangerous." Victoria finally extended the drive. "And because I'm too old and too afraid to do it myself. I've been hiding for thirty years whilst James kept fighting. Maybe he was right. Maybe I've been a coward."

Alex took it. The plastic was warm from Victoria's pocket. It weighed maybe ten grams but felt like holding a bomb.

"What do I do with it?"

"Make copies immediately. Hide them in different places. Then decide—publish it, give it to quantum physicists, give it to police. Just make sure it doesn't disappear again." Victoria pulled out a burner phone, handed that over too. "This has one number programmed— my current phone. Text only, never call. I check it twice a day. If you need me, I'll respond within twelve hours."

"I thought you said you couldn't be contacted."

"I'm not brave enough to stand with you publicly. But I can answer questions. Provide guidance." Victoria managed a sad smile. "Maybe that's better than nothing."

"Thank you."

Victoria looked at Emma and Sophie, still watching from their positions. "Keep your friends close. Trust very few people. The people who funded my research didn't stop when I left. They're still out there. Still trying to control this."

"Who are they?"

"I knew some names in the eighties. Organisations change, but..." Victoria hesitated, glanced around the park again. Lower now, urgent: "The organisation that funded my work used a contract name. Meridian Research Group. I don't know if they still exist under that name or if they've evolved into something else. But Alex - " She met her eyes. "They were willing to kill to protect this research in the eighties. They'll be willing to kill now. If you see that name anywhere—anywhere at all—you need to understand you're in immediate danger."

The words made Alex's skin prickle.

"One more thing," Victoria said. "The Bordeaux conference. June 2025. International Wine Science Conference. Philippe Moreau submitted a paper six months ago—after decades of silence, he's going public. Marcus Webb co-authored. So did Sarah Kimura from New Zealand. They're presenting Elizabeth's research, James's findings, all of it. Making it impossible to ignore."

"The researchers are converging."

"They're tired of hiding. Forty years of dismissal, and now James is dead, and they're angry." Victoria's expression was grim. "Which means everyone presenting will be in danger. If you're going to do something with that data, do it before June. Once that conference happens, everything changes. For better or worse."

She stood slowly, like her joints hurt. "I should go. I've stayed too long already."

"Victoria—" Alex stood too. "Thank you. For this. For finally—"

"Don't thank me. I'm forty years too late." Victoria looked at the memorial tiles gleaming under their shelter. "Sarah Smith. Alice Ayres. Ordinary people who died saving others. That's courage. What I'm doing—handing off my burden and running away again— that's not courage. That's cowardice with a slightly cleaner conscience."

"It's more than nothing."

"Is it?" Victoria managed another sad smile. "I suppose we'll find out."

She walked away, moving quickly for her age, not looking back. Alex watched her disappear through the park entrance, swallowed by Saturday crowds and grey London streets.

Emma appeared at Alex's side immediately, Sophie right behind her.

"What the hell just happened?" Emma demanded. "Who was that? What did she give you?"

Alex held up the USB drive and burner phone. "Victoria Mills. She worked with Dr Chen forty years ago. This is fifteen years of classified research on quantum wine. Everything they've been trying to suppress."

Emma stared at the drive. "And she just... gave it to you? In a public park?"

"She's been hiding for thirty years. She's tired of hiding."

"So she handed the target to you instead?" Emma's voice rose. "Alex, this is insane. We need to go to the police. Right now. Before—"

"Before what?" Sophie cut in. "Before the people who killed Wickham come after us? The police can't protect us from people who've been suppressing this for decades."

"Then what the hell do we do?" Emma looked between them, fear and frustration warring in her face.

Alex closed her hand around the drive. Felt its warmth, its weight. "We make copies. Right now. Multiple copies in different locations. Before something happens to it."

"There's a print shop," Sophie said. "I saw one on King William Street. We passed it walking here."

They left the park together, three women carrying data that could change everything.

Behind them, the memorial tiles gleamed in weak February sunlight. Sarah Smith. Alice Ayres. Ordinary people who'd died saving others, commemorated in Victorian pottery for over a century.

Alex looked down at the USB drive in her hand.

Elizabeth Chen had spent forty years dismissed, alone, documenting truth no one believed.

James Wickham had died three days after trying to force that truth into the open.

Victoria Mills had hidden for three decades before finally finding the courage—or the exhaustion—to hand off her burden.

Now it was Alex's turn. To decide what mattered more: safety or truth. Silence or vindication.

She pocketed the drive and the phone.

Somewhere in London, people who'd killed to protect quantum wine secrets were doing what they did. Watching. Waiting. Planning.

Alex had forty-eight hours, maybe less, before they came for her.

She'd better make them count.

## 7 / THE DATA

SATURDAY, 15 FEBRUARY 2025

1:15 PM

THE PRINT SHOP was called QuickCopy and smelled of toner and recycled paper. It occupied a corner unit on King William Street, one of those anonymous service businesses that survived on corporate accounts and last-minute dissertation printing.

Alex, Sophie, and Emma arrived just after one, the USB drive feeling like a lead weight in Alex's coat pocket.

"We need five copies," Sophie said to the teenager behind the counter. "Printed and saved to USB drives."

The teenager—name tag reading "Josh"—barely looked up from his phone. "Data transfer station's in the back. Three quid per drive, seven pence per page printed. Pay when you're done."

They found the station: an ancient Dell computer surrounded by a rack of blank USB drives in plastic packaging. Emma fed coins into the vending machine, purchased five drives.

"Wait," Alex said, before Sophie could plug in Victoria's drive.

"What if there's tracking software? What if plugging it in sends a signal?"

Sophie's hand froze halfway to the USB port. "Victoria said to make copies immediately. She wouldn't have given it to you if it was tracked."

"She also said people are trying to kill us. We should be paranoid." Alex looked at Emma. "Is there a way to check?"

Emma thought for a moment. "These computers probably have security software. Josh might be able to scan it first."

They called Josh over. He shuffled to the back room with the practised boredom of someone who'd seen everything, inserted the USB drive, clicked through menus. "Running a full scan. Takes like five minutes."

They waited. Alex checked her phone: no messages. No unknown numbers. But she kept glancing at the shop's entrance, watching everyone who walked past on King William Street. Tourists. Office workers. Any of them could be watching.

"All clean," Josh announced. "Just PDF files, Word docs, some Excel spreadsheets. No executables, no weird code. You're good."

Alex exhaled. "Thank you."

"Whatever." Josh returned to his phone.

They opened the first file:

*Quantum_Wine_Overview_VM_1995.pdf*

Alex read the first paragraph aloud, quietly:

*This document represents fifteen years of research (1980-1995) into quantum-coherent phenolic networks in aged wine. The phenomenon documented herein was initially dismissed by mainstream wine science and physics as measurement error or pseudoscience. It is not. Quantum wine is real, replicable under controlled conditions, and has applications far beyond oenology.*

*What follows is the mechanism, the methodology for identification, and the reasons I destroyed my primary research notes and disappeared. If you're reading this, James Wickham has likely made*

*his move. Which means he's likely dead. I'm sorry I wasn't there to protect him. But perhaps you can finish what we started.*
 *—Dr Victoria Mills, March 1995*

Sophie's breath caught. "March 1995. The month she walked away."

Alex scrolled down. The document was 127 pages. Dense scientific writing interspersed with chemical diagrams, statistical analyses, and photographs of wine bottles, vineyards, laboratory equipment.

"We can't read all this now," Emma said practically. "Make the copies first. Read later, somewhere safe."

She was right. Alex copied everything—PDFs, Word documents, Excel spreadsheets—onto all five USB drives. The progress bar crawled across the screen. Three minutes. Five. Seven.

Whilst the files transferred, Alex skimmed the directory:

**Files on Victoria's Drive:**

- Quantum_Wine_Overview_VM_1995.pdf (127 pages)
- Mechanism_Technical_Explanation.pdf (43 pages)
- Terroir_Analysis_QW_Regions.xlsx (Excel spreadsheet)
- Identification_Protocol_90percent.pdf (23 pages)
- Subject_Sensitivity_Study.pdf (31 pages)
- Applications_Memory_Transfer.pdf (56 pages)
- Weaponisation_Research_Notes.docx (89 pages)
- Warning_For_James.pdf (3 pages)
- Apology_To_Elizabeth.pdf (2 pages)
- If_You're_Reading_This.pdf (5 pages)

Plus forty-seven supporting files: photographs, data tables, scanned handwritten notes, chemical analyses.

"Jesus," Sophie whispered. "This is everything. Her entire career in a hundred gigabytes."

The file transfer completed. Alex ejected the drives, pocketed the original and one copy, handed two copies to Sophie and two to Emma.

"Keep them separate," Alex said. "Different locations. If something happens to one—"

"We have backups," Emma finished. "I'll put one in my office, one at my mum's house."

"I'll hide one at work, one at my flat," Sophie said.

Alex kept the original. "I'm reading this tonight. All of it. We need to understand the mechanism before we do anything else."

They paid Josh—£43 for five USB drives and 400 pages of printing—and left the shop carrying three thick folders of paper that could change everything.

Outside, the February afternoon had turned colder. Grey clouds threatened rain. Alex pulled her coat tighter, scanning King William Street.

"Anyone following us?" Emma asked quietly.

"I don't know. I've never done this before." Alex felt absurd—like a character in a spy film, not a wine writer carrying research papers.

But Wickham was dead. Victoria had been terrified enough to hide for thirty years.

"Tube station's nearby," Sophie said. "We should split up. Three different directions. Harder to follow all of us."

"Good thinking." Emma squeezed Alex's hand. "Text when you're home?"

"I will."

They separated at Bank station—Sophie towards the Northern Line south, Emma towards the Circle Line east, Alex towards the Northern Line north. Alex watched them disappear into the crowd, then descended into the Tube.

## 2:30 PM

The platform was moderately busy for a Saturday afternoon. Tourists with shopping bags, couples heading to museums, a busker playing violin badly. Normal London life continuing whilst Alex carried data that powerful people would kill to suppress.

She positioned herself against a pillar where she could watch both entrances. No one seemed to be watching her. No one seemed to care about the woman in the navy coat clutching a folder and shoulder bag.

The train arrived. She boarded, found a seat, opened the folder.

*Quantum Wine Overview* was written in Victoria's precise, scientific prose. Alex read whilst stations blurred past: Bank, Moorgate, Old Street, Angel.

THE MECHANISM (Simplified Version):

*Wine ages through complex chemical reactions. Phenolic compounds—tannins, anthocyanins, flavonoids—polymerise over time, creating larger molecular structures. In conventional wine chemistry, these reactions follow predictable pathways governed by temperature, oxygen exposure, and pH.*

*But in certain wines, under specific conditions, something extraordinary occurs: the phenolic networks achieve quantum coherence.*

*Quantum coherence is the phenomenon whereby particles exist in a superposition of states, maintaining phase relationships across space and time. Until the 1990s, quantum effects were thought confined to near-absolute-zero temperatures and isolated laboratory conditions. But quantum biology has since demonstrated that nature employs quantum mechanics in photosynthesis, bird navigation, enzyme catalysis, and even human olfaction.*

*Wine, it turns out, is an ideal medium for quantum coherence:*

*1. Enclosed system (glass bottle, minimal external interference)*

*2. Dark storage (prevents decoherence from photon interaction) 3.*

*Stable temperature (reduces thermal noise) 4. Complex organic matrix (phenolic networks form quantum-coupled systems) 5. Time (coherence stabilises over 10-40 years)*

*The phenolic molecules in quantum-active wines form entangled networks—not metaphorically entangled, but genuinely quantum-mechanically entangled. Information encoded in one part of the network affects the entire system non-locally.*

*And here's where it becomes astonishing: these networks can store information patterns from the environment during critical formation periods—harvest, fermentation, early ageing. Patterns that include electromagnetic signatures, chemical traces, and (we theorise) consciousness imprints from humans in close proximity.*

*When a sensitive individual consumes quantum wine, the phenolic compounds interact with receptors in the brain—particularly the gustatory cortex, olfactory bulb, and hippocampus. The quantum information encoded in the wine transfers to neural networks, manifesting as vivid sensory memories that feel "real" because, in a quantum sense, they are real. The drinker experiences stored patterns from decades ago.*

*It's not telepathy. It's not magic. It's quantum information transfer through organic chemistry.*

*And it's terrifyingly easy to exploit.*

Alex looked up. She'd missed her stop. Highbury & Islington—one station too far.

She got off, crossed the platform, caught the southbound train back to Angel. Her hands were shaking.

Victoria had done it. She'd explained the mechanism in terms that made sense. Terrifying, paradigm-shifting, revolutionary sense.

Her phone buzzed. Emma:

How are you? Where are you?

Alex:

On my way home. Reading Victoria's
overview. It's... extraordinary.

Emma:

Are you safe?

Alex:

Yes. Going straight home. I love you.

Emma:

Love you too. Be careful.

Alex pocketed her phone, kept reading.

## SATURDAY AFTERNOON, 15 FEBRUARY 2025

## 3:30 PM

## ALEX'S FLAT, ISLINGTON

By the time Alex reached her flat in Islington, she'd read seventy-three pages and her brain felt like it was overheating.

Victoria's research was exhaustive. The technical explanation included quantum field theory equations, spectroscopy data, chemical pathway diagrams. The terroir analysis mapped every known quantum-active wine region: Hunter Valley (volcanic/alluvial sedimentary), Bordeaux (iron-rich gravel), Napa (volcanic), Barossa (ancient schist), Central Otago (schist/quartz).

The common factors Elizabeth Chen had identified were all validated by Victoria's fifteen years of controlled experiments: ancient soils, high transition metals (iron, copper, manganese) plus rare earth elements (lanthanum, cerium, neodymium), minimal intervention winemaking, indigenous yeasts, no filtration, extended ageing in controlled darkness.

And the identification protocol—Victoria's "ninety-percent accuracy" method—was detailed and replicable. Spectroscopic analysis at specific wavelengths, quantum entanglement tests using EPR correlation measurements, even a tasting protocol for human subjects.

*Subject Sensitivity Study* explained why only some people experienced quantum wine effects:

*Approximately 8-12% of the population possesses heightened sensitivity to quantum-coherent compounds. This correlates with:*

*1. Professional wine tasters (trained palate, enhanced olfactory sensitivity) 2. Individuals with enhanced gustatory receptors (supertasters) 3. People with synesthesia or other cross-modal sensory processing 4. Genetic variants in TAS2R bitter taste receptors and OR olfactory receptors*

*Sensitivity can be enhanced through training, but baseline genetic predisposition is required. Not everyone can experience quantum wine, just as not everyone has perfect pitch.*

That explained why only Alex and Sophie—and possibly a few others at Wickham's tasting—had experienced the 1986 Tyrrell's. They were genetically sensitive. Trained tasters. The right biology meeting the right wine.

Alex was so absorbed she didn't notice the man across the street until she was at her front door, keys in hand.

He stood on the opposite pavement. Perhaps forty, dark coat, holding a newspaper. Not reading it. Just standing there. Looking directly at her building.

Watching.

Alex's blood went cold. She forced herself not to stare. Unlocked the door with shaking hands, stepped inside, closed it. Counted to five. Then looked through the door's glass panel.

The man was still there. Same position. Same newspaper. Same fixed attention on her building.

Meridian. It had to be.

She climbed the stairs to Flat 3, fumbled with the second lock. The flat was empty—Emma wouldn't be home for hours. She'd gone to her office in Shoreditch first to hide one USB, then on to her mum's in Islington with the other.

Alex locked the door, engaged the chain, checked every window.

The man was still across the street. Pretending to read. Watching.

She pulled the curtains closed, double-checked all the locks, then called Sophie.

"Did you get home okay?" Alex asked.

"Just walked in. Alex, there's a black car parked outside my building. Two men inside. They've been there since I arrived."

"Same here. One man across the street. They're watching us."

"Christ." Sophie's voice was tight. "What do we do?"

"I'm reading everything now. All of Victoria's research. Understanding what we have."

"Can you come here? Bring your copies. We'll go through it together, decide what to do."

"Give me forty-five minutes. I'll come through the back streets, see if I can lose anyone following."

"Be careful."

"You too."

Alex hung up, made tea with shaking hands, settled at the kitchen table with Victoria's printed research.

She kept reading.


4:30 PM

*Applications_Memory_Transfer.pdf* was fascinating and horrifying in equal measure.

Victoria had been tasked with exploring how quantum wine could be used for intelligence gathering, interrogation, psychological manipulation. The theory: if wine could store memories, could it be engineered to extract specific information from a target? Could false memories be implanted through carefully designed quantum-active wines?

Victoria's fifteen years had produced mixed results:

*Memory extraction through quantum wine is theoretically possible but practically unreliable. The information encoded in wine is ambient—environmental patterns, emotional states, sensory data from the vineyard and winemaking process. It's not targeted. You cannot engineer a wine to extract, for example, nuclear launch codes from a subject's mind.*

*However, emotional manipulation is frighteningly effective. Quantum wines encode emotional states from their creation environment. A wine made during fear, anger, or joy will transfer those emotional patterns to sensitive drinkers. Applications include:*

*1. Interrogation (inducing anxiety, compliance, trust) 2. Negotiation (creating positive emotional states) 3. Psychological warfare (trauma implantation) 4. False confession generation (subjects "remember" events that never occurred)*

*I refused to continue this research in 1995 when I realised what they intended. They wanted to create wines that could make subjects believe they had committed crimes, witnessed events, experienced abuse. Perfect tools for destroying reputations, generating false testimony, manipulating legal proceedings.*

*I destroyed my most dangerous findings. But the theoretical framework remains. Someone with sufficient resources and amorality could recreate my work.*

*That's why I disappeared. That's why quantum wine must remain secret until proper ethical frameworks exist. The applications are too dangerous.*

*But James believes transparency is the only defence. Make it public, make it impossible to monopolise. Perhaps he's right. Perhaps I've been a coward.*

Alex set down the paper, feeling sick.

Wickham had tried to make it public. He'd assembled quantum wines, invited sensitive tasters, created proof.

And they'd killed him for it.

They—Meridian, or whoever they were—wanted quantum wine kept secret. Wanted control of the knowledge, the wines, the applications. Wanted to use it for interrogation, manipulation, control.

Victoria had escaped. But she'd given Alex the keys to everything.

Which meant Alex was now a target.

## 5:20 PM

The buzzer rang.

Alex jumped, nearly spilling her tea. She checked the intercom camera: Sophie, looking pale and frightened.

She buzzed her up, unchained the door, stood in the doorway until Sophie appeared on the landing.

"They're still there," Sophie said without preamble. "The two men. I watched from my window for ten minutes—they never moved."

"Did they see you leave?"

"I went out the back way, through the service entrance. Took side streets the whole way." Sophie shook her head. "But Alex, they know where we live. They know everything."

They locked themselves in. Checked the curtains were still closed, checked windows. Then spread Victoria's research across the kitchen table.

"What have you read so far?" Sophie asked.

"Overview, mechanism, sensitivity study, memory transfer applications." Alex pushed the weaponisation file towards her. "This one's the worst. What they wanted Victoria to create. What they're still trying to create."

Sophie picked it up, started reading. Her face went progressively paler.

Ten minutes later: "Bloody hell. They wanted to use wine to implant false memories? To extract information? To manipulate emotions?"

"That's why they killed Wickham. Why they'll kill anyone who tries to expose this. They want monopoly control over weaponised quantum wine."

"We can't let them have it."

"We can't. Which means we go public. All of it. Make it impossible for them to control."

Sophie set down the file. "What about the dangers? What Victoria wrote about weaponisation being too easy once the knowledge is public?"

"If we don't go public, Meridian completes the work in secret. If we do, at least there's transparency. Oversight. Other scientists can work on defences, regulations." Alex met Sophie's eyes. "It's not perfect. But it's better than monopoly."

Sophie nodded slowly. "Agreed. So what's our plan?"

"We need scientific validation. Someone credible who can verify Victoria's work. Someone who gives us legitimacy."

"The researchers Victoria mentioned—Moreau, Webb, Kimura. They're presenting at the Bordeaux conference. They're ready to fight."

Alex opened Victoria's final file on her laptop: *If_You're_Reading_This.pdf*. Contact information for all three researchers.

"We try calling them. See who answers. Build an alliance." Alex checked the time: 5:35 PM. "France is an hour ahead—6:35 PM there. Australia is eleven hours ahead—4:35 AM Sunday. New Zealand is thirteen hours ahead—6:35 AM Sunday."

"Try France first. Then New Zealand."

Alex dialled Philippe Moreau.

The phone rang. And rang. And rang. No answer. No voicemail.

"He might be at dinner," Sophie said.

Alex tried Sarah Kimura in New Zealand. The phone rang once, then straight to automated message: "The number you have dialled is not available."

"That's odd." Alex tried again. Same result.

"Technical issue maybe?"

"Maybe." But Alex's stomach was tight with unease.

She opened her laptop, pulled up Marcus Webb's contact info from Victoria's files. "I'm going to email Webb. Australia's the middle of the night, but we can't wait."

She typed carefully:

*Dr Webb,*

*My name is Alex Hartley. I'm a wine writer in London. Victoria Mills gave me her complete research files today—everything from her fifteen years at the private lab. I experienced quantum wine myself on Thursday at James Wickham's tasting (1986 Tyrrell's Vat 1). So did Sophie Chen, Elizabeth Chen's granddaughter.*

*We need your help. We're going public with Victoria's research but need scientific validation. Can you provide secure file transfer method? This is urgent.*

*—Alex Hartley*

She added her phone number, hit send.

"Now what?" Sophie asked.

"We keep reading. Understand everything. Be ready to move fast when Webb responds."

They read together for the next forty-five minutes. Victoria's *Weaponisation_Research_Notes* was eighty-nine pages of classified work organised by application:

***Memory Extraction (65% success rate):*** *Wines fermented under specific emotional conditions enhanced recall of corresponding* *memories. Stress-fermented wines amplified stress memories. Joy-harvest wines amplified happy memories.*

***Emotional Manipulation (78% success rate):*** *By controlling harvest environment and fermentation conditions, Victoria had created wines that reliably induced specific emotional states—trust, fear, compliance, euphoria.*

***False Memory Implantation (43% success rate):*** *The most disturbing. In about half her trials, Victoria had created wines that implanted false sensory memories. Subjects would "remember" events that never occurred.*

***Memory Suppression (31% success rate):*** *Some quantum wines suppressed access to specific memories, creating temporary amnesia.*

***Dependency Creation (Failed—abandoned as too dangerous):*** *Victoria had detected early signs that quantum wines could create psychological dependency. She'd abandoned this line. But the theoretical framework remained.*

"Christ," Sophie whispered. "These aren't wines. They're weapons."

"Which is exactly why we need to go public. Make it impossible for them to weaponise in secret."

## 6:20 PM

Alex's phone rang. Unknown number.

Her stomach dropped. She answered on speaker.

A woman's voice, professional and cold: "Ms Hartley. Ms Chen. I assume you're together—we saw Ms Chen enter your building an hour ago."

Alex's blood froze. They'd been watching. Tracking Sophie's arrival.

"Who are you?" Alex demanded.

"My name is Dr Caroline Reeves. I'm Director of Research Acquisition for Meridian. Dr Mills gave you materials that belong to us. Materials created under contract during her employment from 1980 to 1995. We want them back."

"Victoria destroyed her notes when she left."

"She destroyed her lab notes. But she kept personal copies. Copies she had no legal right to retain." Dr Reeves's voice was utterly calm, utterly reasonable. "We're not unreasonable people, Ms Hartley. We'll compensate you for your time and trouble. Fifty thousand pounds each. Cash. In exchange for all copies of Dr Mills's research. The USB drives, the printed documents, any digital files. Everything."

"That's a bribe," Sophie said.

"That's compensation for stolen property." A pause. "We know you've read enough to understand what's at stake. This research has national security implications. Applications beyond wine science. We need to ensure it doesn't fall into the wrong hands."

"Your hands sound like the wrong hands," Alex said.

Dr Reeves laughed—oddly genuine. "You have spirit. I appreciate that. But Ms Hartley, Ms Chen—you're out of your depth. This isn't about wine anymore. This is about technology that could reshape intelligence gathering, legal proceedings, diplomatic negotiations. Technology worth billions. Technology that powerful governments would kill to possess."

"Like you killed James Wickham?"

Silence. Then: "Mr Wickham died of a heart attack. Natural causes. The police will confirm this eventually."

"Morrison said it was suspicious."

"Detective Inspector Morrison is thorough. I respect that. But she'll find no evidence connecting his death to Meridian. We're very careful." The implicit threat was clear: *We killed him and got away with it.*

"Monday, five PM," Dr Reeves continued. "Bring all copies to the following address." She rattled off a location in Canary Wharf. "Fifty thousand pounds each. You walk away wealthy and alive. Or you keep the research, and we take other measures. Your choice."

"What other measures?" Alex asked.

"The kind involving lawyers, lawsuits, frozen bank accounts, destroyed careers, criminal charges for theft of classified materials. We have very good lawyers, Ms Hartley. We've been protecting this research for forty years. We're not going to let two wine enthusiasts compromise national security."

"You're threatening us."

"I'm offering you a generous exit. Take it." Dr Reeves's voice hardened. "You have until Monday, five PM. Use your time wisely."

The call ended.

Alex and Sophie stared at each other.

"National security," Sophie said. "If they can prove government contracts, classified status—"

"We'd be criminals. Theft of state secrets." Alex felt the trap closing. "We can't give them the data. But if we don't, they'll destroy us legally. Or just kill us."

"Then we go public before Monday. Upload everything tonight. Make it impossible to suppress."

"Without scientific validation? Anonymous internet posts get dismissed as conspiracy theories." Alex shook her head. "We need Webb. We need credibility."

"We might not have time for credibility."

Alex's phone buzzed. Emma:

> Should I come home? It's after six. What's happening?

Alex typed:

Don't come home tonight. Please. Men are
watching this building. Stay at your mum's.
I'll explain tomorrow. I love you.

Emma:

You're scaring me.

Alex:

I know. I'm sorry. Stay safe. Please.

Long pause. Then:

Fine. But tomorrow morning we're calling
Morrison. First thing. Promise me.

Alex:

I promise. I love you.

Emma:

I love you too.

Alex set down her phone. Tomorrow. Less than forty hours until
Meridian's Monday deadline. They needed Webb's help now.

"Let me check email," Sophie said, pulling her laptop closer.

Nothing from Webb.

"It's the middle of the night there," Alex said. "He won't see it
until morning."

"Then we keep reading. Understand everything. Be ready."

They pulled up the next file: *Warning_For_James.pdf*. Only three
pages. Dated February 10, 2025—three days before the tasting.

Alex read aloud:

*James,*

*I'm writing this because I know you won't listen if I call. You never did listen when you thought you were right.*

*Don't do the tasting. Don't assemble those wines. Don't invite those people. You're painting a target on everyone who experiences the quantum effect. They're watching for exactly this kind of gathering. They've been hunting quantum-active wines for thirty years. A vertical tasting at your residence? With two dozen witnesses? They'll know. They'll come.*

*I understand why you want to go public. I understand your logic: transparency as protection, proof as defence. Make it impossible to suppress by making it undeniable. But James, they don't need to suppress the science. They just need to suppress the scientists.*

*They killed Philippe Moreau's assistant in 1998. Made it look like a car accident. They killed Sarah Kimura's research partner in 2016. "Suicide." Sarah herself disappeared shortly after—we never confirmed whether they got to her or whether she went into hiding. They've been eliminating anyone who gets too close for forty years.*

*If you do this tasting, if you prove quantum wine to two dozen witnesses, you're signing your own death warrant.*

*Please. I'm begging you. Don't do this. Wait. Let the Bordeaux conference happen in June. Let Philippe and Marcus present their findings. You don't have to be the martyr.*

*But if you're reading this, you've already made your decision. Which means I'm probably too late. Which means you're probably already dead.*

*I'm sorry I wasn't brave enough to stand with you. I'm sorry I hid for thirty years whilst you kept fighting.*

*I hope whoever you chose to inherit this research is braver than I was.*

*—Victoria*

Sophie stared at the screen. "She warned him. Three days before. And he did it anyway."

"He chose to be the martyr. To force quantum wine into the open even if it cost his life."

"And now we've inherited that burden."

They sat in silence, surrounded by forty years of suppressed research.

"We should try Moreau and Kimura again," Alex said.

Sophie nodded. Alex tried both numbers. Moreau: no answer. Kimura: phone not available.

"Same as before." Alex's unease was growing. "Something's wrong."

"Maybe they're just unavailable. Weekend, different time zones—"

"Or Meridian got to them first."

The words hung in the air.


## 7:15 PM

Sophie's laptop chimed. "Email. From Webb."

She opened it:

*Ms Hartley,*

*Received your message. Victoria alive—that's good news. I'm devastated to hear about James.*

*I can help. Here's a secure file transfer service—Tor-routed, end-to-end encrypted, no metadata trail. Upload everything there. I'll distribute to trusted colleagues (quantum physicists, biochemists) through similar channels. If Victoria's science is solid, we'll have preliminary verification by Sunday afternoon your time.*

*Be careful. Meridian doesn't negotiate in good faith. Don't trust them. Don't meet them.*

*More soon. Stay alive.*

*—Marcus Webb*

The email included a link and access credentials.

"He's in," Sophie said. "He's helping."

"Upload everything. Now. Before something happens."

Sophie began the upload whilst Alex kept reading. Her eyes were burning from staring at documents, her brain overloaded with quantum mechanics and weaponisation protocols and forty years of suppressed science.

At 7:25, Alex's phone buzzed. Text from unknown number:

> Ms Hartley. You left QuickCopy on King William Street at 1:47 PM with five USB drives and 400 printed pages. Documents that don't belong to you. Dr Mills had no right to share that research. Return all copies by Monday 5 PM or face legal action. We know you kept one copy, gave two to Ms Chen, two to Ms Lawson. This is your only warning. —Legal representative of Meridian Research Group

Alex screenshot it, showed Sophie.

"They've been watching," Sophie whispered. "Everything. They know exactly what we did."

"Real-time surveillance." Alex stared at the message. Sophie's upload bar showed 87% complete. "They know where the copies are."

Alex replied:

> We don't have what you're looking for.

Response within seconds:

> Don't insult our intelligence. We have CCTV footage from QuickCopy. We know Ms Lawson has two copies—one at her office in Shoreditch, one at her mother's house in Islington. Return the data. No one gets hurt. Keep it, you'll regret it.

Not a legal threat. A physical one.

Alex's stomach lurched. They'd followed Emma. Tracked her across London—to her office, to her mum's house. They knew everywhere she'd been. And Emma was still there. At a location Meridian had identified.

She grabbed her phone, texted Emma:

> Are you safe? Lock the doors. Don't go out tonight.

No immediate reply.

"That's it," Alex said, voice shaking. "We're targets. All of us. They've been following Emma too—they know exactly where she went this afternoon."

"Then we work faster." Sophie's upload completed. "Webb has everything. His colleagues can verify overnight."

"And then what? We go public Monday night before their deadline?"

"If the science holds up, yes. Coordinated release across multiple platforms. Make it impossible to suppress."

Alex checked the time: 7:35 PM.

She pulled up news sites, searching for anything about quantum wine researchers. Scrolled through French sources.

There.

Posted at 6:47 PM (5:47 PM UK time):

**BREAKING: Prominent Wine Researcher Found Dead in Bordeaux**

*Dr Philippe Moreau, 71, a respected wine scientist at ISVV Bordeaux, was found dead in his home Friday evening. French authorities are investigating. Dr Moreau was scheduled to present research at the upcoming International Wine Science Conference in June.*

*Colleagues describe Dr Moreau as dedicated and passionate. The cause of death has not been released.*

Alex's hands went numb.

"Sophie. Look."

Sophie read the article. Her face drained of colour.

"They killed him," she whispered. "Philippe Moreau. One of the original researchers. They killed him Friday evening—the day after Wickham."

"Before he could present at the Bordeaux conference." Alex's mind raced. "They're eliminating everyone. Wickham Thursday. Moreau Friday. If they're following the pattern—"

"Kimura's next. And Webb."

"We need to warn Webb. Now."

Alex pulled out her phone, checked the time: 7:45 PM London. That made it 6:45 AM Sunday in Sydney.

Early, but not obscenely early. Webb might be awake.

She found his number in Victoria's files.

"What are you doing?" Sophie asked.

"Calling for help. Warning Webb. Building an alliance before they eliminate everyone."

She dialled Marcus Webb in Australia.

⬜

## 8 / ALLIANCE



7:47 PM

THE PHONE RANG four times before a man answered, his voice tense, carrying an Australian accent.

"Yeah?"

"Dr Webb? It's Alex Hartley. We just got your email—the secure transfer details."

"Good. Use them." A pause. "But I'm guessing that's not why you're ringing at this hour."

"No. Philippe Moreau is dead."

Sharp intake of breath. Then silence.

Alex could hear movement—Webb walking somewhere private, a door closing.

"When?" His voice had gone hard.

"Friday evening. They're saying heart attack. But—"

"Bollocks. Philippe ran marathons. Fittest bloke I knew." Webb's voice went hard. "They killed him."

"We think so. The same people who killed James Wickham. The

same people who've been suppressing quantum wine research for forty years."

"And you're ringing me why? To tell me I'm next on the list?" Webb's voice was bitter. "I already know. I've had a car parked outside my house since Thursday. Two men, shifts every eight hours. They're not even hiding anymore."

"Because we're going to fight back," Alex said. "Victoria gave me everything. The mechanism, the terroir analysis, the identification protocols, the weaponisation research. Everything they've been trying to keep secret. And we're going public with it."

Webb laughed—a short, harsh sound. "You're going to get yourself killed."

"Maybe. But I'm going to prove quantum wine exists first. And I need your help."

"What makes you think I can help? I stopped publishing twelve years ago. I keep my head down. I teach undergrads about phenolic compounds and pH levels. I'm no threat to anyone."

"But you were. You published in 2008. You documented quantum correlations in Semillon ageing. You're one of the original researchers. You know it's real."

"Knowing and proving are different things." A pause. "What do you want from me?"

"Your data. Your expertise. And I want you to co-author what we publish. You, me, Sophie Chen—Elizabeth's granddaughter—and whoever else will stand with us. We make it impossible to dismiss by making it comprehensive."

"Wait—Sophie Chen is Elizabeth's granddaughter?" Webb's voice softened. "I saw her name on the email but didn't make the connection. Christ, I haven't thought about Elizabeth in years. How is she?"

"Dead. Cancer, 2022."

"Bugger." Genuine grief in his voice. "Elizabeth was brilliant. Best wine scientist I ever met. They destroyed her for telling the truth."

"Which is why we're going to vindicate her. Publicly. Scientifically. Before anyone else dies." Alex looked at Sophie, who was watching intently. "Dr Webb, you have a choice. Hide and hope they leave you alone. Or help us prove Elizabeth was right."

Silence stretched. Alex could hear Webb breathing, thinking.

"If I do this," he said finally, "I'm dead. You understand that? The moment I go public, I'm a target. They'll come for me like they came for Philippe."

"Probably. But you're a target anyway. The car outside your house proves that. At least this way, your death would mean something."

"That's a hell of a pitch."

"It's the only pitch I have."

Webb was quiet for another moment. Then: "What's your plan? Specifically. I'm not committing academic suicide without knowing the strategy."

Alex glanced at Sophie, who nodded encouragingly. "We have until Monday 5 PM London time to decide. That's when Meridian Research Group wants Victoria's data returned. We're either giving it back and taking their money, or we're going public before they can stop us."

"Meridian. Jesus. You've really pissed off the wrong people."

"Do you know them?"

"Know of them. Private research firm. Government contracts. Intelligence community connections. They're the ones who've been hunting quantum wines since the eighties. They funded Victoria's work. And when she left, they made sure no one else could continue openly."

"How do you know this?"

"Because they approached me in 2009. Right after my paper. Offered me funding, lab space, whatever I needed. All I had to do was stop publishing and work for them exclusively." Webb's voice hardened. "I said no. Two months later, my lab flooded. 'Accident.'

Lost ten years of samples. Lost my funding. Lost my reputation when I couldn't replicate my results without the samples."

"They destroyed your career."

"They sent a message. Stay quiet or face consequences. I stayed quiet. Taught classes. Kept my head down. And I'm still alive, which is more than I can say for Philippe."

"Which is why going public might actually be safer. Make yourself too visible to kill quietly."

"Or make yourself an irresistible target." Webb sighed. "But you're right. I'm already a target. At least this way, I go down swinging."

"So you'll help?"

"I'll help. But Hartley—if we're doing this, we do it right. Proper peer review. Multiple independent verifications. We don't just dump data on the internet and hope people believe us. We make it scientifically bulletproof."

"Which takes time we don't have."

"Then we compress the timeline. My colleagues—the ones I mentioned in the email—they'll review Victoria's work fast. If the data's strong enough, we get preliminary verification. Then we go public with scientific backing, not just anecdotal evidence."

"You really think they'll help?"

"I think they owe me favours. But Hartley—this is a long shot. Most scientists won't touch anything that sounds like pseudoscience. Quantum wine has been dismissed for forty years. Convincing people otherwise in forty-eight hours? Nearly impossible."

"Nearly impossible is better than completely impossible."

Webb laughed. "I like you. You're either very brave or very stupid."

"Probably both."

"Good. You'll need both." A pause. "Use that secure link I sent—upload everything as soon as we're off the phone. And Hartley? Watch your back. Meridian will do anything to get that research back."

"They've already offered us money. Fifty thousand pounds each."

"Don't take it. It's a trap." Webb's voice went cold. "You show up to collect that money, you disappear. Tragic accident. Happens all the time. Understood?"

"Understood."

"Good. Now let me get to work. If the science is solid—if Victoria's work holds up under review—we'll have a chance. If not..." He didn't finish the sentence. "Thank you, Dr Webb. Seriously. Thank you."

"Don't thank me yet. We're all probably going to die. But at least we'll die proving Elizabeth was right." He paused. "Tell Sophie—Elizabeth's granddaughter—tell her I'm sorry. Sorry we couldn't protect her grandmother. Sorry the field treated Elizabeth the way they did. She deserved better."

"You can tell her yourself. She's right here."

Alex handed the phone to Sophie.

"Dr Webb?" Sophie's voice was tight with emotion. "This is Sophie Chen."

"Sophie. Good God. I remember when Elizabeth used to bring you to conferences when you were small. You can't have been more than five or six."

Sophie's eyes filled with tears. "I remember. Barely. The smell of wine labs. Grandmother letting me taste grape juice from the press. She'd explain fermentation like it was magic."

"She loved you very much. Talked about you constantly. You were her hope—proof that her work would outlast the dismissal, that someone would carry it forward." Webb's voice caught. "I'm sorry I lost touch with her after they destroyed her career. I should have done more. Should have stood with her."

"You're standing with her now. That's what matters." Sophie wiped her eyes. "Dr Webb, I grew up watching people dismiss my grandmother. Watching her work alone, believing something no one else would believe. Watching it slowly kill her spirit even before the cancer came. And now I know she was right. We both experienced it

—Alex and I. We stood in that vineyard with her. We heard her voice. We know quantum wine is real."

"Then we make the world know it too. Get me that data. We'll make Elizabeth's legacy count for something."

"Thank you. That means more than you know."

Sophie handed the phone back to Alex. Webb's voice was gruff: "Take care of that girl. She's carrying a hell of a burden."

"I will."

"And Hartley? One more thing. Sarah Kimura. The New Zealand researcher. Have you contacted her?"

"We tried. The number in Victoria's files is disconnected."

"That's her old university line. I have her mobile." Webb paused. "I think she'll be dead by tomorrow if we don't warn her. She was Philippe's co-author on the conference paper. If they killed him, they'll kill her next. She needs to know she's in danger. I'll text you her number. Ring her. Now. Don't wait."

The line went dead.

Alex looked at Sophie. "Kimura. Webb thinks she's next."

Sophie checked the time. "It's eight AM Sunday morning in New Zealand." Her phone buzzed. "That's her number now."

Alex dialled immediately.

The phone rang. And rang. And rang.

Voicemail: *You've reached Dr Sarah Kimura. I'm unable to take your call. Please leave a message.*

"Dr Kimura, this is Alex Hartley ringing from London. I'm a wine writer investigating quantum wine research. Philippe Moreau has been killed. We believe you may be in danger. Please ring me back immediately. It's urgent."

She left her number, ended the call.

"She might just be sleeping," Sophie said. "Or out. It's Sunday morning."

"Or she's already dead." Alex set down her phone. "Three of the original researchers. Wickham, Moreau, maybe Kimura. That leaves

Webb and Victoria. Webb has surveillance outside his house. Victoria's in hiding."

"And us. We're researchers now too, whether we wanted to be or not." Sophie pulled up her laptop. "I'm uploading to Webb's secure link now." The progress bar crawled across the screen. Forty-seven files. Three gigabytes of data. Victoria's entire career being transmitted through encrypted channels.

Whilst the upload ran, Alex checked her phone. A text from Emma:

> Staying at Mum's tonight. Went to the office
> first, then here. Doors locked. Are you
> okay? What's going on?

The "Doors locked" meant Emma had got her earlier message. Small comfort — Meridian knew that address. But telling Emma she'd been followed would only terrify her more. Better one night of ignorance than one night of panic.

Alex typed:

> I'm safe. Sophie's here. Stay there tonight.
> I'll explain everything tomorrow morning. I
> promise.

Long pause. Then:

> Okay. But we're calling Morrison first thing.
> You promised.

> I know. First thing. I love you.

> Love you too. Please be careful.

Alex set down her phone, feeling the weight of that promise.

"Done," Sophie said after ten minutes. "Webb has everything."

"Now we wait."

"And write." Sophie pulled up their draft paper. "If Webb's

colleagues verify the science, we need to be ready to publish immediately. Monday afternoon at the latest. That gives us until tomorrow evening to make this paper perfect."

They worked through the evening. Alex drafted sections on the mechanism whilst Sophie compiled Elizabeth's observational data spanning forty years. They cross-referenced Victoria's experimental results with Webb's 2008 paper, building a comprehensive picture of quantum wine research from multiple independent sources.

Sophie paused mid-sentence, staring at her screen. "Wait—Alex, look at this." She angled her laptop. "I've been mapping Elizabeth's observations against Victoria's experimental data. Every quantum-active wine Elizabeth documented corresponds to specific harvest conditions Victoria identified—temperature spikes above thirty-five degrees, rapid fermentation starts, specific phenolic concentrations. It's not random. There's a formula here." She pulled up three spreadsheets side by side. "If we can identify the exact parameters, we could predict which vintages will develop quantum coherence. Elizabeth knew this. She was documenting the pattern for forty years."

Alex leaned over, studying the correlations. The pattern was undeniable—Elizabeth's forty years of observations weren't just documentation, they were systematic data collection proving specific environmental conditions created quantum-active wines. "This needs to go in the paper. This is the bridge between Elizabeth's field observations and Victoria's lab results. This is the proof it's replicable."

"If we can predict it," Sophie said slowly, "we can control it. We can tell winemakers exactly what conditions create quantum wine." She met Alex's eyes. "That's what my grandmother wanted. Not just to prove it exists, but to understand it well enough to harness it."

At 9:15, they tried calling Kimura again. Same result—straight to voicemail.

At 10:30, Alex's phone buzzed. Text from Marcus Webb:

Got the files. Distributing to six colleagues
now—three quantum physicists, two
biochemists, one neuroscientist. All sworn
to secrecy until we verify. They're running
their own analyses overnight. We'll have
preliminary verification by tomorrow evening
GMT. If this holds up, we go public Monday
afternoon. Coordinated announcement
across multiple universities simultaneously.
They can't suppress us all. Stay alive until
then. —MW

Alex showed Sophie. "He's doing it. Six independent reviewers overnight."

"My grandmother waited forty years for this. Now we might have verification in twenty-four hours." Sophie's voice shook. "It's happening so fast."

"Because we don't have time for slow. Meridian's deadline is Monday at five. We need to beat it."

They kept writing. By midnight, the paper was eighteen pages. Single-spaced. Dense with citations, chemical formulae, quantum mechanics explanations.

**Title:** *Quantum Coherence in Aged Wine: Mechanism, Evidence, and Implications for Memory Transfer*

**Authors:** Alexandra Hartley, Sophie Chen, Dr Marcus Webb (pending confirmation)

**Abstract:**

*We present evidence for quantum-coherent phenolic networks in aged wines and demonstrate that these networks can store and transfer information patterns including sensory memories and emotional states. This phenomenon, previously dismissed as measurement error or pseudoscience, is supported by fifteen years of controlled experiments (Mills, 1980-1995), forty years of observational data (Chen, 1978-2022), and independent verification from multiple researchers (Moreau 1997, 2002; Webb 2008; Kimura*

*2015). We describe the mechanism, the conditions required for quantum wine formation, the implications for wine science, and the potential applications and dangers of this technology. Given the weaponisation potential and suppression history, we argue for immediate public disclosure and international regulation.*

"It's good," Alex said, reading through one more time. "Really good."

"It's amateur," Sophie said. "We're a wine writer and a sommelier playing at being scientists."

"We're witnesses. We experienced quantum wine. We have Victoria's data. We have Elizabeth's notebooks. We'll have Webb backing us up. That's more than enough."

"If Webb's colleagues verify the science."

"They will." Alex saved the document, backed it up to three different cloud services. "We should sleep. Tomorrow's going to be intense."

Sophie nodded, settled on the sofa with a blanket. "Alex? Thank you. For doing this. For risking everything to vindicate my grandmother."

"Thank you for trusting me with her research."

They turned off the lights. Alex lay in bed, Emma's side empty and cold, staring at the ceiling.

Somewhere in Australia, six scientists were reviewing Victoria's research, deciding whether quantum wine was real or pseudoscience.

Somewhere in London, Meridian was planning their next move.

And somewhere in Alex's mind, the memory of that 1986 Tyrrell's Vat 1 still echoed—Elizabeth Chen's voice in the vineyard, quantum information encoded in wine, impossible and undeniable.

Alex fell asleep somewhere around two AM, dreaming of vineyards and entangled molecules and truth too dangerous to speak.

## SUNDAY, 16 FEBRUARY 2025

### 9:15 AM

Alex woke to grey Sunday morning light and Emma's side of the bed still empty. She'd slept—somehow—from two AM until now, seven hours of exhausted unconsciousness.

Sophie was awake on the sofa, laptop open, refreshing her email every few seconds. Checking for Webb's verification.

Nothing yet. Just waiting.

Alex made coffee, checked her own phone. No messages from Webb. No word from Kimura. Just one text from Emma, sent at 7:30 AM:

> It's Sunday morning. You promised we'd
> call Morrison first thing. Are we doing that?

Alex's stomach dropped. The promise. She'd said "tomorrow morning" meaning Sunday morning. And now it was Sunday morning and they hadn't called.

She rang Emma.

"Hi," Emma answered, voice tight.

"I know. I promised Sunday morning. But Emma—we need to wait for Webb's verification first. We can't go to Morrison with claims that sound insane. We need proof."

"So you're breaking your promise."

"I'm adapting it. We'll still call Morrison. Just... later. After we have scientific validation. Then we go with something she can actually use."

Silence on the line. Then: "You're choosing quantum wine over me again."

"That's not fair."

"Isn't it? Yesterday you promised Sunday morning. Now it's Sunday morning and you're making excuses." Emma's voice cracked. "I can't do this, Alex. I can't keep watching you choose danger over safety. Choose proving something over staying alive."

"Emma, please—"

"I'm still at my mum's. And I need space—to think about whether I can do this. Whether I can watch you self-destruct for quantum wine." A pause. "Call me when you've decided what matters more. The truth you're chasing or the people who love you."

The line went dead.

Alex stood in the kitchen, phone in hand, feeling like she'd been punched.

"She's right," Sophie said quietly. "We did promise. And we're breaking it."

"Because we need proof first."

"Or because we want to be the ones who prove it." Sophie met Alex's eyes. "My grandmother spent forty years dismissed. I want to vindicate her. But Emma's right—we're choosing that over everything else. Over safety. Over the people who love us."

Alex sat down heavily. "What would you do?"

Sophie thought for a long moment. "I'd wait for Webb. Publish with proof. Then go to police." She managed a sad smile. "Which makes me as reckless as you."

Alex texted Emma:

> You're right. I'm sorry. I'm choosing quantum wine over us and it's not fair to you. But I have to finish this. I have to make sure Elizabeth's work means something. I love you.

No response.

The morning dragged on. Alex and Sophie sat at the kitchen table, laptops open, refreshing email every few minutes. Waiting for Webb's verification.

At 11:30, Alex tried calling Kimura again. It rang six times, then voicemail. She didn't leave another message.

"Still no answer," Sophie said. "That's not good."

"Maybe she's ignoring unknown numbers. Or out hiking. It's Sunday."

"Or Meridian got to her first."

They didn't say more. Just kept waiting.

Lunch was sandwiches neither of them wanted. Afternoon tea was tea neither of them drank.

At 2:15 PM, Alex found herself reading Victoria's *Apology_To_Elizabeth.pdf* file. Just two pages. Undated but clearly written during Victoria's years in hiding.

*Elizabeth,*

*I'm sorry.*

*I'm sorry I took Meridian's money when you were being destroyed. I'm sorry I watched them dismiss you as a fraud whilst I continued the research in secret. I'm sorry I built my career on your suffering.*

*You were right. About all of it. Quantum wine is real. The mechanism is exactly what you proposed in 1979. You saw it first, understood it first, published it first. And they destroyed you for it whilst I stayed silent and safe.*

*I told myself I was protecting the research by keeping it classified. That someone needed to continue the work properly, with resources, with scientific rigour. But really I was protecting myself. Protecting my reputation, my funding, my comfort.*

*I'm a coward. I watched you suffer for forty years and did nothing.*

*This apology is worthless. You'll never read it—I'm too afraid to send it. But writing it down feels necessary. An acknowledgment of what I did. Of what I failed to do.*

*I don't expect forgiveness. I don't deserve it.*

*—Victoria*

Alex set down the paper, throat tight.

"What is it?" Sophie asked.

"Victoria wrote an apology to your grandmother. Never sent it. Just kept it in her files for thirty years."

"Can I see?"

Alex handed it over. Sophie read in silence, tears streaming down her face.

"She was ashamed," Sophie whispered. "All those years. Knowing she'd abandoned Grandmother. Knowing she'd chosen safety over truth."

"Like we're doing. Choosing to wait for verification instead of going to police like we promised."

"Maybe. Or maybe we're choosing to finish what they started." Sophie wiped her eyes. "Grandmother died dismissed. Victoria lived in hiding. Now we have a chance to make their sacrifices mean something. To prove they were right."

"At what cost?"

"I don't know. But I know doing nothing would cost more."

They sat with that thought.


5:47 PM

Alex's phone buzzed.

Email from Marcus Webb. Subject: VERIFICATION COMPLETE.

Alex's hands shook as she opened it.

*Hartley,*

*Verification done. Six independent reviewers—three quantum physicists, two biochemists, one neuroscientist. All confirm: mechanism is theoretically sound, data is robust, conclusions are justified.*

*Quantum wine is real.*

*We're going public tomorrow, Monday, 4:30 PM GMT. I'm coordinating with two journals (arXiv preprint, open-access physics journal) and three universities for simultaneous release. Maximum visibility, maximum impact. I've cc'd you on submission emails. Add your paper as co-publication.*

*This is it. Tomorrow we prove Elizabeth Chen was right. Tomorrow we change wine science forever.*

*But Hartley—once this is public, everything changes. Meridian will come at us hard. So will government agencies, corporate interests, everyone who wants to control quantum wine. Don't meet with them. Don't take their money. And the moment the papers go live, go to the police. Tell them everything. Get protection.*

*See you on the other side.*

*—Marcus Webb*


Alex looked up at Sophie. "He did it. Webb verified everything. We're publishing tomorrow at half four."

Sophie's eyes filled with tears. "My grandmother was right. For forty years she was right. And tomorrow the world will know."

"Tomorrow we go public. Beat Meridian's five PM deadline by half an hour. Then we go straight to police with published proof."

Alex texted Emma:

> Webb verified everything. Publishing tomorrow 4:30 PM. Then police immediately after. I'm sorry for breaking my promise. But we have proof now. Scientific validation. Morrison will have to take us seriously. I love you.

Response came after five minutes:

> I'm glad you have proof. I'm still angry you broke your promise. But I understand why. Come home tomorrow. Alive. Please.

Alex:

> I will. This time I promise. And I mean it.

Emma:

**I love you too. Be careful.**

Sophie was already working, finalising the paper format. "We submit tomorrow morning when arXiv opens. Nine AM our time. Papers go live around four-thirty."

"And then we go to Morrison. With published papers, scientific verification, everything she needs to take us seriously."

"Assuming we survive that long."

"Assuming that."

They worked through Sunday evening, polishing the paper one final time. Every citation checked. Every claim verified. Every formula double-checked.

At 8:00 PM, they ordered takeaway. Neither ate much.

At 9:30 PM, the paper was perfect. Ready to submit Monday morning.

"You should stay here tonight," Alex said. "Safer together. And we need to be ready to move fast tomorrow."

Sophie nodded, settled back on the sofa. "I keep thinking about Grandmother. How she'd feel knowing tomorrow her research goes public. After forty years of dismissal. After dying without vindication."

"I think she'd be proud. Of the work. Of you. Of all of us."

"I hope so."

They tried to sleep. Alex lay in bed, mind racing with everything that could go wrong tomorrow. Meridian could get an injunction. The journals could refuse publication. MI5 could intervene.

Or it could work. The papers could go live. The world could learn quantum wine existed. Elizabeth Chen could be vindicated.

At 11:47 PM, Alex finally fell asleep, phone in hand, waiting for Monday.

PART 2
SUPPRESSION

MONDAY, 17 FEBRUARY 2025

6:15 AM

ALEX WOKE to her phone buzzing insistently. Grey Monday morning light filtered through the curtains. Sophie was already awake on the sofa, laptop open, staring at her screen.

Alex grabbed her phone. Messages from Marcus Webb, time-stamped from three hours ago when it was evening in Australia:

> Final coordination complete. All institutions ready. All journals ready. ArXiv submission opens 9 AM your time. We submit simultaneously—you in London, me in Sydney.

> Papers go live around 4:30 PM GMT. That's half an hour before Meridian's deadline. Perfect timing.

This is it, Hartley. We're proving quantum
wine exists. We're vindicating Elizabeth
Chen. We're changing wine science forever.
And we're painting massive targets on our
backs.

Don't meet with Meridian. Don't take their
money. And once the papers are live, go to
the police immediately. Tell them everything.
Get protection before Meridian can retaliate.
Good luck. See you on the other side. - MW

Alex sat up, heart pounding. This was it. Today. In ten hours,
quantum wine would be public knowledge.

"You saw Webb's message?" Sophie asked from the sofa, voice
tight with nerves.

"Just now. Are you ready?"

"No. But we're doing it anyway."

Alex checked her other messages. One from Emma, sent at
5:30 AM:

Can't sleep. Too worried. Please be safe
today. Call me the moment you're done. I
love you.

Alex replied:

Emma. Today's the day. Publishing at 4:30,
then straight to police like I promised. I
know you're angry. But I love you. And I'm
coming to you tonight. I promise.

The response came immediately:

I'm not angry anymore. Just scared. Be
safe. Call me the moment you can. I love
you too.

Alex set down her phone, throat tight. Emma at her mum's house,
unable to sleep, terrified. And Alex here, about to publish research

that would make them both targets.

"Coffee?" Sophie asked, already in the kitchen.

"God, yes."

They made coffee in tense silence. Strong, bitter, necessary. Neither of them had slept well—Alex had woken repeatedly through the night, checking her phone, checking the time, imagining everything that could go wrong.

At 7:15 AM, Alex showered, changed into clean clothes. Needed to look professional for the journalist calls that would inevitably come. Navy jumper, good jeans. Presentable for video interviews.

Sophie was already dressed, had been since she woke. She looked exhausted—dark circles under her eyes, hands shaking slightly as she refreshed her email for the hundredth time.

"Still nothing new from Webb?" Alex asked.

"Just the message from last night. Everything's set. We just have to execute." Sophie closed her laptop, looked at Alex. "Before we do this—before we make this public and can't take it back—are you absolutely certain?"

"I'm certain," Alex said immediately. "Your grandmother spent forty years on this. She died dismissed. We're not letting her research die with her."

"Okay." Sophie opened her laptop again. "Then let's finish this."

They reviewed the paper one final time. Eighteen pages of quantum mechanics, wine chemistry, and forty years of suppressed research. Title, authors, abstract—everything perfect.

At 8:30 AM, Alex made more coffee. Her hands were shaking.

At 8:45 AM, Sophie pulled up the arXiv submission portal. "Fifteen minutes."

Alex paced the small kitchen. This was it. The moment where everything changed. Once they submitted, there was no going back. The research would be public. Reviewers would see it. By afternoon, the world would know.

"Alex." Sophie's voice pulled her back. "It's time. Portal's open."

Alex sat beside her on the sofa. "Do it."

Sophie filled in the submission form with practised precision. Title: *Quantum Coherence in Aged Wine: Mechanism, Evidence, and Implications for Memory Transfer*. Authors: Hartley, A.; Chen, S.; Webb, M. The abstract summarised forty years of Elizabeth's research —quantum-coherent phenolic networks, terroir requirements, experimental validation from six independent researchers. Primary category: Quantum Physics. She uploaded the eighteen-page PDF.

Sophie's cursor hovered over the "Submit" button.

"Ready?" she asked.

Alex nodded.

Sophie pressed enter.

The upload bar crawled across the screen. 47%. 68%. 84%. 100%.

Upload complete.

Submission ID: 2502.07845

Status: Pending moderation.

"Done," Sophie whispered. "It's submitted."

Alex felt lightheaded. They'd done it. Quantum wine research was in the arXiv queue. By this afternoon, it would be public.

Her phone rang. She checked the screen—Emma.

"Em?"

"Did you do it? Did you submit?" Emma's voice was strained.

"Just now. Nine AM. Papers should go live around four-thirty."

"I'm coming home. I can't sit here at Mum's waiting. I need to be with you."

"Em, it might not be safe—"

"I don't care. You said the papers go public this afternoon. Once they're out, we go to Morrison together. All of us. Until then, I'm not leaving you alone with this." Emma's voice softened. "I'll be there by lunchtime. We'll wait together."

Alex felt relief flood through her. "Okay. Thank you."

"I love you. See you soon."

Alex ended the call, set down her phone. Looked at Sophie. "Emma's coming home. She'll be here by midday."

"Good," Sophie said quietly. "We shouldn't be alone for this."

Alex nodded. "Now the waiting."

The longest seven hours of Alex's life.

## MORNING - THE WAITING

By half past nine, Alex was pacing the flat like a caged animal.

The paper was submitted. Status: Pending moderation. The arXiv moderators were reviewing, checking for obvious errors, spam, inappropriate content. Usually took twenty-four to forty-eight hours. But Webb had arranged for priority review—called in favours, cited urgent scientific importance.

Sophie sat at the kitchen table, refreshing the arXiv page every thirty seconds.

At 10:15 AM, Alex tried calling Kimura one final time. It rang through to voicemail again. She didn't leave another message.

"Still not answering," Alex said, setting down her phone. "Straight to voicemail every time since Saturday night."

"You think they got to her?" Sophie's voice was small.

"I don't know. But Philippe's dead. Wickham's dead. And Kimura was co-author on the Bordeaux paper with Philippe." Alex felt cold. "Webb's under surveillance. Victoria's in hiding. We're next on the list if this publication doesn't protect us."

"Maybe we should call the New Zealand police. Report her missing."

"With what evidence? Unanswered calls? They'd think we're paranoid." Alex rubbed her face. "We'll try again after the papers go live. If she still doesn't answer by tonight, we tell Morrison everything. Let her coordinate with international police."

Sophie nodded, but she looked sick.

They went back to waiting. Refreshing the arXiv page. Watching the clock crawl towards publication time.

Sophie made tea neither of them drank. Alex tried to work on other things—respond to emails, review tasting notes for her Decanter column—but couldn't concentrate.

At noon, her phone rang. Jancis Robinson.

Alex answered immediately. "Jancis."

"Alex. My phone's been ringing all afternoon. Something about quantum wine research being published today? ArXiv preprint?" Jancis's voice was carefully neutral. "Is this real?"

"It's real. Papers go live at half four. Six independent scientists verified the mechanism. Everything's been peer-reviewed and validated."

Silence on the line. Then: "I want to experience it. Myself. First-hand. No more reading papers—I need to taste quantum wine and confirm this phenomenon exists."

"I'd be honoured to arrange that."

"Good. Monday next week. Berry Bros. & Rudd, private tasting room. Just you, Sophie Chen, and myself. Bring quantum-active wines. I'll provide controlled conditions, proper documentation. If I experience what you describe, I'll write about it for the Financial Times."

"You'd stake your reputation on this?"

"My reputation is built on rigorous evaluation. If quantum wine is real, the wine world needs to know. If it's not, the wine world needs to know that too." A pause. "Will you come?"

"Yes. Absolutely."

"Good. I'll send details. And Alex? Be careful. You've just made yourself very visible. Not everyone will be pleased."

She ended the call.

Alex looked at Sophie. "Jancis Robinson wants to taste quantum wine. Next Monday. Private tasting at Berry Bros."

Sophie's eyes filled with tears. "That's... that's everything Grandmother wanted. The most respected wine critic in the world taking quantum wine seriously."

"So we're doing it."

"We're absolutely doing it."

## 1:00 PM

Emma arrived just after one o'clock, letting herself in quietly. She carried a Pret bag—sandwiches neither Alex nor Sophie had thought to buy—and her laptop case.

"You both look terrible," she said, setting down the food. Then she crossed to Alex and wrapped her arms around her. "How are you holding up?"

"Barely." Alex held on tightly. "Thank you for coming."

"Where else would I be?" Emma pulled back, studied Alex's face. "When did you last eat?"

"I don't remember."

"Right. Eat. Both of you." Emma unpacked sandwiches, distributed them with the efficient care of someone who knew they'd be ignored otherwise. "Then we wait. Together."

Sophie managed a small smile. "It's good you're here."

"Of course I'm here." Emma sat down at the table, pulled out her own laptop. "Now, what's the status?"

## MONDAY AFTERNOON

## 3:30 PM

By half three, the tension in the flat was unbearable. Alex stood at the window, watching the street below for any sign of surveillance. Sophie sat at the kitchen table, refreshing the arXiv page every thirty seconds. Emma made her fourth pot of tea—none of them were drinking it, but the ritual gave her something to do with her hands.

The papers were still in moderation. Status: Pending. The arXiv moderators were reviewing, checking for obvious errors, spam, inappropriate content. Usually took twenty-four to forty-eight hours. But Webb had arranged for priority review—called in favours, cited urgent scientific importance.

Alex's phone rang. Webb.

"Status check," he said without preamble. "Papers still pending your end?"

"Yes. You?"

"Same. But I just spoke to the arXiv admin. They're finishing review now. Should go live by four PM GMT. Be ready."

"We're ready."

"Hartley—once this is public, everything changes. You understand that? We'll be targets. Meridian, government agencies, corporate interests. Everyone who wants to control quantum wine will come after us."

"I know."

"Good. Just wanted to make sure." A pause. "Elizabeth would be proud. You know that, right? You're doing what she couldn't. Making her research impossible to ignore."

"I hope so."

"I know so. See you on the other side."

He ended the call.

3:47 PM.

Sophie refreshed the page. Still pending.

3:51 PM.

Refresh. Pending.

3:56 PM.

Refresh. Pending.

Alex couldn't watch any more. She went to the window, stared out at Islington's Monday afternoon. Normal people living normal lives. Going to work, picking up shopping, completely unaware that in minutes, the scientific understanding of wine would fundamentally change.

"Alex." Sophie's voice, tight with tension. "It's live."

Alex spun round. Sophie's laptop screen showed the arXiv page:

Paper ID: 2502.07845 Title: *Quantum Coherence in Aged Wine: Mechanism, Evidence, and Implications for Memory Transfer*

Authors: Hartley, A.; Chen, S.; Webb, M. Status: PUBLISHED
Submitted: 17 Feb 2025 Published: 17 Feb 2025, 16:02 GMT

"It's live," Sophie repeated, her voice cracking. "My grandmother's research is live. Public. Real."

Alex's phone buzzed. Email notification from the physics journal:

*Your paper "Quantum Memory Transfer in Aged Wines: Experimental Validation" has been published in the Journal of Quantum Biology, Volume 47, Issue 2.*

Another notification. Then another. The press releases were auto-sending, triggered by publication.

Alex's phone started ringing. Unknown number. She answered.

"Alex Hartley? This is James Barrett, Nature News. I've just read your quantum wine paper. Is this real? Can I quote you?"

"It's real. Verified by six independent researchers. The mechanism—"

"Can we do an interview? Video call? I want to run this tomorrow morning but I need quotes—"

Another call coming through. Alex put Barrett on hold. "Hello?"

"Ms Hartley, BBC Science desk. We're seeing reports about quantum coherence in wine. Can you provide comment?"

Alex's head spun. It was happening. The wine world, the science world, everyone was seeing the papers. Reacting. Questioning. Believing.

Sophie's phone was ringing too. So was Emma's—journalists somehow finding any number connected to Alex Hartley.

"Emma—can you handle the BBC? Sophie, take the Guardian. I'll deal with Nature News." Alex put Barrett back on. "Sorry. Yes, I can provide quotes. The mechanism is quantum-coherent phenolic networks that form during wine ageing under specific terroir conditions—"

The next hour was chaos.

Alex fielded seven journalist calls. Gave four video interviews. Responded to thirty-three emails from scientists, wine professionals, academics. Sophie did the same. Emma, bless her, took notes, tracked who'd contacted them, managed the flood of incoming information.

At 4:47 PM, Alex refreshed the arXiv page.

Paper downloads: 234 Views: 612

She refreshed again. 247 downloads. 629 views.

"It's spreading," Sophie said, watching over her shoulder. "Look —Nature News just tweeted the link. Science Magazine too."

Alex kept refreshing. Every thirty seconds, the numbers jumped:

5:03 PM: 441 downloads 5:11 PM: 782 downloads

5:24 PM: 1,340 downloads

"We're trending on Science Twitter," Sophie said, scrolling through her phone. "Number three globally. Behind only a Mars probe landing and a cancer breakthrough."

By 5:35 PM, the count had passed 2,000. By six o'clock: 3,847 downloads, 12,293 views.

Emma pulled up the Guardian's website. "They've already posted an article. 'Wine as Memory Storage: Scientists Claim Quantum Breakthrough.' Published fourteen minutes ago."

The Guardian article quoted their paper extensively. Explained the mechanism in accessible terms. Included sceptical quotes from two Oxford physicists ("interesting but requires replication") and enthusiastic quotes from a quantum biologist at MIT ("if verified, paradigm-shifting").

Fair. Balanced. Real.

"Financial Times is running it," Sophie said. "So is the New York Times. Science Magazine. New Scientist. Everyone's picking it up."

## MONDAY EVENING

### 5:15 PM

At twenty past five, Alex's phone rang. Unknown number.

She almost didn't answer—she'd been fielding calls for ninety minutes, journalists and scientists blurring together. But something made her pick up.

"Ms Hartley." The voice was calm, professional, female. "Dr Caroline Reeves, Meridian Research Group. Congratulations on your publication. Very thorough. Very public. Very problematic."

Alex's blood went cold. "Dr Reeves."

Sophie looked up sharply.

"I wanted to give you one final opportunity before this becomes... complicated." Dr Reeves's tone was almost friendly. "We know about Dr Webb's verification. We know about your press releases. We know you're planning further disclosures. Here's what's going to happen if you proceed: within the hour, we'll file injunctions in UK, US, and Australian courts claiming theft of classified research. Your bank accounts will be frozen. Your assets seized. Criminal charges filed under the Official Secrets Act."

"You can't classify research that was never formally classified."

"We can try. And whilst we're trying, you'll be in legal limbo. No income. No access to funds. Facing prison time." Dr Reeves's voice hardened. "Or, you issue a retraction. Contact every journalist you spoke to today. Tell them you were mistaken, the research was flawed, you regret the premature publication. We'll want the USB drives back. And we'll pay you. Fifty thousand pounds each. Same offer as before. Final chance to take it."

"No."

"You're certain? Because once we file these injunctions—"

"We're certain. Quantum wine is public knowledge now. Verified by independent scientists. Downloaded thousands of times. You can't suppress it."

Silence on the line. Then: "You're making a serious mistake, Ms Hartley. One you'll regret."

"I've made worse mistakes."

"Not like this." Dr Reeves ended the call.

Alex set down her phone, hands shaking.

"That was them," Sophie said. Not a question.

"Meridian. Dr Caroline Reeves. She's threatening legal action. Official Secrets Act charges. Bank account freezing. Same deal as before—fifty thousand each to retract everything."

"They're desperate," Sophie said. "The research is already public. They can't put that genie back in the bottle. They're bluffing."

"Maybe. Or maybe they have enough legal leverage to destroy us anyway." Alex stood. "Which is why we're going to Morrison. Right now. We tell her everything—Meridian's threats, Victoria's research, Wickham's death. All of it."

They gathered evidence: printed papers, USB drives, screenshots of Meridian's threats, recordings of today's journalist interviews. Everything that proved quantum wine was real and Meridian wanted it suppressed.

At 5:32 PM, they left the flat.

A black car was parked across the street. Two men inside, watching.

"Meridian," Sophie whispered.

"Probably." Alex pulled out her phone, photographed the car, the number plate. Evidence. "Let's go. Don't look at them. Just walk normally."

They walked to the Tube station. The black car didn't follow. But Alex felt eyes on her back the entire way.

MONDAY EVENING

CHARING CROSS POLICE STATION

6:03 PM

Charing Cross Police Station was busy—Monday evening, the usual chaos. Drunk and disorderly from the weekend. Domestic disturbances. Petty theft. Normal police work.

Alex gave her name at the desk.

"DI Morrison is expecting you," the desk sergeant said. "But she's running late. Can you wait?"

They sat in the waiting area. Hard plastic chairs. Health and safety posters. A young man with a bleeding nose. An older woman arguing quietly with a uniformed officer.

Normal. Everything normal.

Except Alex had just published research that would change wine science forever, and a private research firm was threatening to destroy her life for it.

Her phone buzzed. Text from an unknown number:

> Ms Hartley. Lying to the police earlier was
> unwise. Coming to them now is worse.
> Leave. Go home. Forget quantum wine.
> Last warning. —VM

Alex stared at the message. VM. Victoria Mills's initials.

But this couldn't be Victoria. Victoria had given Alex the research specifically TO go public. She'd wanted Elizabeth vindicated. Why would she now tell Alex to "forget quantum wine"?

Unless it wasn't Victoria. Unless someone had intercepted the burner phone Victoria had given her. Unless Meridian was spoofing VM's identity to frighten her.

Alex quickly checked her contacts. The burner phone number

Victoria had given her at Postman's Park—this text wasn't from that number. Different number entirely.

Someone was impersonating Victoria.

Alex deleted the message without responding. Meridian's psychological games wouldn't work.

"Ms Hartley?" A uniformed officer stood in the waiting room doorway. "DI Morrison can see you now. All three of you."

They followed him up two flights, down a corridor, to Morrison's office.

Morrison was on the phone, looking harassed. She waved them in, gestured to chairs.

"—yes, I understand. But I need more time. The Wickham case has complications." She listened, frowning. "Tomorrow morning, then. Thank you, sir."

She hung up, turned to Alex, Sophie, and Emma. Her expression was carefully neutral.

"Ms Hartley. Ms Chen. And this is?"

"Emma Lawson. My partner," Alex said.

"Right. You said you have information about James Wickham's death. I'm listening."

Alex took a breath. This was it. The moment where they either convinced Morrison to take quantum wine seriously, or where they became suspects in a murder investigation.

"James Wickham died because he was trying to prove quantum wine exists. He assembled quantum-active wines, invited sensitive tasters, created undeniable proof. And a research organisation called Meridian Research Group killed him to suppress that proof."

Morrison's pen paused. "Quantum wine."

"I know how it sounds. But it's real. Scientifically validated as of ninety minutes ago." Alex pulled out her phone, showed Morrison the arXiv papers, the press releases, the verification from six independent researchers. "Published. Public. Verified by physicists and biochemists at three universities."

Morrison read. Her expression didn't change, but Alex saw her eyes widen slightly.

"You're saying wine can store memories."

"Quantum-coherent phenolic networks store information patterns from the environment during fermentation and ageing. Including sensory data and emotional states from humans in proximity. When certain genetically sensitive individuals consume these wines, they experience vivid sensory recall of those stored patterns." Alex spoke quickly, precisely. "It sounds impossible. But the mechanism is scientifically sound. Multiple researchers have documented it. And Meridian has been trying to suppress and weaponise it for forty years."

"Weaponise wine."

"Memory extraction. False memory implantation. Emotional manipulation. All documented in research files we obtained from Dr Victoria Mills, who worked for Meridian from 1980 to 1995." Alex handed Morrison a USB drive. "This contains everything. The mechanism, the applications, the threats we've received. Meridian wants this research back. They've threatened us with legal action and physical violence. We believe they killed Wickham, Philippe Moreau in Bordeaux, and possibly Dr Sarah Kimura in New Zealand."

Morrison took the USB drive, turned it over in her hands. "This is a serious accusation."

"It's a serious crime. Murder. Possibly multiple murders. And they're still hunting anyone who knows about quantum wine." Alex met Morrison's eyes. "We went public today because it was the only way to protect ourselves. Make the knowledge so widespread they can't suppress it. But we're still in danger. And we need police protection."

Morrison was quiet for a long moment. Then she picked up her phone, dialled. "This is DI Morrison. I need you to look into an organisation called Meridian Research Group. Start with corporate registrations, directors, government contracts." She listened. "Yes, immediately. And flag any connections to the Wickham case."

She hung up, looked at Alex. "I'm going to need formal statements from both of you. Everything you know about Wickham, about Meridian, about these... quantum wines. We'll need the original USB drive, not just copies. We'll need contact information for Dr Mills and Dr Webb. And you'll need to stay available for further questioning."

"We can do that."

"Good. Because if what you're telling me is true—if a private research organisation has been killing people to suppress scientific research—this becomes a major investigation. Possibly national security implications." Morrison stood. "Wait here. I'm going to speak with my supervisor. This is above my pay grade."

She left the office. Alex, Sophie, and Emma sat in silence.

"Do you think she believes us?" Sophie asked.

"I think she's taking us seriously. Whether she believes quantum wine exists..." Alex shrugged. "The scientific validation helps. But Morrison's a detective, not a physicist."

Emma squeezed Alex's hand. "You did the right thing. Going to the police. Going public. All of it."

"I hope so."

They waited. Ten minutes. Fifteen. Through the office window, Alex could see Morrison in the corridor, speaking with a grey-haired man in a suit. Both looked serious. Both kept glancing back at Morrison's office.

Finally, Morrison returned. But she wasn't alone.

The grey-haired man followed her in. Behind him, three more men in dark suits. Not police. Something else.

Something that made Morrison's expression go tight and professional.

The lead man held up credentials. "DCI James Caldwell, MI5 Counter-Terrorism. We're taking custody of Ms Hartley and Ms Chen under the Official Secrets Act. DI Morrison, you've been briefed?"

Morrison's jaw tightened. "Sir, these are witnesses in an active murder investigation—"

"Which is now a matter of national security. You'll receive formal notification within the hour." Caldwell turned to Alex and Sophie. "Ms Hartley. Ms Chen. You're coming with us. Don't resist. Don't attempt to contact anyone. Your phones will be confiscated."

"Wait—" Emma stood. "You can't just take them. They haven't been charged with anything."

"We're not charging them. We're protecting them." Caldwell's voice was calm, professional. Practised. "There are credible threats against their safety. We're placing them in protective custody until those threats are assessed."

"For how long?" Alex asked, her voice steadier than she felt.

"As long as necessary. Days. Possibly weeks." Caldwell gestured to his colleagues. "Please. This will be easier if you cooperate."

Alex looked at Morrison. "Is this legal?"

Morrison's expression was pained. Helpless. "If they're invoking the Official Secrets Act... yes. I don't have jurisdiction."

"Emma—" Alex turned to her partner.

"I'll get a solicitor. I'll call everyone I know. I'll—" Emma's voice broke. "I'll get you out."

"Don't." Caldwell's voice hardened. "Attempting to interfere with a national security matter will result in your own arrest, Ms Lawson. Go home. Say nothing to anyone. Wait for official notification."

Two MI5 officers moved forward, flanking Alex and Sophie. Not grabbing them, but making it clear resistance wasn't an option.

"Phones," Caldwell said.

Alex's hands shook as she surrendered her phone. All those journalist contacts. All that evidence. All those download notifications from arXiv showing quantum wine spreading across the scientific world.

Gone.

Sophie handed over her phone too, her face pale.

"This way."

They were led out of Morrison's office, down a back stairwell Alex hadn't known existed, into an underground car park. Three black Range Rovers waited, engines running, exhaust ghosting in the cold air.

"Separate vehicles," Caldwell said. "Ms Hartley in the first. Ms Chen in the second. Security protocols."

"Where are you taking us?" Sophie asked.

"Thames House. MI5 headquarters. You'll be debriefed, assessed, and assigned protective custody." Caldwell opened the door of the first Range Rover. "Get in, Ms Hartley."

Alex looked back. Emma stood in the stairwell doorway, Morrison beside her, both watching with identical expressions of helpless concern.

Then the door closed. The engine hummed. The convoy pulled out of the car park, into London evening traffic.

Through the tinted windows, Alex watched the city blur past. Normal London. Normal Monday evening. People finishing work, heading home, heading to pubs, living normal lives.

Six hours ago, Alex had published research that proved quantum wine existed.

Now she was in MI5 custody, being taken to Thames House, separated from Emma, her phone confiscated, her freedom gone.

Everything had changed.

The Range Rover drove in silence. No radio. No conversation. Just the hum of the engine and London's traffic sounds muffled through armoured glass.

Alex tried to track their route—Strand, Trafalgar Square, Whitehall—but after a few turns she lost orientation. Intentional, probably. Disorient the detainee.

Finally, the convoy pulled into an underground car park. Concrete. Fluorescent lights. Security barriers requiring multiple clearances.

Thames House. MI5 headquarters.

"Out," Caldwell said, opening Alex's door.

She stepped into the car park. Sophie was being led from the second vehicle, looking small and frightened between two large MI5 officers.

Their eyes met across twenty feet of concrete. Sophie mouthed: *Are you okay?*

Alex nodded. Lied.

"This way."

They were led through security doors, down corridors, through checkpoints requiring biometric scans. Everything sterile, institutional, designed to intimidate.

Processing was clinical. Photographs from five angles. Fingerprints, both hands. Retinal scan. DNA swab. A woman in a grey suit confiscated Alex's belongings—wallet, keys, watch, the USB drive she'd been carrying, everything except the clothes she was wearing.

"You'll get these back when you're released," the woman said. Not unkind, just professional. Detached.

"When will that be?"

"That depends on your cooperation."

Alex and Sophie were separated. Alex watched Sophie being led down a different corridor, both of them looking back until doors closed and sight was lost.

Then Alex was alone with two officers—one man, one woman, both wearing the same grey suits that seemed to be uniform here.

"This way."

More corridors. More security doors. Everything beige and fluorescent and deliberately disorienting. Finally, they stopped at a numbered door: B-47.

The male officer unlocked it, gestured inside. "Your quarters. Don't attempt to leave. The door is locked and monitored. Someone will bring you dinner at eight. Debrief tomorrow morning, seven-thirty. Someone will bring you dinner shortly."

"What about Sophie? Is she—"

"We can't discuss other detainees."

The door closed. The lock clicked.

Alex was alone.

The room was small—three metres by four—containing a single bed, a desk, a chair, and an ensuite bathroom. Institutional beige walls. No windows to the outside. A camera in the ceiling corner, red light blinking steadily.

Alex sat on the bed. It creaked. The mattress was thin, institutional. The kind designed for temporary accommodation, not comfort.

A digital clock on the desk blinked 7:14 PM. Her watch was gone. Her phone was gone. But at least she could track time.

She'd been in custody for just over an hour. It felt like days.

Emma would be frantic. Going home alone, no idea where Alex had been taken, unable to help.

And Sophie—somewhere in this building, alone in another beige room, probably terrified.

Alex lay back on the bed, stared at the ceiling. The camera blinked. Always watching.

She'd published quantum wine research. Made it public. Proved Elizabeth Chen had been right for forty years.

And six hours later, she was in MI5 detention.

Was this what winning looked like?

Footsteps in the corridor. Alex sat up, pulse jumping.

The lock clicked. The grey-suited woman entered, carrying a tray.

"Dinner," she said, setting it on the desk. "You have forty-five minutes. Someone will collect the tray at nine."

The woman turned to leave.

"Wait. Please. Is Sophie okay? Sophie Chen? She was brought in with me."

"I can't discuss other detainees."

"Can you at least tell her I'm okay? That I'm not hurt?"

The woman's expression softened slightly. "She's fine. Safe. Being treated the same as you. That's all I can say."

She left. The lock clicked again.

Alex looked at the tray: shepherd's pie, peas, a bread roll, water in a plastic cup. Institutional food. She ate mechanically, tasting nothing.

The fluorescent lights hummed. The camera watched. The door stayed locked.

Alex had no idea what tomorrow would bring.

But she knew one thing: quantum wine was public now. Published. Downloaded thousands of times. Spreading across universities, research labs, wine professionals worldwide.

They'd won that battle.

Even if it meant losing everything else.

▭

## 10 / THAMES HOUSE



DAY 1 - MORNING

A LEX WOKE to grey light filtering through reinforced glass, disoriented for several seconds before memory crashed back: MI5 custody. Thames House. Detention.

The digital clock on the desk read 6:47 AM.

She sat up slowly, muscles aching from the thin mattress. The camera in the ceiling corner blinked its red eye. Always watching.

Alex tried to reconstruct the previous evening: the convoy from Charing Cross, the underground car park, processing, the confiscation of her belongings, the long walk through identical corridors to this beige cell. Sophie being led away down a different corridor, both of them looking back until doors closed and sight was lost.

How long ago? Six hours? Eight?

She stood, tested the door. Locked. Went to the ensuite bathroom—small, functional, a single mirror bolted to the wall. She looked terrible: dark circles under her eyes, hair tangled, still wearing yesterday's clothes.

She splashed water on her face, tried to think.

Quantum wine was public. The papers had been downloaded thousands of times before MI5 took her phone. Journalists had quoted her. Scientists were already discussing it on Twitter. That couldn't be undone.

So why was she here?

Protective custody, Caldwell had said. But protection from whom? Meridian? Or protection of Meridian's interests by keeping Alex isolated and silent?

The lock clicked. Alex turned as the door opened.

A woman in a grey suit—different from last night—entered with a tray. "Breakfast. You have forty-five minutes. Someone will collect you at 7:30 for debriefing."

"Where's Sophie Chen? Is she—"

"I can't discuss other detainees." The woman set the tray on the desk. "Eat. You'll need your strength."

She left. The lock clicked.

Alex looked at the breakfast: toast, butter, jam, tea in a paper cup. Institutional. She ate mechanically, watching the clock: 7:04. 7:11. 7:23.

At exactly 7:30, the lock clicked again. A man this time, young, military bearing. "Ms Hartley. Come with me."

He led her through corridors that all looked identical. Up two flights of stairs, through security checkpoints requiring his badge at each one, finally to a small interview room.

DCI Caldwell sat behind a table, laptop open. He looked well-rested, alert. Everything Alex wasn't.

"Ms Hartley. Please sit."

Alex sat. The room was windowless, like her cell. A camera in the corner. Recording equipment on the table.

"For the record." Caldwell pressed a button. "Interview with Alexandra Hartley, Tuesday 18 February 2025, 08:32 hours. Present: DCI James Caldwell, MI5, and Ms Hartley. Ms Hartley, you understand you're here under protective custody pursuant to the Official Secrets Act?"

"I understand you said protective custody. But I'm locked in a cell. I can't contact anyone. This feels more like arrest."

"It's protective custody. There's a difference." Caldwell's voice was patient. Practised. "You're not charged with any crime. You're being protected from credible threats whilst we assess the national security implications of your actions."

"What credible threats?"

"Meridian Research Group has substantial resources and no apparent moral compunctions about eliminating threats to their research programme. You went public with classified material. That makes you a target." Caldwell folded his hands. "We're protecting you from them. And, potentially, from yourself."

"From myself?"

"From making further disclosures that could compromise national security." He opened a folder, pulled out printed pages. Alex recognised them immediately: her quantum wine paper, printed and annotated in red ink.

"'Quantum Coherence in Aged Wine,'" Caldwell read. "Very thorough. Very detailed. Very dangerous."

"Dangerous to whom? Meridian? Or dangerous to the government agencies that want to control quantum wine?"

"Dangerous to the United Kingdom. The research you publicised —quantum memory transfer, emotional manipulation, false memory implantation—has significant intelligence and defence applications. Applications that are now public knowledge because you decided to bypass proper classification procedures."

Alex felt anger rising. "That research was never properly classified. Victoria Mills left Meridian thirty years ago. Elizabeth Chen published in open journals. Marcus Webb published in 2008. This was public domain research."

"It was classified the moment Dr Mills signed her employment contract with Meridian in 1980." Caldwell pulled out another document: a contract, yellowed with age, Victoria Mills's signature at the bottom. "That contract included non-disclosure agreements, classified materials clauses, and national security restrictions. When she left in 1995, she violated those agreements by retaining research materials. When you published them, you became an accessory to that violation."

Alex stared at the contract. Forty-five years old. But apparently still binding.

"She destroyed her lab notes. The files she gave me were personal copies—"

"Which she had no legal right to possess. Classified means classified, Ms Hartley. You can't just decide something should be public because you think it's morally right."

"So what—you're charging me with violating the Official Secrets Act?"

"We're deciding whether to charge you. That depends on your cooperation." Caldwell leant forward. "Here's the situation. Quantum wine research is now public knowledge. We can't suppress the papers—they've been downloaded thousands of times. But we can control further disclosures. We can ensure no additional classified materials are released. And we can determine who has access to the remaining research."

"The USB drives."

"All five copies. We want them. The printed documents. Everything Dr Mills gave you. We want to know who else has copies. Dr Webb. Dr Mills herself. Anyone you've shared the research with."

"And if I cooperate?"

"No charges. You'll be released with conditions—no further publications about quantum wine, no interviews beyond what you've already given, no contact with other researchers in this area. You go back to your life. Write about Portuguese whites or whatever it is wine writers write about. Pretend this never happened."

Alex laughed bitterly. "Pretend I didn't publish papers with my name on them? Pretend I didn't go on record with Nature News and the BBC?"

"You can say you were mistaken. That further analysis showed the phenomenon was less significant than you initially believed. That you regret the premature publication." Caldwell's voice hardened. "Or you can refuse to cooperate, and we'll charge you under the Official Secrets Act. Two to fourteen years in prison, depending on severity. Your choice."

"This is extortion."

"This is national security." Caldwell stood. "You have twenty-four hours to think about it. Tomorrow morning, same time. You'll give me your answer then."

"I want to speak to a solicitor."

"You're not under arrest. You don't have a right to legal counsel during protective custody."

"Then I want to speak to Emma. My partner. She doesn't know where I am, if I'm safe—"

"She knows you're in protective custody. She'll receive official notification today. Beyond that, no contact until you've been fully debriefed and cleared." Caldwell gestured to the door. "Use the time wisely, Ms Hartley. Think about what you're willing to lose."

They took her back to her cell. The lock clicked behind her.

Alex sat on the narrow bed, head in her hands.

Twenty-four hours. One day to decide: betray everything she'd worked for, or face prison.

Neither option was acceptable.

## WEDNESDAY, 19 FEBRUARY 2025

## DAY 2

Wednesday began the same way: grey light, 6:47 AM, the camera's red eye blinking.

But Alex had barely slept. She'd spent the night staring at the ceiling, running through arguments, trying to find a way out that didn't exist.

The problem was simple: Caldwell was right. Victoria's contract was binding. The research was classified. Alex had published it anyway. That was a crime.

The only question was whether Alex would cooperate in damage control or face prosecution.

Breakfast arrived at seven. Different grey-suited woman, same institutional food. Alex forced herself to eat, knowing she needed energy for whatever today would bring.

At 7:30, they collected the tray. At 7:45, the young officer came to escort her.

"Where are we going?" Alex asked.

"Debrief. Same as yesterday."

But it wasn't the same interview room. This one was larger, with a proper table, four chairs. And Caldwell wasn't alone.

A woman sat beside him—mid-fifties, severe suit, the kind of face that suggested decades of dealing with unpleasant decisions.

"Ms Hartley," Caldwell said. "This is Commander Patricia Wilkes, Counter-Terrorism Command. She has some questions about your relationship with Dr Victoria Mills."

Alex's stomach dropped. "My relationship?"

"Sit down, Ms Hartley." Wilkes's voice was clipped, efficient. "We need to establish exactly how Dr Mills contacted you, what information she provided, and where she is now."

"I don't know where she is. She gave me the research and disappeared—"

"When?"

"Saturday. The fifteenth. Postman's Park."

"What time?"

"Noon."

"And she gave you a USB drive containing classified materials."

"She said they were personal copies. From research she did forty years ago—"

"Research funded by Her Majesty's Government under classified programmes. Research she had no legal right to possess or distribute." Wilkes pulled out a tablet, showed Alex a photograph. "Is this Dr Mills?"

It was Victoria. Older than in the 1971 photo from UC Davis, but unmistakably her. Silver hair, wire-rimmed glasses, the same intelligent eyes.

"Yes. That's her."

"When was this photograph taken?"

Alex looked closer. The background showed Postman's Park. The memorial tiles. "Saturday. When we met."

"We have CCTV footage showing this meeting. Dr Mills approaching you. Handing you something. Leaving separately." Wilkes swiped through images: Victoria walking into the park, Victoria standing by the memorial, Victoria leaving. "We've been hunting Dr Mills for thirty years. She's a fugitive, Ms Hartley. Wanted for theft of classified materials, violation of the Official Secrets Act, and potentially more serious charges."

"She was in hiding. From Meridian. Because they wanted to weaponise her research—"

"She was in hiding from us. Because she stole classified research and disappeared." Wilkes leant forward. "Where is she now?"

"I don't know. She said she was going somewhere they—you— couldn't find her."

"Did she mention any locations? Any safe houses? Any contacts who might be helping her?"

"No. Nothing."

"What about Dr Webb? Did Dr Mills contact him?"

"I don't know. You'd have to ask Webb."

"We will. He's being questioned by Australian authorities right now." Wilkes made a note. "What about Ms Chen? Sophie Chen. What did she know about Dr Mills?"

"Nothing. Sophie never met Victoria. She only had her grand-mother's notebooks—"

"Elizabeth Chen's notebooks. Also containing classified research. Where are those notebooks now?"

Alex realised the trap too late. "Sophie has them. They're her inheritance—"

"They're classified materials. We'll need to confiscate them." Wilkes closed her tablet. "Ms Hartley, here's what's going to happen. You're going to provide a complete inventory of every piece of quantum wine research you possess. Every USB drive, every printed page, every notebook. You're going to identify everyone you've shared this research with. And you're going to tell us everything Dr Mills said about her current location."

"I've told you everything—"

"I don't believe you." Wilkes stood. "You have until tomorrow morning. Think very carefully. Because if we discover you've lied to us—if Dr Mills contacts you again and you don't immediately report it—the charges will be much more severe."

They took Alex back to her cell. 8:47 AM.

The rest of the day stretched ahead, empty and oppressive.

The afternoon stretched ahead. Alex paced—three metres by four, twelve steps one way, fifteen the other—then ate the lunch they brought at noon, then lay on the bed staring at the ceiling, trying to think.

They wanted everything. Not just cooperation—complete surrender. Every USB drive, every document, Elizabeth Chen's note-books. Confiscate forty years of research and lock it away again—exactly what had happened to Elizabeth the first time.

Could Alex let that happen?

At three PM, the lock clicked. Alex sat up, expecting the grey-suited woman with tea.

Instead, Caldwell entered. He looked tired. The camera stayed on—red light blinking steadily.

"Ms Hartley. We need to talk."

He sat on the desk chair, rubbed his face. When he looked at Alex, his expression was serious but not unkind.

"I've been doing this job for fifteen years. Counter-terrorism. National security. I've interrogated actual terrorists. Actual threats to national security." He paused. "You know what you are, Ms Hartley?"

"A wine writer who published scientific research?"

"Someone who's about to destroy her life over principle." Caldwell's voice was matter-of-fact. "Here's what I know about you. You're three years into the Master of Wine programme. Exam scheduled for June. You've worked for Decanter for six years. You're in a relationship with Emma Lawson—architect, together six years. You rent a flat in Islington. No children. No serious financial problems. Good life."

"Why are you telling me this?"

"Because tomorrow morning, you're going to make a decision that determines whether you keep that life or lose it." Caldwell leant forward. "If you cooperate—give us the USB drives, stop publishing about quantum wine, sign the documents—you go home. Back to Emma, back to wine writing, back to your MW programme. With restrictions, yes. But free."

"And if I refuse?"

"We charge you. Official Secrets Act, theft of classified materials, possibly conspiracy charges. You'll be remanded in custody awaiting trial. Months in prison before trial even starts. Your flat lease expires —Emma can't afford it alone. Your Decanter position ends. Your MW candidacy is suspended."

Alex felt the walls closing in. "You'd destroy everything—"

"You'd destroy everything. By refusing to cooperate." Caldwell stood. "I'm not threatening you. I'm telling you what happens. I've seen idealists destroy themselves over principle before. They always think principle matters more than their life. Then they're in prison, years passing, and they realise—principle doesn't keep you warm at night."

He moved to the door, then turned back. "Your colleague. Ms Chen. Sophie. She cooperated. We released her this morning. Eight AM. She signed the documents, handed over the notebooks, went home with a warning. She made the smart choice."

Alex's breath caught. "Sophie's free?"

"Since this morning. Gave us everything we asked for. Now she's home, safe, getting on with her life." Caldwell's voice was calm. "You could be home by tomorrow if you make the same choice. Or you could stay here—in this cell, or one like it—for months. Years, maybe. Your choice."

He left. The door locked.

Alex sat on the bed, trembling.

Sophie was free. Had cooperated. Had given them Elizabeth's notebooks—forty years of her grandmother's research, confiscated by the same government that had suppressed it the first time.

Sophie had capitulated. And was home.

Alex could do the same. Sign the documents. Go home to Emma. Keep her career, her life, her future. Or refuse. Stand on principle. Face prison.

She thought about Elizabeth Chen, spending forty years fighting alone. About James Wickham, choosing to prove quantum wine even though it killed him. About Victoria Mills, living with thirty years of guilt for staying silent.

And she thought about herself. About what kind of person she wanted to be. But was there a third way?


Alex lay on the bed, staring at the ceiling, thinking.

What if she cooperated—signed their documents, accepted their restrictions—but used those restrictions strategically? The government wanted to control quantum wine research. But they also needed expertise. Someone who understood the mechanism, who'd experienced it firsthand, who could advise on countermeasures.

What if Alex became that someone? Cooperated enough to get

released, but positioned herself to stay connected to quantum wine research from inside the system?

It wasn't martyrdom. It wasn't pure principle. It was strategic compromise.

Elizabeth had fought alone and lost. Alex didn't have to fight alone. She had Webb, Sophie, journalists who'd already written about quantum wine, scientists who were already studying it. The research was public. That couldn't be undone.

Alex just had to survive long enough to see what came next.

At five PM, they brought dinner. Chicken, rice, vegetables. Alex ate, barely tasting it.

At seven PM, the lights dimmed slightly. Simulating evening.

At nine PM, Alex lay on the bed, her decision made.

She'd cooperate. Not because she'd given up—because she'd realised there were multiple ways to fight. Staying free, staying connected, staying relevant was worth more than martyrdom. Elizabeth would understand. Elizabeth, who'd been practical and scientific, who'd hidden her research when continuing meant death.

## THURSDAY, 20 FEBRUARY 2025

### DAY 3 - MORNING

Thursday morning, Alex woke with her decision solid.

Not surrender. Strategy.

At 8:30, they brought her to a different interview room. Larger. Better furnished. Caldwell was waiting, but he wasn't alone.

A woman sat beside him—late sixties, elegant, wearing a black suit. Silver hair pulled back. Wire-rimmed glasses.

"Ms Hartley," Caldwell said. "This is Dr Patricia Thornton. Scientific Adviser to the Home Office. She's been reviewing your case over the past two days."

The woman—Thornton—nodded. "Ms Hartley. I've read your

quantum wine papers with great interest. And reviewed Dr Mills's classified research files."

Alex's stomach tightened. Another interrogator.

"Dr Thornton is here," Caldwell continued, "to assess the scientific validity of your claims and the national security implications."

"It's real," Alex said. "Six independent researchers verified—"

"I know what they verified." Thornton's voice was crisp, professional. "I've reviewed the verification reports. I've also reviewed Dr Mills's original research files. The mechanism is theoretically sound. Quantum coherence in phenolic networks is plausible. The terroir requirements make sense."

She paused. "But the weaponisation applications—memory extraction, false memory implantation, emotional manipulation—those concern me greatly."

"They should concern everyone. That's why we went public. To prevent monopolisation—"

"You went public," Thornton interrupted, "without considering the consequences. Quantum wine research is now available to hostile intelligence services, terrorist organisations, anyone with a chemistry lab and access to the right wines."

"Or we've made it impossible for any one group to weaponise it. Transparency creates accountability—"

"Transparency creates vulnerability." Thornton removed her glasses, rubbed her eyes. She looked suddenly tired. "Ms Hartley, I've spent forty years advising governments on scientific threats. Chemical weapons. Biological agents. Nuclear proliferation. And now this —quantum memory manipulation through wine. Do you understand how difficult this will be to regulate?"

"That's not my problem to solve."

"It became your problem when you published it." Thornton put her glasses back on. "Here's what's going to happen. The government will classify all future quantum wine research retroactively. Public papers will remain public, but new research will require security clearances. Meridian's weaponisation programme will be shut down and their research confiscated."

She folded her hands. "And you, Ms Hartley, will have a choice. Face prosecution for violating the Official Secrets Act. Or accept employment with the Home Office as a scientific consultant on quantum wine countermeasures."

Alex blinked. "You're offering me a job?"

"We need expertise. You experienced quantum wine firsthand. You understand the mechanism. You've studied Dr Mills's weaponisation research. That makes you valuable." Thornton's expression was unreadable. "We can prosecute you, or we can employ you. Your choice."

A job. Working for the government on quantum wine countermeasures. It was almost absurd—she'd tried to expose classified research, and now they wanted to hire her to protect it.

But it was also exactly what Alex had been thinking about last night. A way to stay connected. A way to stay relevant.

"What would the job involve?"

"Monitoring scientific literature for quantum wine research. Identifying potentially quantum-active wines before they reach hostile actors. Advising on defensive countermeasures—how to detect if someone's been subjected to quantum wine manipulation. Developing protocols for safe handling." Thornton pulled out a document. "Twelve-month contract initially. Renewable annually. Starting salary £65,000. Full security clearance. Flexible hours—you'd work from home mostly, come to the office for monthly briefings."

"And I could still write about wine? For Decanter?"

"As long as you don't publish classified information. Your existing quantum wine papers are public—you can discuss those. But nothing new without clearance."

"What about the MW programme? The exam in August?"

"Your candidacy continues. The Institute has been notified that you're cooperating with a national security investigation. No black marks on your record."

It was everything Caldwell had threatened to take away. Offered back as reward for cooperation.

"And if I refuse?"

"Prison. Career destruction. Everything DCI Caldwell has already outlined." Thornton stood. "You have until tomorrow morning. Think carefully."


## THURSDAY EVENING

That evening, Alex lay on the narrow bed and thought about Elizabeth Chen.

Elizabeth had spent forty years fighting. Documenting quantum wine. Publishing despite dismissal. Working alone, dying without vindication.

What would Elizabeth do in Alex's position?

The answer came immediately: Elizabeth would refuse. Would go to prison. Would die fighting rather than work for the people who'd suppressed her research.

But Elizabeth had lost. Forty years of fighting, and she'd died dismissed. No vindication. No recognition. Nothing.

Alex had already won. Published the research. Made it public. Given Elizabeth the vindication she'd never got in life.

That was enough. That had to be enough.

And if accepting a government job—even a job protecting classified quantum wine research—meant Alex could keep her life, keep Emma, keep her career, stay connected to the work... wasn't that better than dying a martyr?

More than that: working inside the system gave Alex access. Information. Influence. She could shape how quantum wine research developed. Could ensure it wasn't just used for weapons. Could advocate for ethical frameworks from within.

Elizabeth had fought alone from outside. Alex could fight from inside. Different strategy. Same goal.

Elizabeth would understand. Elizabeth, who'd been practical and scientific, who'd hidden her research when continuing meant death, who'd spent forty years working alone because that was what survival required.

Elizabeth would understand that sometimes survival meant compromise. And compromise meant continuing the fight another way.

Alex made her decision.

Tomorrow morning, she'd sign everything. Take the job. Go home to Emma. Live her life within constraints.

But she wouldn't stop fighting. She'd just fight differently.


## FRIDAY, 21 FEBRUARY 2025

### DAY 4 - MORNING

Friday morning, 8:30 AM. The interview room. Caldwell, Thornton, and a new person—a man in a grey suit carrying a stack of documents.

"Ms Hartley," Caldwell said. "This is Mr Davies, from the Government Legal Department. He has contracts for your review."

Davies slid documents across the table. "Official Secrets Act declaration. Non-disclosure agreement covering all quantum wine research. Consultancy contract with the Home Office, twelve-month initial term, renewable annually. Starting salary £65,000, plus security clearance benefits."

Alex stared at the papers. Ten pages. Dense legal text. Her professional life restructured, constrained, controlled.

But also: her freedom. Her career. Her future with Emma.

"If you sign," Thornton said, "all charges are dropped. Your MW candidacy continues. You'll be released this afternoon. But Ms Hartley—understand this. Once you sign, you're bound by these agreements. Future violations of the Official Secrets Act carry significantly harsher penalties. This is your only chance to walk away clean."

Clean. As if signing this made her clean.

But what was the alternative? Prison? Losing everything?

Alex picked up the pen. Her hand shook slightly.

She thought about Wickham, dead for trying to prove quantum wine. About Moreau, killed for planning to go public. About Elizabeth Chen, spending forty years dismissed.

Alex had proved them right. Published the research. Made quantum wine impossible to suppress.

That was victory, even if it came with conditions.

She signed.

Her signature looked shaky, uncertain. But it was done.

Caldwell witnessed. Thornton witnessed. Davies collected the contracts, placed them in a folder, offered his hand.

"Welcome to the Home Office Scientific Advisory Council," he said. "You start Monday."

Alex couldn't speak. Just nodded.

"You'll be released at four PM," Caldwell said. "Processing takes a few hours. Someone will drive you home. And Ms Hartley? You made the right choice."

Had she?

Alex couldn't tell any more.


## FRIDAY AFTERNOON - RELEASE

Processing for release took three hours.

They returned her belongings: wallet, keys, her watch still showing Monday's time.

Alex reset the date. Friday, 21 February, 3:47 PM. Four days she'd been detained. Four days gone.

"Where's the USB drive?" Alex asked.

The grey-suited woman handed her a receipt. "Retained as evidence in an ongoing investigation. Classified materials."

Alex stared at the receipt. Victoria's research—forty years of work

—reduced to: *"One (1) USB storage device. Contents: Classified. Status: Retained."*

They'd copied it, analysed it, and now they were keeping it to ensure she couldn't distribute additional copies. Control the information. Control the threat.

Fine. The research was already public. By now the papers must have been downloaded thousands of times. Tens of thousands, maybe. Universities worldwide would be examining it, replicating the findings, building on Elizabeth's work. MI5 could keep the drive. The knowledge was already out there.

The woman was waiting, pen poised. Alex signed the receipt.

They gave her papers: copies of the contracts she'd signed, a welcome packet for the Home Office Scientific Advisory Council, a phone number to call on Monday morning. Her new handler would be Dr Thornton. Monthly briefings, quarterly reviews, annual contract renewal pending satisfactory performance.

At 3:47 PM, the grey-suited woman who'd brought her breakfast four days ago escorted Alex to the underground car park.

"Your transport's here. Someone will drive you home."

A civilian car this time. Not the black Range Rovers from Monday night. Just a normal sedan with a driver who didn't speak.

Alex got in the back seat, and the car pulled out of Thames House, into London afternoon traffic.

It was Friday. Late afternoon. The city was alive with people finishing work, heading to pubs, starting their weekends. Normal life. Normal Friday.

Alex watched it all through the car window, feeling disconnected. Like she'd been underwater for four days and surfaced to find the world unchanged whilst she'd fundamentally transformed.

The car drove through familiar streets—Millbank, Embankment, Strand. Towards Islington. Towards home.

Alex's throat tightened. Home. Emma. Real life.

The car pulled up outside her building at 4:23 PM. The driver said nothing, just unlocked the doors.

Alex got out. The car drove away immediately.

She stood on the pavement, staring at her front door. Four days. She'd left Monday evening in MI5 custody. Now she was back. Free. Employed. Constrained.

Alive.

Alex climbed the stairs, legs unsteady. Unlocked the flat door.

Emma was sitting on the sofa, laptop open, phone pressed to her ear. She looked exhausted—dark circles under her eyes, hair unwashed, wearing the same jumper she'd worn Monday.

She looked up when Alex entered. Went completely still. Then she ended the call without saying goodbye and crossed the room in three strides.

"Alex—"

Emma wrapped her arms round Alex so tightly Alex could barely breathe. Neither of them spoke. They just held each other, standing in the doorway, whilst four days of fear and separation and helplessness finally broke through.

Alex felt tears she'd been suppressing since Monday finally come. Emma was crying too. Both of them shaking, clinging to each other like drowning people finding solid ground.

"You're okay," Emma whispered. "You're home. You're okay."

"I'm okay." Alex's voice broke. "I'm home. I'm sorry. I'm so sorry."

"Don't apologise. Don't you dare apologise." Emma pulled back, held Alex's face in both hands. "What happened? Where were they keeping you?"

"Thames House. MI5 headquarters. Protective custody, they called it. Really just detention whilst they decided whether to charge me."

"Did they hurt you?"

"No. Just... interrogation. Psychological pressure. Threats." Alex pulled away gently, moved to the sofa, collapsed onto it. "They offered me a deal."

Emma sat beside her, took her hand. "What kind of deal?"

"Drop the charges, let me keep my MW candidacy, hire me as a consultant. In exchange, I sign non-disclosure agreements and work for the government on quantum wine countermeasures."

"You took the deal."

"I took the deal." Alex looked at their joined hands. "Prison or employment. It wasn't really a choice."

"I'm glad you took it. I'm so glad you're home." Emma squeezed her hand. "I tried everything. Called solicitors, called Morrison, called everyone I could think of. No one could help. National security—once they invoke that, there's no recourse."

"I know. Sophie told me—" Alex stopped. "Wait. Have you spoken to Sophie?"

"She rang Wednesday night. They'd released her that morning. She signed everything they wanted—handed over her grandmother's notebooks, agreed to non-disclosure, everything." Emma's voice was gentle. "She was terrified, Alex. She didn't know what else to do. They told her the same thing they told you—cooperate or face charges."

"She did the right thing. We both did. Survival is better than martyrdom."

"Is it?" Emma studied her face. "You don't sound convinced."

"I'm not. But I'm here. Free. With you. And I have a plan." Alex looked at Emma. "The job—it's not surrender. It's positioning. I'll be inside the system. I'll have access to quantum wine research. I can shape how it develops. Make sure it's not just weaponised. Advocate for ethics, transparency, proper frameworks."

"You're going to fight from inside."

"Exactly. Elizabeth fought from outside for forty years and lost. I'm going to fight from inside and maybe—maybe—actually change things." Alex managed a weak smile. "Strategic compromise instead of martyrdom."

Emma leaned her head on Alex's shoulder. "I think that's brave. Smarter than dying on principle."

They sat in silence for a moment.

"The quantum wine papers are still up," Emma said finally. "Still public. Downloaded over 80,000 times now. Universities worldwide are discussing it. You won that battle.”

“Did I? I published research and ended up in government custody. I signed away my freedom to publish anything else. I’m working for the same people who suppressed Elizabeth’s research forty years ago.” Alex set down the water glass Emma had given her. “That doesn’t feel like winning.”

“You proved Elizabeth was right. That’s winning. The rest—the job, the constraints—that’s just surviving.” Emma took Alex’s hand again. “Elizabeth fought alone and lost. You fought with allies and survived. That’s a different kind of victory.”

Alex wanted to believe that.

Her phone—returned by MI5 along with her other belongings— buzzed. She’d charged it whilst Emma made tea. Now messages flooded in: Emma (dozens from the past four days), Sophie (seventeen), Morrison (three), Jancis Robinson (five), Marcus Webb (two), editors, colleagues, journalists.

Alex opened Jancis’s messages first. The most recent, sent this morning:

> Alex, I heard through colleagues that you were taken into protective custody. I hope you’re safe and well. The tasting offer stands whenever you’re ready. Monday, 24 February, Berry Bros. & Rudd. Just you, Sophie, and myself. If quantum wine is real —and I believe it might be—the wine world needs credible evaluation from respected sources. I’m willing to provide that if you’ll trust me. Let me know. —Jancis

Monday. Three days away.

Alex showed Emma the message.

“Are you going to go?” Emma asked.

“I don’t know. I just signed government contracts. Non-disclosure agreements. I’m not supposed to discuss quantum wine publicly—“

“You’re not publishing new research. You’re participating in a professional wine tasting. That's what wine writers do." Emma's voice was firm. "Check your contract. I bet there's nothing preventing you from attending tastings or discussing already-published information."

Alex pulled out the contract Davies had given her. Read through the restrictions section carefully.

Emma was right. The restrictions covered publishing classified research, conducting unauthorised experiments, making public statements about classified programmes. But attending wine tastings—even quantum wine tastings—wasn't explicitly forbidden.

"Jancis wants to experience it herself," Alex said slowly. "If she does—if she writes about it for the Financial Times—that's the kind of validation the wine world will actually believe."

"Then you should go. You, Sophie, and the most respected wine critic in the world. Proving quantum wine is real." Emma smiled. "That's exactly the kind of vindication Elizabeth deserved."

Alex picked up her phone, replied to Jancis:

> Jancis, I'm home and safe. I'd be honoured to participate in your tasting. Monday, Berry Bros. & Rudd. Sophie will bring her grandmother's 1986 Tyrrell's Vat 1. Let me know what time. —Alex

The response came within minutes:

> Excellent. 2 PM. Private room, controlled conditions. I'll document everything. If this is real—and I suspect it is—the world needs to know. See you Monday. —JR

Alex set down her phone, looked at Emma.

"So. Three days to recover. And then we find out if Jancis Robinson—the Jancis Robinson—experiences quantum wine and believes it's real."

"No pressure."

"None at all."

They smiled at each other. First genuine smiles in days.

Alex still didn't know if she'd made the right choice. Didn't know if working for the government whilst pretending to be free was victory or capitulation.

But she was home. She was safe. And in three days, Jancis Robinson would taste quantum wine.

Maybe that was enough.

Maybe that was vindication after all.

## 11 / BERRY BROS. & RUDD

MONDAY, 24 FEBRUARY 2025

MORNING

MONDAY MORNING. Alex woke at 6:30 AM, two hours before her alarm, heart already racing.

Today. Today Jancis Robinson would taste quantum wine.

Emma stirred beside her. "Can't sleep?"

"Nervous. What if it doesn't work? What if the 1986 Tyrrell's doesn't show the effect with Jancis?"

"It worked with you. It worked with Sophie. It'll work with Jancis." Emma rolled over, propped herself up on one elbow. "She's genetically sensitive—professional taster, decades of training, one of the most refined palates in the world. If anyone can experience quantum wine, it's her."

"But what if—"

"Alex. Stop." Emma kissed her forehead. "You've already proved quantum wine exists. Published papers. Got independent verification. This tasting with Jancis isn't about proving anything. It's about sharing Elizabeth Chen's discovery with someone who'll appreciate it. Someone who'll write about it with the respect it deserves."

"You're right. I know you're right."

"Of course I'm right. I'm always right." Emma smiled. "Now. Breakfast. You need to eat. Can't have you fainting in front of Jancis Robinson because you were too nervous to have toast."

They ate breakfast together. Alex couldn't taste anything, her stomach in knots. She'd laid out her clothes the night before—smart trousers, white shirt, navy blazer. Professional but not too formal. Wine writer, not government employee.

Although she was both now. The Home Office contracts sat in a drawer, signed and binding. She'd start officially next Monday. But today—today she was still just a wine writer participating in a private tasting.

At 10 AM, Sophie rang. "Are you ready?"

"No. Terrified. You?"

"Same. I've been awake since five. I keep checking the bottles—what if they've oxidised? What if they've lost the quantum effect? What if—"

"Sophie. Breathe. The bottles are fine. You've been storing them properly. They'll work."

"How do you know?"

"I don't. But we have to believe they will." Alex paused. "Are you bringing your grandmother's notebooks?"

"Some of them. The ones documenting the 1986 vintage specifically. I thought Jancis might want to see Elizabeth's actual handwriting, her observations from that harvest." Sophie's voice caught. "My grandmother documented this forty years ago. Today, Jancis Robinson reads those notes and then experiences exactly what my grandmother described. That's... that's everything."

"It is. We'll see you at Berry Bros. Quarter to two?"

"I'll be there at 1:30. I need time to settle my nerves."

They ended the call. Alex looked at Emma. "She's bringing Elizabeth's notebooks. Original documentation from 1986."

"Good. Jancis will appreciate the historical context. The continuity between Elizabeth's observations and your experience." Emma checked the time. "You should leave by one. Traffic on a Monday afternoon can be unpredictable."

"Come with me."

"What?"

"Come with me. To Berry Bros. You won't be in the tasting—Jancis wants just the three of us—but you could wait nearby. Moral support." Alex took Emma's hand. "I want you there. Even if you're just sitting in a café. Knowing you're close."

Emma squeezed her hand. "Of course I'll come. Let me change into something suitable for St James's."


MONDAY AFTERNOON

1:45 PM

ST JAMES'S, LONDON

Berry Bros. & Rudd occupied a narrow seventeenth-century building at 3 St James's Street, sandwiched between shops selling bespoke suits and handmade shoes. The oldest wine merchant in Britain—founded 1698, royal warrant holders since George III.

Alex had been here once before, years ago, touring the historic cellars that ran beneath Pall Mall. Vaulted brick ceilings, dim lighting, thousands of bottles sleeping in the cool darkness. Napoleon III had kept wine here. Lord Byron. Winston Churchill. The cellars held history.

Today, they'd hold something new: Jancis Robinson experiencing quantum wine.

Emma squeezed Alex's hand. "I'll be at the café across the street. Text me when you're done. And Alex? You've got this. Just be yourself. Trust the wine."

"Thank you. For everything. For believing me when this all sounded insane."

"You're welcome. Now go. Don't keep Jancis waiting."

Alex crossed St James's Street, pushed open the heavy wooden door of Berry Bros. & Rudd.

The shop was tiny—barely six metres wide, more like someone's private library than a commercial space. Dark wood panelling. Antique furniture. A massive set of scales from the eighteenth century, used historically to weigh customers (a tradition maintained today—Alex had been weighed on her previous visit, her weight recorded in a leather-bound ledger alongside Byron's and Churchill's).

A young man in a suit looked up from behind a desk. "Ms Hartley?"

"Yes."

"Ms Robinson is expecting you. This way."

He led Alex through the shop, past racks of fine wine with hand-written labels, through a door marked Private, down a narrow staircase. The temperature dropped with each step. They descended into the cellars—vaulted brick, dim lighting, the smell of old stone and sleeping wine.

The cellars were larger than the shop above—a labyrinth of interconnected rooms stretching beneath Pall Mall. The young man navigated confidently, turning left at a rack of Burgundy, right at a corridor of Bordeaux, finally stopping at a heavy wooden door.

"The Napoleon Room," he said, opening it. "Ms Robinson's already inside. Can I bring you anything? Water? Coffee?"

"Water would be lovely. Thank you."

Alex stepped through the door.

The Napoleon Room was small and intimate—perhaps four metres square, with a vaulted brick ceiling and walls lined with old wine racks. A round table stood in the centre, covered with a white cloth. Three chairs. Three settings of wineglasses—six at each place. A notebook and pen at each setting.

And Jancis Robinson, standing beside the table, examining a bottle of wine.

She looked up when Alex entered. Silver hair, intelligent eyes behind stylish glasses. She wore simple black trousers and a grey jumper—practical, professional. No jewellery except a watch.

"Alex. Thank you for coming." Jancis's voice was warm but serious. "This room is as controlled as I could manage—constant temperature, minimal light, no external interruptions. We'll have complete privacy."

"It's perfect. Thank you for hosting this."

"Thank you for trusting me." Jancis set down the bottle—Alex recognised it as Tyrrell's Vat 1, though not the 1986. "I've assembled a small vertical of Hunter Semillon. 2018, 2014, 2008, 2004, 1998. And Sophie is bringing the 1986. I want context before we taste the quantum-active wine. Want to understand what normal Hunter Semillon tastes like at various ages."

"That's very thorough."

"If I'm going to write about quantum wine for the Financial Times, I need to be thorough. My readers trust me to be rigorous and sceptical. If I tell them wine can store consciousness, they need to believe I've evaluated it properly."

The door opened. Sophie entered, carrying a padded wine bag and a leather portfolio. She looked nervous but determined.

"Sophie Chen," Jancis said, extending her hand. "I'm so glad you could join us. And thank you for bringing your grandmother's bottles."

"Thank you for taking this seriously. For being willing to experience what my grandmother documented." Sophie's voice was tight with emotion. "She spent forty years being dismissed. Having someone of your stature actually taste quantum wine, actually consider its validity—that would have meant everything to her."

"MI5 had taken most of my grandmother's notebooks," Sophie said, setting the portfolio on the table. "But they let me keep the personal ones — the harvest diaries that document her vineyard observations. No classified material. Just a woman writing about wine."

"I hope I can do her research justice." Jancis gestured to the table. "Please, sit. Both of you. Let me explain how this will work."

They sat. Sophie carefully removed two bottles from the padded bag: 1986 Tyrrell's Vat 1, both with perfect fill levels, both looking like they'd been stored impeccably for four decades.

"We'll taste chronologically," Jancis said. "Youngest to oldest. I want to experience the development arc of Hunter Semillon. Understand what's normal for these wines at ten, fifteen, twenty, twenty-seven years of age. Then we'll taste the 1986—thirty-nine years old. If I experience something different, something unusual, I'll know it's not just the normal character of aged Hunter Semillon."

"That makes sense," Alex said.

"I'm not going to tell you what I'm experiencing during the tasting. I'll make my notes privately. After we've finished all six wines, we'll compare observations. See if we experienced the same things. If there's alignment—if we all describe unusual sensory experiences with the 1986 and not the other wines—that's evidence. Replicable, documented evidence."

"You're treating this like a proper scientific experiment," Sophie said.

"Because it is. If quantum wine is real—if your grandmother was right—this isn't just a wine story. It's a neuroscience story. A quantum biology story. Possibly the biggest story in wine since phylloxera." Jancis smiled. "So yes, I'm being scientific about it."

The young man returned with a tray: three bottles of water, three clean spittoons, a basket of plain crackers for palate cleansing.

"We won't be disturbed," he said, and left, closing the door behind him.

Jancis checked her watch. "It's 2:03. Let's begin."

She picked up the first bottle—2018 Tyrrell's Vat 1—and poured small measures into each of their first glasses.

"This wine is seven years old," Jancis said. "Still quite young for

Hunter Semillon. I'm expecting high acidity, citrus character, minimal development. Let's see."

Alex went through her ritual: appearance (pale gold, bright), nose (lemon, lime, struck match, flinty minerality), palate (high acid, lean, very tight, not ready to drink). She made notes. Professional tasting notes. Wine critic mode.

Jancis made notes too, writing quickly in precise handwriting.

Sophie tasted, made notes, looked like she was barely breathing.

They spat. Cleansed palates with water and crackers.

"Second wine," Jancis said. "2014. Eleven years old."

She poured. They tasted. Alex noted: developing honeyed character now, still high acid, beginning to show the complexity that made Hunter Semillon age so well.

They worked through the vertical methodically. 2008—seventeen years old, showing toast and lanolin. 2004—twenty-one years old, honeyed and complex but still vibrant. 1998—twenty-seven years old, extraordinarily developed yet somehow fresh.

Each wine was remarkable. But each was recognisably just wine. Good wine. Great wine. But normal wine.

Nothing unusual. No sensory experiences beyond what great aged Semillon should provide.

Jancis made detailed notes at each stage, her expression neutral, professional.

Finally, only one glass remained empty at each setting.

Jancis picked up the first bottle of 1986 Tyrrell's Vat 1. Examined it in the dim cellar light. The wine was deep gold, almost amber.

"This is it," Sophie whispered. "The vintage my grandmother was documenting. The harvest she witnessed in January 1986. The wine that proved her theory."

Jancis nodded. "Before we taste this—Sophie, may I see your grandmother's notebooks? The ones documenting this vintage specifically?"

Sophie opened the leather portfolio, carefully removed three notebooks. Old, worn, the covers faded. She opened the first to a page marked with a ribbon.

*January 15, 1986. Harvest day. Tyrrell's Vat 1 vineyard, Pokolbin.*

*Weather: Clear, hot. Temperature reached 38°C by midday. Started picking at 5:47 AM to avoid heat. Grapes perfect—sugar levels optimal (11.2 Baumé), acidity high (pH 3.04). Everything as predicted.*

*This is it. The vintage that will prove them all wrong.*

*If the quantum coherence theory is correct, these grapes—picked today, fermented this week—will encode the conditions of this harvest. The heat. The light. My certainty. In forty years, someone will taste this wine and access this moment. They'll experience what I'm experiencing right now.*

*I stood in the vineyard at dawn. Watched the sun rise over the Brokenback Range. Felt the heat building. Heard the cicadas starting. I thought: this is the moment. This is proof.*

*They'll taste this wine and they'll know I was right.*

Jancis read slowly, carefully. Her expression shifted—surprise, interest, something that might have been awe.

"Your grandmother predicted this," Jancis said softly. "Forty years ago. She predicted that someone would taste this wine in 2025 and experience her harvest memory."

"She made this prediction on harvest day itself," Sophie said. "January 15, 1986. Standing in the vineyard as the grapes were being picked, predicting that forty years later, someone would taste the wine made from those grapes and experience this exact moment. And she was right."

Jancis set down the notebook. Picked up the bottle of 1986 Tyrrell's Vat 1. Looked at Alex and Sophie.

"Are you both ready?"

Alex's heart hammered. "Yes."

"Sophie?"

"Ready."

Jancis poured.

The wine was deep gold, viscous, coating the glass. Alex lifted hers, inhaled.

The aroma was extraordinary—all the characteristics of aged Hunter Semillon magnified: honey, toast, beeswax, lanolin, preserved lemon, something like hay baking in summer sun. And underneath, that other sensation. Not a smell. A feeling.

Heat. Bright sun. The sound of cicadas.

Alex looked across the table. Sophie had gone very still, her glass raised, her eyes wide.

Jancis brought the glass to her lips. Tasted.

For a moment, nothing. Just the three of them in the Napoleon Room, tasting wine in silence.

Then Jancis's expression changed. Her eyes widened. Her breathing quickened. The professional mask cracked completely.

She set down her glass very carefully. Sat very still. Her hands were trembling.

"Jancis?" Alex asked quietly. "Are you all right?"

Jancis didn't answer immediately. She was staring at her glass like it had just spoken to her.

Finally, she looked up. Met Alex's eyes. Then Sophie's.

"I was in a vineyard," she said, her voice barely above a whisper. "Australian vineyard. Early morning. The sun just rising. Hot— already hot, even at dawn. I could feel it on my skin. I could hear cicadas. I could smell eucalyptus." She paused. "And a woman's voice. Very clear. Saying: 'This is the vintage that will prove them all wrong.'"

Sophie made a small sound—half sob, half laugh. "That's my grandmother. That's Elizabeth. That's what Alex experienced. That's what I experienced. That's the quantum memory."

"It felt completely real," Jancis continued. "Not like imagination. Not like a hallucination. Real. I was there. In that vineyard. Forty years ago. Experiencing someone else's memory." She picked up her glass again, stared at the wine. "My God. Your grandmother was right. It's real. Quantum wine is real."

Alex felt tears prick her eyes. "You experienced it. You actually experienced it."

"I did. And I—" Jancis stopped, took a breath. Her hands were still shaking. "I've tasted thousands of wines. Forty-five years as a professional taster. I've experienced extraordinary wines that moved me emotionally. Wines that brought back memories of places I'd been, people I'd known. But this—this wasn't my memory. This was someone else's. And it was as real as anything I've ever experienced."

She set down her glass, picked up her pen, started writing. Her handwriting was shaky now, not the precise script from the earlier wines.

They sat in silence whilst Jancis wrote. Alex and Sophie exchanged looks—relief, vindication, disbelief that this was actually happening.

Finally, Jancis set down her pen. "I need to taste it again. To confirm. To see if I experience the same thing."

She lifted her glass. Tasted again.

This time, Alex watched her face. Saw the exact moment the quantum experience hit—Jancis's eyes unfocused, her breathing stopped for a heartbeat, her expression shifting to something distant, transported. She was there. In the vineyard. In January 1986.

When she came back, tears were running down her face.

"Your grandmother," Jancis said to Sophie, her voice thick. "She was there. I felt her certainty. Her determination. Forty years of working alone, being dismissed, and in that moment—standing in the vineyard at dawn—she knew. She knew she was right and everyone else was wrong."

Sophie was crying too. "That's exactly what she felt. That's what the notebook says. 'This is the vintage that will prove them all wrong.' She knew. And now you know. You've experienced what she experienced."

Jancis wiped her eyes. "I need to document this properly. Every detail. Because I'm going to write about this for the Financial Times, and my readers need to understand—this isn't fantasy. This isn't new age mysticism. This is quantum biology. Real. Replicable. Extraordinary."

She wrote for ten minutes. Filled three pages with detailed notes—every sensory detail, every aspect of the experience, comparing it to the five other wines they'd tasted.

When she finished, she looked at Alex and Sophie. "Tell me your experiences. Both of you. What you felt when you first tasted the 1986."

Alex described the Wickham tasting. The vineyard. The heat. The magpie call. The woman's voice. The certainty.

Sophie described the same experience. Identical details. The harvest morning. The vindication.

Jancis listened, made notes, nodded. "Alignment. Complete alignment across three independent tasters. That's replicable evidence."

"What are you going to write?" Sophie asked.

"The truth. That quantum wine exists. That your grandmother spent forty years documenting something real. That I experienced it myself, under controlled conditions, with independent witnesses." Jancis paused. "But I also need to write about the implications. What this means for wine science. For consciousness research. For understanding memory and time."

"And the dangers," Alex added. "Victoria Mills's weaponisation research. The applications for memory manipulation. The reasons Meridian has been trying to suppress this."

"I'll be careful about that," Jancis said. "I don't want to give anyone a manual for weaponising wine. But yes—the world needs to know this exists. Needs to understand both the wonder and the danger."

She stood, picked up the bottle of 1986 Tyrrell's Vat 1, examined it in the cellar's dim light. "This is the most extraordinary wine I've ever tasted. Not because of its flavour—though it's remarkably well-preserved—but because of what it contains. Forty years of stored memory. A woman's vindication, preserved in glass."

She placed it carefully back on the table, as if it were something sacred.

"When will your article publish?" Alex asked.

"I'll write it this week. Submit to the Financial Times Friday. They'll want to fact-check, verify, possibly interview their own scientists. Publication probably next Monday or Tuesday." Jancis looked at both of them. "Are you prepared for what happens after? Once the most respected wine publication in the world confirms quantum wine exists?"

Alex thought about her Home Office contracts. Her restrictions. The government job starting in one week.

"I'm prepared. As much as anyone can be."

"Good. Because this will change everything. The wine world. The scientific world. Everything." Jancis smiled. "Your grandmother would be very proud, Sophie. What she couldn't achieve in forty years—recognition, credibility, vindication—you've achieved in two weeks."

"We achieved it," Sophie corrected. "Alex published the research. Marcus Webb provided verification. You're providing validation from the wine world. My grandmother's vindication required all of us."

"Elizabeth fought alone," Alex said quietly. "But she doesn't have to be vindicated alone. That's the difference."

They packed up the bottles carefully. Jancis kept detailed notes— weights, measurements, photographs of the labels, everything documented for her article.

As they climbed the stairs from the cellar back to the shop, Alex felt something shift. A weight lifting. She'd proved quantum wine existed. Published the research. Brought Jancis Robinson to experience it herself. Made Elizabeth Chen's forty years of dismissed work impossible to ignore.

That was victory. Even with the government job, even with the restrictions, even with everything she'd signed away.

That was vindication.

They emerged into the shop. The young man looked up. "How did it go?"

"Extraordinary," Jancis said simply. "Truly extraordinary. Thank you for the use of the Napoleon Room."

"My pleasure, Ms Robinson. Same time next week?"

"Actually, I think once was enough for this particular experiment. But thank you."

They stepped out onto St James's Street. Late afternoon sun, February cold, London traffic rumbling past. Normal world. Normal Monday.

Except nothing was normal any more.

Emma was waiting at the café across the street. She looked up when they emerged, saw Alex's face, and smiled.

"How did it go?" she mouthed.

Alex gave her a thumbs up. Emma's smile widened.

Jancis shook hands with both Alex and Sophie. "I'll send you the article before publication. Make sure I've got the science right. And thank you—both of you—for trusting me with this. For letting me experience what your grandmother documented."

"Thank you for believing it was possible," Sophie said. "For taking quantum wine seriously when you had every reason to dismiss it."

"I'm a critic. My job is to evaluate wine rigorously and honestly. Today, I evaluated the most extraordinary wine of my career." Jancis's expression was serious. "Your grandmother was right, Sophie. And now the world will know."

She walked off down St James's Street, already pulling out her phone, probably already composing notes for her article.

Alex and Sophie looked at each other.

"We did it," Sophie said.

"We did."

"My grandmother spent forty years fighting. And we vindicated her in two weeks."

"Not we. You. You preserved her notebooks. You contacted me after the Wickham tasting. You were brave enough to pursue this even when it seemed insane." Alex squeezed Sophie's hand. "Elizabeth would be proud."

"I hope so." Sophie wiped her eyes. "I really hope so."

Emma crossed the street, wrapped Alex in a hug. "You look happy. Actually happy. First time since you got out of Thames House."

"I am happy. Jancis experienced it. The quantum effect. Exactly what Elizabeth documented. Exactly what Sophie and I experienced. She's writing about it for the Financial Times." Alex pulled back, looked at Emma. "We won. Despite everything—the government job, the restrictions, all of it—we won. Elizabeth's vindication is happening."

"I'm so proud of you." Emma kissed her. "Both of you. What you've accomplished in two weeks is extraordinary."

Sophie's phone buzzed. She checked it. "Text from Marcus Webb."

She read aloud: "'Jancis just emailed me. She experienced it? The quantum effect? Is this real? Call me ASAP—doesn't matter what time.'"

Sophie immediately called him, put it on speaker. "Dr Webb?"

"Sophie. Alex. Tell me. Did Jancis experience quantum wine?"

"It's true. We just finished the tasting. She experienced the 1986 Tyrrell's Vat 1. Elizabeth's harvest memory. Everything."

Webb was quiet for a moment. When he spoke again, his voice was thick with emotion. "Elizabeth's vindicated then. Finally. Forty years late, but vindicated."

"She is. Thanks to you. Your verification made publication possible."

"No. Thanks to all of us. You published. I verified. Jancis validated. That's how science works—collaboration, replication, independent verification." He paused. "There's going to be a conference. June. Bordeaux. International Wine Science Conference. They've invited me to present on quantum wine. I'm going to dedicate the presentation to Elizabeth. Would you both consider co-presenting?"

Alex's stomach tightened. "I've got government restrictions now. I signed contracts—"

"For publishing new classified research. Not for presenting already-public research at academic conferences." Webb's voice was firm. "Check your contracts. I bet presenting public research is permitted. And if it is—if you can come to Bordeaux—we make Elizabeth's vindication complete. Present her work to the international wine science community. Get her the recognition she deserved when she was alive."

Alex looked at Sophie. Sophie nodded.

"We'll check the contracts," Alex said. "If we're permitted—we'll be there."

"Good. I'll send details. And Hartley? Chen? You did good. Elizabeth would be proud. Hell, I'm proud. You took on governments and corporations and suppression, and you won. That's not nothing."

He ended the call.

Alex, Sophie, and Emma stood on St James's Street as afternoon faded towards evening. Monday traffic. Normal London. Normal lives being lived all round them.

But for Alex, nothing was normal any more.

She'd published research that proved quantum wine existed. She'd brought Jancis Robinson to experience it firsthand. She'd vindicated Elizabeth Chen's forty years of dismissed work.

And in June, she'd present that vindication to the international wine science community.

Despite the government job. Despite the restrictions. Despite everything she'd signed away.

She'd won.

Not the way she'd expected. Not without costs.

But vindication nonetheless.

"I need wine," Sophie said. "Actual wine. Normal wine. No quantum effects. Just celebration."

"I know a place," Emma said. "Islington. Good wine list. Let's celebrate properly."

They walked towards the Tube station, three women who'd fought governments and corporations and forty years of suppression.

And won.

Behind them, in the cellars of Berry Bros. & Rudd, bottles of quantum wine slept in the darkness.

Waiting for the next person to discover them.

Waiting for the next story to unfold.

Waiting for science to finally catch up with what Elizabeth Chen had known for forty years:

Wine could store consciousness.

Memory could be bottled.

Time could be tasted.

And the impossible was real.

## 12 / CONSEQUENCES



Tuesday morning, Alex woke to her phone buzzing incessantly. She checked the time—7:23 AM—and saw seventeen missed calls, forty-three text messages, and sixty-seven emails.

Something had happened.

She opened the most recent text. From Jancis Robinson, sent ten minutes ago:

> Alex. My article published early. Financial
> Times ran it this morning, front page of the
> business section. Reaction is... significant.
> Call me when you're up. —JR

Alex's heart hammered. She opened her browser, navigated to the Financial Times website.

The headline dominated the page:

QUANTUM WINE: TASTE, MEMORY, AND THE IMPOS-
SIBLE MADE REAL By Jancis Robinson MW

Below it, a subtitle:

*The world's most respected wine critic experiences quantum consciousness transfer through aged wine. What she found will change science forever.*

Alex read:

*Yesterday afternoon, in the historic cellars of Berry Bros. & Rudd, I experienced something impossible. I tasted a 39-year-old wine—1986 Tyrrell's Vat 1 Hunter Valley Semillon—and accessed someone else's memory. Not metaphorically. Not poetically. Actually, physically, neurologically experienced a memory that wasn't mine.*

*I was transported to an Australian vineyard on a January morning in 1986. I felt the heat. I heard cicadas. I smelled eucalyptus. And I heard a woman's voice—Dr Elizabeth Chen, the oenologist who documented this phenomenon for forty years—saying: "This is the vintage that will prove them all wrong."*

*Dr Chen was right. And forty years after she began documenting quantum coherence in aged wines, her vindication has arrived.*

The article was 2,500 words. Detailed. Rigorous. Describing the controlled tasting conditions, the five non-quantum wines for comparison, the identical experiences across three independent tasters.

Jancis described the mechanism—quantum-coherent phenolic networks, information storage, memory transfer. She cited Alex's published papers, Webb's verification, Victoria Mills's research.

She described Elizabeth Chen's forty years of dismissed work. The 1979 paper that destroyed her career. The decades of lonely documentation. The death in 2022 without recognition.

And she described the vindication:

*Dr Chen's granddaughter, Sophie Chen, preserved her notebooks. Wine writer Alexandra Hartley published her research. Quantum physicist Dr Marcus Webb provided verification. And yesterday, I experienced what Dr Chen documented: quantum wine is real.*

The article ended:

*This is not the end of quantum wine research. It's the beginning. Scientists worldwide must now grapple with the implications: wine can store consciousness. Memory can be transferred through molecules. The impossible is possible.*

*Dr Elizabeth Chen spent forty years trying to tell us this. She was dismissed, mocked, destroyed professionally for her honesty. History will remember her differently. As the woman who discovered something extraordinary. As the scientist who was right when everyone else was wrong.*

*As the person who proved that wine is more than fermented grapes. It's memory. It's time. It's consciousness in a bottle.*

*And it's real.*

Alex set down her phone, hands shaking.

Jancis had done it. Written about quantum wine with the full weight of her authority. Published in the Financial Times, one of the world's most respected publications.

Elizabeth's vindication was complete.

Emma stirred beside her. "What's wrong? You're vibrating."

"Jancis's article published. Front page of the Financial Times business section. She's calling quantum wine real. She's vindicating Elizabeth Chen. She's—" Alex's voice broke. "She's telling the world everything we proved."

Emma sat up, took the phone, read the article. Her expression shifted from sleepy to alert to awed.

"This is extraordinary. Jancis Robinson—THE Jancis Robinson—

is calling quantum wine real in the Financial Times. That's—" Emma looked at Alex. "That's going to change everything."

"I know."

"No, I mean everything. Your government job. The restrictions. The scientific community. The wine world. This article legitimises quantum wine completely. There's no dismissing it now."

Alex's phone rang. Jancis.

"Jancis. I just read it. The Financial Times piece—it's extraordinary. Thank you for taking this seriously. For writing about Elizabeth with such respect."

"She deserved respect. She deserved recognition forty years ago." Jancis's voice was firm. "The article published at midnight. By six AM, it had been shared 50,000 times. By seven, I'd received interview requests from BBC, Sky News, CNN, Nature, Science Magazine. Everyone wants to talk about quantum wine."

"What are you telling them?"

"The truth. That I experienced it myself. That it's real. That Dr Chen was right." A pause. "But Alex, you need to know—your name is in the article. Your papers are cited. People will want to interview you. And I know you have government restrictions now—"

"I'll handle it. I published research. That's public record. I can discuss published research. I just can't publish new classified information." Alex thought about her Home Office contracts. "I start the government job Monday. Until then, I'm still just a wine writer. I can give interviews."

"Good. Because the wine world needs to hear from you. You're one of three people who've experienced quantum wine and published about it. Your voice matters."

They spoke for ten more minutes—logistics, interview requests, how to handle the media attention. When Alex finally hung up, her phone immediately started ringing again.

BBC Science. She answered.

"Ms Hartley? We'd like to interview you about quantum wine.

This morning if possible. We're doing a segment for BBC Breakfast at eight AM. Would you be available?"

"I—yes. Where?"

"We can send a crew to you—they're already mobile and can be there by 7:45. Where are you?"

"Islington. But I'd need time to prepare—"

"Forty-five minutes should work. We'll be there at 7:45. Thank you, Ms Hartley. This is going to be extraordinary television."

Alex ended the call, looked at Emma. "BBC wants to interview me. At 7:45. For BBC Breakfast. I need to shower. And dress. And figure out what to say."

"Say the truth. That quantum wine is real. That Elizabeth Chen was right. That science needs to take this seriously." Emma was already pulling clothes from the wardrobe. "Wear the navy blazer. White shirt. Professional but not stiff. And Alex—" She turned, her expression serious. "This is it. This is your moment. Don't waste it being modest or apologetic. Own what you've discovered."

Alex showered, dressed, tried to calm her racing heart.

At 7:43, the buzzer rang. BBC crew. Two people with cameras, lights, and the kind of efficient professionalism that came from doing breakfast television every morning.

They set up in the living room—lights positioned, camera angled, a small microphone clipped to Alex's blazer.

"We're going live at 8:07," the producer said. "Three minutes, max. The hosts will ask about quantum wine, your experience, what this means for science. Just be natural. Tell your story."

At 8:07 exactly, the camera's red light blinked on.

Alex took a breath, steadied herself.

She heard the host's voice through her earpiece: "This morning, we're joined by wine writer Alexandra Hartley, who recently published research claiming that wine can store and transfer consciousness. Ms Hartley, is that really what you're suggesting? That wine has memory?"

Alex looked at the camera. Thought about Elizabeth Chen, forty years of lonely work. Thought about Wickham, dead for this truth. Thought about Victoria Mills, hiding for thirty years.

"Yes," Alex said clearly. "That's exactly what I'm suggesting. And it's not just suggestion—it's verified scientific fact. Wine can develop quantum-coherent molecular structures that store information patterns from the environment during ageing. When certain people consume these wines, they experience vivid sensory recall of those stored patterns. Including memories from decades ago."

"You experienced this yourself?"

"I did. I drank a 39-year-old Hunter Valley Semillon and accessed a memory from the 1986 harvest. I felt Australian heat. Heard cicadas. Experienced a moment from forty years ago as if I was physically there." Alex leant forward slightly. "And yesterday, Jancis Robinson—one of the world's most respected wine critics—experienced the same wine and had an identical experience. Under controlled conditions. With witnesses. This isn't fantasy. This is quantum biology."

"But how is that possible? How can wine store memory?"

"The same way birds navigate using quantum effects in their eyes. The same way plants use quantum coherence for photosynthesis. Quantum mechanics operates in biological systems all the time— we're just beginning to understand it. Wine, stored in darkness for decades, provides ideal conditions for quantum coherence. Phenolic networks form entangled states. Information gets encoded and preserved."

"And someone drinking the wine can access that information?"

"About eight to twelve per cent of the population—people with genetic sensitivity and trained palates—can experience quantum wine effects. Professional tasters, mostly. The rest of the population just tastes good wine. But for those who are sensitive, the experience is profound."

The interview lasted four minutes. When it ended, the producer was grinning. "That was excellent. Really excellent. Natural, authoritative, fascinating. Thank you, Ms Hartley."

They packed up quickly. By 8:15, they were gone.

Alex sat on the sofa, suddenly exhausted.

Emma sat beside her, took her hand. "You were brilliant. Confident. Clear. You made quantum wine sound real and scientifically rigorous, not new age mysticism."

"I hope so. Because now everyone's going to have an opinion about it."

Her phone rang again. Sky News. Then Channel 4. Then CNN.

By noon, Alex had given seven interviews. BBC, Sky News, Channel 4, CNN International, two for science podcasts, one for Nature News.

Every interviewer asked the same questions: Is quantum wine real? What did you experience? What does this mean for science?

And Alex gave the same answers: It's real. I experienced stored memory. This changes everything.

At 2 PM, her phone rang. Unknown number. Alex almost ignored it—she'd been fielding calls all morning, most from journalists or scientists or curiosity seekers.

But something made her answer.

"Ms Hartley. Dr Patricia Thornton. We need to talk."

Alex's stomach dropped. Her Home Office supervisor. Already.

"Dr Thornton. Hello."

"I've been watching your interviews. BBC, Sky News, CNN. Very articulate. Very convincing." Thornton's voice was neutral. "But we need to discuss your contractual obligations. You start work Monday. I need to know—are you planning to continue giving interviews? Making public statements?"

"I'm discussing already-published research. The contracts don't forbid that—"

"The contracts require discretion. Consultation with your supervisor before making public statements." Thornton's voice hardened slightly. "You've given seven interviews this morning without consulting me. That's concerning."

"The Jancis Robinson article published this morning. Journalists started calling at seven AM. I didn't have time to consult—"

"Then you should have declined the interviews until we'd discussed appropriate messaging." A pause. "Ms Hartley, I understand you're excited about quantum wine validation. But you work for the government now. We have equities in this research. We need to control the narrative."

"Control the narrative? Elizabeth Chen spent forty years having her narrative controlled—dismissed, suppressed, destroyed. I'm not doing that to her memory."

"You're employed to protect classified research, not publicise it."

"I'm publicising already-public research. There's a difference."

Thornton was quiet for a moment. "We'll discuss this Monday. When you come in for your first day. But Ms Hartley—be careful. Enthusiasm for quantum wine is one thing. Becoming a public spokesperson for something the government considers classified is another."

She ended the call.

Alex set down her phone, feeling the weight of constraints settling back over her shoulders.

Emma watched her. "Problem?"

"Thornton. She's not happy about the interviews. Says I should have consulted her first. That I need to be discreet about quantum wine."

"You published papers about quantum wine. Jancis Robinson just validated it in the Financial Times. Half the scientific world is discussing it. How are you supposed to be discreet?"

"I don't know. But I start the government job Monday. Until then —" Alex picked up her phone. "Until then, I'm going to do as many interviews as I can. Make quantum wine as public as possible. Make Elizabeth's vindication so complete that even the government can't suppress it."

## WEDNESDAY, 26 FEBRUARY 2025

Wednesday morning brought more interview requests. And something else: an email from the Institute of Masters of Wine.

Alex opened it with trepidation.

*Dear Ms Hartley,*

*We've reviewed your recent publications regarding quantum wine research and your media appearances discussing these findings. Whilst we note concerns raised by government authorities regarding classified research, we've determined that your MW candidacy may continue.*

*However, your practical examination scheduled for August 2025 will include questions about quantum wine. As this phenomenon is now part of the public discourse on wine science, MW candidates must be prepared to discuss it knowledgeably and objectively.*

*Please continue your studies. We look forward to your examination.*

*Regards, The Institute of Masters of Wine*

Alex read it twice, hardly believing it.

Her MW candidacy was safe. The examination would proceed. They were even incorporating quantum wine into the examination questions.

Recognition. Official recognition from the wine world's highest authority.

She showed Emma the email.

"They're taking it seriously," Emma said. "The Institute of Masters of Wine is acknowledging quantum wine as legitimate wine science. That's—Alex, that's enormous."

"I know. Elizabeth spent forty years trying to be taken seriously by the wine establishment. Now the MW programme is testing candidates on quantum wine." Alex felt tears prick her eyes. "She did it. We did it. Quantum wine is real wine science now."

Her phone buzzed. Text from Sophie:

> Did you see the FT piece trending on Twitter? 500,000 shares. Jancis's validation is everywhere. Universities worldwide are requesting research access. My grandmother's notebooks are being cited in scientific papers. This is really happening.

Alex replied:

> It's happening. Elizabeth's vindication is complete.

Another text, from Marcus Webb:

> Bordeaux conference confirmed. June 15-18. You and Sophie are listed as co-presenters on my quantum wine session. "The Research of Dr Elizabeth Chen: Quantum Coherence in Aged Wines." 300-person auditorium. This is the big stage, Hartley.

Alex stared at the message. June. Four months away. The international wine science conference. Presenting Elizabeth's research to the global wine community.

The ultimate vindication.

She replied:

> We'll be there. For Elizabeth.

Webb:

> For Elizabeth. And for everyone who's ever been dismissed for telling the truth.

## THURSDAY, 27 FEBRUARY 2025

Thursday brought media saturation. Quantum wine was everywhere.

The Guardian ran a feature: "Wine, Memory, and Quantum Mechanics: The Discovery That Changes Everything."

Nature published a perspective piece: "Quantum Biology in Aged Wines: Implications for Consciousness Research."

The New York Times: "A Wine Writer's Discovery: How Quantum Physics Explains the Impossible."

Every article cited Alex's research. Every piece mentioned Elizabeth Chen. Every discussion acknowledged forty years of dismissed work now vindicated.

At 3 PM, Alex's phone rang. Sophie.

"Have you seen the latest?" Sophie's voice was high with emotion. "UC Davis—where my grandmother worked—they're creating an endowed research position. The Dr Elizabeth Chen Chair in Quantum Oenology. Fully funded. They're soliciting applications now."

"Sophie, that's—"

"They're naming a research chair after her. At the university that destroyed her career forty years ago. They're commemorating her. Recognising her contribution." Sophie was crying now. "She spent her whole life fighting for recognition from UC Davis. And now—now she's going to have a chair named after her."

"She deserves it. She deserves all of it."

"I know. I just wish she was alive to see it."

"Maybe she can. If consciousness can be stored in wine—"

"Don't. I can't think about that right now." Sophie took a breath. "There's something else. The Australian Wine Research Institute contacted me. They want to acquire my grandmother's notebooks. Not confiscate them—acquire them properly. For their archive. They'll digitise them, make them available to researchers worldwide. Preserve her work."

"That's wonderful."

"I said yes. On one condition—that the collection be called the Elizabeth Chen Quantum Wine Archive. That her name be on every page. That everyone who uses her research knows exactly who discovered this."

"Perfect. That's exactly what she'd want."

They talked for another twenty minutes. Sophie was getting interview requests too. Nature wanted to profile her as "the granddaughter who vindicated a dismissed scientist." Science Magazine wanted a piece about preserving and publishing family research.

Elizabeth Chen, dismissed for forty years, was becoming a scientific hero.


## FRIDAY, 28 FEBRUARY 2025

Friday morning, Alex woke to an email from Jancis Robinson:

*Alex - my article has been downloaded 2.5 million times. Financial Times website crashed twice from traffic. I've received over 10,000 emails, most supportive, some sceptical, all engaged. Quantum wine is the biggest wine story in decades. Well done. You changed the world. —JR*

Alex showed Emma. "Two and a half million downloads. Jancis's article is the most-read Financial Times piece in years."

"Because it's extraordinary. A respected critic confirming something impossible. That's news." Emma poured coffee. "How do you feel? Ready for Monday?"

Monday. The government job. Her first day working for the Home Office Scientific Advisory Council.

"No. But I don't have a choice."

"You always have a choice. You could refuse the job. Take the consequences."

"Which are prison and career destruction. Not really a choice." Alex sipped coffee. "I'll make it work. I'll do the government job, follow the restrictions, and still find ways to advance quantum wine research within constraints."

"That's not victory. That's compromise."

"Sometimes compromise is victory. Elizabeth fought alone and lost. I'm fighting with constraints but surviving. That's different." Alex set down her cup. "And I'm presenting at Bordeaux in June. That's my real work. That's Elizabeth's full vindication—presenting her research to the international wine science community. The government can't stop that."

"Can't they? You signed contracts—"

"For not publishing new classified research. Presenting already-public research at an academic conference is different. I checked the contract language. It's permitted."

"So June is your line in the sand. The moment where you make Elizabeth's vindication complete."

"Yes. And until then, I survive. I work within constraints. I navigate government supervision. But in June—in June I stand on that stage in Bordeaux and tell the world exactly who Elizabeth Chen was and what she discovered."

Emma smiled. "Then let's get you to June."

## SATURDAY, 1 MARCH 2025

The weekend was quiet. Alex deliberately avoided interviews, ignored her phone, tried to decompress before Monday's job start.

She and Emma walked through Regent's Park. Cold March morning, early spring flowers just beginning to show. Normal life. Normal Saturday.

"I've been thinking," Emma said as they walked. "About what you said. That Elizabeth fought alone and lost, but you're fighting with constraints and surviving. That's true. But there's another difference."

"What's that?"

"Elizabeth spent forty years trying to prove she was right. You spent two weeks proving she was right. That's not the same fight. You're not recreating her struggle—you're completing it. Finishing what she started."

Alex thought about that. "So I'm not compromising. I'm just... taking a different path to the same destination."

"Exactly. Elizabeth needed vindication. You provided it. The method doesn't matter—published papers, Jancis's article, the Bordeaux conference. What matters is the outcome: Elizabeth Chen is recognised as the scientist who discovered quantum wine. That's victory."

"Even if I'm working for the government that suppressed her research?"

"Especially then. You're inside the system now. You can change it from within. Make sure future Elizabeth Chens aren't dismissed and destroyed. That's legacy work."

Alex squeezed Emma's hand. "How did I get so lucky? Finding someone who understands all this?"

"You didn't get lucky. You just dated an architect. We understand structure, foundations, long-term building projects. Your quantum wine work is the same—you're building something that will last decades. Elizabeth laid the foundation. You're constructing the framework. Future researchers will build on top of that. It's all part of the same structure."

They walked in comfortable silence, London waking up round them.

Alex thought about Monday—the government job, Thornton's restrictions, the weight of classified research. But also June. Bordeaux. Standing on that stage presenting Elizabeth's research to three hundred wine scientists.

Completing what Elizabeth had started.

That was victory, even if the path there wasn't straight.

## SUNDAY, 2 MARCH 2025

Sunday evening, Alex prepared for Monday. Laid out clothes—professional, conservative, appropriate for a government office. Reviewed her contracts, highlighting the permitted activities versus forbidden ones.

Her phone rang. Victoria Mills.

Alex answered immediately. "Victoria. Are you safe?"

"Safe enough. I saw Jancis's article. Saw your interviews. Saw the scientific community validating quantum wine." Victoria's voice was warm. "You did it, Alex. You proved it exists. Made it impossible to suppress."

"We did it. Your research made publication possible."

"My research spent thirty years hidden. You made it public. That's courage." A pause. "I heard you signed government contracts. Working for the Home Office."

"I did. Starting tomorrow. Restrictions on publishing, requirements to consult before public statements. But I can still present at conferences, still discuss published research."

"That's good. That's workable." Victoria sounded thoughtful. "Government restriction is better than prison. And you can do more inside the system than outside it. Trust me—I spent thirty years hiding outside the system. It achieves nothing."

"I'm presenting at Bordeaux. June. Elizabeth's research. Full vindication."

"Good. Do that. Make her legacy complete." Victoria's voice softened. "I failed Elizabeth. I hid when she needed allies. I chose safety over truth. But you didn't. You chose truth even when it was dangerous. Elizabeth would be proud."

"I hope so."

"I know so. Now go. Start your government job. Navigate the restrictions. And in June, stand on that Bordeaux stage and tell the world exactly who Elizabeth Chen was."

"I will. I promise."

"Good. And Alex? Thank you. For finishing what Elizabeth and I started. For making quantum wine real."

Victoria ended the call.

Alex sat on her bed, contract printouts spread round her, feeling the weight of tomorrow.

Government employee. Classified research consultant. Restricted speech. Monitored activities.

But also: wine writer. MW candidate. Quantum wine researcher. Elizabeth Chen's vindicator.

She could be both. Had to be both.

Elizabeth had fought alone and lost.

Alex would fight within constraints and survive.

Different battles. Different outcomes.

But the same truth at the centre: quantum wine was real.

And nothing—not government restrictions, not corporate suppression, not forty years of dismissal—could change that now.

---

PART 3
VINDICATION

MONDAY, 16 JUNE 2025

BORDEAUX, FRANCE

THE INTERNATIONAL WINE Science Conference occupied the entire Grand Théâtre de Bordeaux—an eighteenth-century masterpiece of neoclassical architecture in the heart of the city. Twelve Corinthian columns fronted the building. Inside, gilded ceilings, red velvet seats, and the kind of grandeur that made every presentation feel historically significant.

Alex stood backstage, watching through a gap in the curtain as three hundred wine scientists filled the auditorium. Researchers from forty countries. Oenologists, viticulturists, chemists, quantum physicists who'd pivoted to wine science after February's publications. Everyone who mattered in wine research was here.

And in ninety minutes, Alex would stand on that stage and present Elizabeth Chen's life's work.

Sophie appeared beside her, equally nervous. "I can't do this. I can't stand up there and talk about my grandmother in front of three hundred people."

"Yes, you can. We practised. You know the material. And Marcus will be there—he's presenting first, setting up the science. We just tell Elizabeth's story."

"Just tell the story of decades of dismissed research. Just vindicate a woman who died thinking she'd failed. Just—" Sophie's voice broke. "What if I cry?"

"Then you cry. Your grandmother spent her entire professional life being dismissed. You're allowed to be emotional about her vindication." Alex squeezed Sophie's hand. "We're doing this for her. She would want us to be honest, not perfect."

Marcus Webb emerged from the green room, looking uncomfortable in a suit. He was more used to teaching undergraduates in Sydney than presenting at international conferences.

"Ready?" he asked.

"No," Alex and Sophie said simultaneously.

"Good. Neither am I. But we're doing it anyway." Marcus looked out at the auditorium. "Three hundred people. Christ. I've never presented to this many people."

"You've verified quantum wine for six independent researchers. You've published in peer-reviewed journals. You've taught for twenty years. You can do this." Alex forced confidence into her voice. "We're telling the truth. That's all. The truth about Elizabeth Chen's research. The truth about quantum wine. Truth doesn't require performance—just honesty."

A conference organiser appeared. "Dr Webb? You're on in five minutes. Ms Hartley, Ms Chen—you'll be introduced immediately after Dr Webb's presentation. Questions at the end—all three of you on stage together."

Five minutes.

Alex's stomach churned. She'd given dozens of interviews over the past three months. Appeared on BBC, CNN, written articles for Decanter and Nature. But this was different. This was the wine science establishment. The same community that had dismissed Elizabeth Chen for forty years.

If they accepted Elizabeth's research today—if they acknowledged quantum wine as legitimate science—that would be complete vindication.

If they dismissed it again, even after all the evidence…

"Don't think like that," Emma had said this morning before Alex left the hotel. "You've already won. Quantum wine is verified. Published. Real. This presentation isn't about proving anything. It's about honouring Elizabeth. Remember that."

Honouring Elizabeth.

Alex could do that.

The lights in the auditorium dimmed. The conference chair—a distinguished French oenologist in his seventies—walked to the podium.

"Ladies and gentlemen, we now begin our session on quantum phenomena in aged wines. This is perhaps the most extraordinary development in wine science in decades—the discovery that certain wines can maintain quantum coherence and store information patterns across time. Our first presenter is Dr Marcus Webb, Senior Lecturer in Wine Science at the University of Sydney, who has spent eighteen years studying quantum correlations in Hunter Valley Semillon ageing. Dr Webb."

Applause. Respectful, curious.

Marcus walked onto the stage. Stood at the podium. Looked out at three hundred faces.

For a moment, Alex thought he might freeze.

Then he began.

"Thank you. I'm here to talk about quantum wine—a phenomenon I've studied for eighteen years and dismissed for seventeen of them. Because quantum wine shouldn't exist. By all conventional wine chemistry, quantum coherence in room-temperature phenolic networks is impossible. And yet, it exists. And the person who discovered it forty years ago—Dr Elizabeth Chen—spent her entire career trying to tell us this. We didn't listen. Today, I want to explain why we should have."

The next forty minutes were masterful. Marcus presented the mechanism: quantum-coherent phenolic networks, entangled molecular structures, information storage through quantum states. He showed spectroscopic data, EPR measurements, independent verification from six researchers. He explained why certain terroirs produced quantum-active wines whilst others didn't—soil composition, mineral matrices, the role of rare earth elements in stabilising quantum coherence.

He cited Elizabeth Chen's 1979 paper—dismissed at the time, vindicated now. He showed how her observations predicted everything they'd discovered in the past four months.

"Dr Chen was right," Marcus concluded. "For forty years, she was right. We dismissed her because quantum wine seemed impossible. But quantum biology—photosynthesis, bird navigation, enzyme catalysis—is real. Nature uses quantum mechanics constantly. Why wouldn't wine? Dr Chen asked that question in 1979. We're finally answering it in 2025. Forty years too late for her to see her vindication. But not too late for us to acknowledge it."

Applause. Stronger this time. Engaged.

Marcus stepped back from the podium. The conference chair returned.

"Thank you, Dr Webb. We'll now hear from Alexandra Hartley and Sophie Chen, who will present on Dr Elizabeth Chen's research and the personal implications of quantum wine discovery. Ms Hartley."

Alex walked onto the stage. Sophie beside her. The lights were bright, the audience a blur of faces.

Alex reached the podium, adjusted the microphone, looked out at three hundred wine scientists.

"My name is Alex Hartley. I'm a wine writer and Master of Wine candidate. Four months ago, I experienced quantum wine for the first time—a 1986 Hunter Valley Semillon that carried me to an Australian vineyard forty years earlier. I felt the heat. I heard cicadas. I experienced a harvest morning from January 1986 as if I was physically there. And I heard a woman's voice saying: 'This is the vintage that will prove them all wrong.'"

She paused. The auditorium was completely silent.

"That woman was Dr Elizabeth Chen. Oenologist. Quantum wine researcher. The person who discovered what we're all discussing today. And she's not here to receive your recognition. Because she died in 2022, three years before quantum wine was finally validated. She died dismissed. Alone. Convinced she'd failed."

Alex felt her throat tighten. Pushed through.

"I'm here to tell you that Dr Chen didn't fail. She was right. About everything. Quantum coherence in wine. Memory storage through phenolic networks. The terroir requirements. The sensitivity patterns. Everything she documented over four decades has been proven correct. She didn't fail. We failed her. The wine science community failed her. We dismissed her research. Destroyed her career. Left her to work alone for her entire professional life."

Sophie stepped forward, stood beside Alex at the podium.

"My name is Sophie Chen. Elizabeth Chen was my grandmother. I grew up watching her work—documenting wines, running experiments, publishing papers that no one read. Everyone thought she was crazy. Including, sometimes, me. I was embarrassed by her research. Embarrassed that my grandmother was the family eccentric who believed wine had consciousness."

Sophie's voice broke. She took a breath, continued.

"I never got to apologise to her. Never got to tell her I believed her research was real. She died thinking she'd failed. Thinking forty years of work had been for nothing. But it wasn't for nothing. It was for this. This moment. Three hundred wine scientists in Bordeaux acknowledging that quantum wine is real. UC Davis creating the Dr Elizabeth Chen Chair in Quantum Oenology. The Australian Wine Research Institute preserving her notebooks in the Elizabeth Chen Quantum Wine Archive. My grandmother didn't fail. She succeeded. We just didn't recognise it until she was gone."

Alex took over. "I want to show you something."

She nodded to the tech operator. A slide appeared on the screen behind them—a photograph of Elizabeth Chen in her laboratory, perhaps fifty years old, holding a wine glass, smiling at the camera.

"This is Dr Chen in 1984. At UC Davis. The year before her career was destroyed by dismissive reviewers who refused to consider that quantum wine might be real." Alex's voice was steady now, certain. "She's holding a glass of wine. Making observations. Doing science. Being brilliant. And she's happy—because at this moment, she still believed the scientific community would eventually listen to her."

Another slide. A page from Elizabeth's notebook, handwriting precise and careful.

"This is from January 1986. The harvest that produced the wine I tasted in February. Dr Chen documented every detail—temperature, humidity, picking time, fermentation parameters. And she documented something else: the quantum signature. The moment when she knew this wine would store information. Would preserve her consciousness. Would prove her right."

Another slide. Elizabeth Chen in old age, perhaps 2019, standing in a vineyard.

"This is Dr Chen in 2019, three years before she died. Still working. Still documenting. Still believing, despite decades of dismissal, that quantum wine was real. She never gave up. Never stopped researching. Never compromised her integrity by pretending her observations were wrong just to regain professional acceptance."

Alex looked out at the audience. Three hundred faces, all watching, all listening.

"Today, we're telling you that Dr Elizabeth Chen was right. And we're asking you—the wine science community—to ensure that her name is attached to every quantum wine discovery from this day forward. Not as a footnote. Not as a historical curiosity. But as the person who discovered this phenomenon. The scientist who was right when everyone else was wrong. The researcher who deserves recognition she never received whilst alive."

Sophie stepped forward again. "My grandmother left forty-three notebooks documenting quantum wine. Thousands of observations. Hundreds of analyses. A lifetime of careful, rigorous science. The Australian Wine Research Institute is preserving those notebooks. Digitising them. Making them available to researchers worldwide. Her work will never be lost again. Her voice will never be silenced again."

Alex nodded to the tech operator. The final slide appeared—Elizabeth's words from the January 1986 notebook, enlarged so everyone could read:

*This is the vintage that will prove them all wrong. In forty years, someone will taste this wine and experience what I'm experiencing right now. They'll feel the heat. They'll hear the cicadas. They'll know I was right. And they'll make sure everyone else knows too.*

The auditorium was completely silent.

"She was right," Alex said quietly. "In forty years, someone did taste that wine. I tasted it. Sophie tasted it. Jancis Robinson tasted it. We all experienced exactly what Dr Chen predicted. We all accessed her memory from January 1986. And we're making sure everyone knows she was right."

Sophie's voice was thick with emotion. "My grandmother spent forty years fighting alone. She died alone. But she doesn't have to be vindicated alone. That's what today is about. Three hundred wine scientists acknowledging that Dr Elizabeth Chen discovered something extraordinary. That her life's work matters. That she deserves recognition."

Alex looked directly at the audience. "Quantum wine is real. Dr Elizabeth Chen proved it. And we—all of us in this auditorium—have a responsibility to ensure her legacy is honoured. Thank you."

They stepped back from the podium.

For a moment, nothing. Silence.

Then someone in the front row stood. Started clapping.

Someone else stood. More applause.

Within seconds, the entire auditorium was standing. Three hundred wine scientists—including elderly professors in the front row who might have been the very reviewers who'd dismissed Elizabeth's 1979 paper—giving Elizabeth Chen the recognition she'd never received whilst alive. The wine establishment itself acknowledging its failure.

Alex felt tears running down her face. Sophie was openly crying. Marcus, standing at the side of the stage, wiped his eyes.

The applause continued. Two minutes. Three. Finally, the conference chair returned to the podium.

"Thank you. That was... extraordinary. We'll now take questions."

Hands shot up across the auditorium.

The chair pointed to a woman in the third row. "Professor Dubois, University of Bordeaux."

The woman stood. "My question is for Ms Chen. You mentioned your grandmother's notebooks are being preserved. Will they be available for research? Can we access her original observations?"

Sophie nodded. "Yes. The Australian Wine Research Institute is digitising everything. They'll be available online by September. Complete access. Free to any researcher."

More hands.

"Dr Schmidt, Technical University of Munich." A man in the middle rows. "Dr Webb, your verification included quantum measurements. Can you share your methodology? We'd like to replicate your findings."

"Absolutely," Marcus said. "I'll publish detailed protocols next month. But the basic approach is EPR spectroscopy at specific wavelengths—I can provide exact parameters after the session."

More questions. Methodology, replication, terroir analysis, sensitivity studies. Every question serious, engaged, treating quantum wine as legitimate science.

Finally, a woman in the back row. "Dr Patterson, University of

Cambridge. My question is for Ms Hartley. You work for the UK government now, consulting on quantum wine countermeasures. Does that create conflicts? Being both a researcher and someone working to restrict research?"

Alex had expected this question. Had prepared for it.

"It creates tension, yes. But also opportunity. I'm inside the system now. I can advocate for transparent research, ethical frameworks, proper regulation. Dr Chen worked outside the system and was destroyed. I'm working inside it, trying to prevent that from happening to future researchers." She paused. "But to be absolutely clear: I believe quantum wine research should be public and accessible. The government employs me to help develop safety protocols, not to suppress research. If those roles ever conflict—if I'm asked to suppress legitimate science—I'll resign."

"Even if that means prosecution?"

"Even then. Because Dr Chen spent her entire career being suppressed. I won't contribute to that happening to anyone else."

Applause. Genuine, supportive.

The conference chair checked his watch. "We have time for one more question."

An elderly man in the front row raised his hand slowly. The chair nodded.

"Professor Moreau, University of Bordeaux."

Alex's breath caught. Moreau. Philippe Moreau—the researcher killed in February—this must be his father.

The old man stood slowly, using a cane. He looked at Alex and Sophie.

"My son," he said, his voice carrying through the auditorium, "Philippe Moreau, was researching quantum wine. He was planning to present at this conference. In February, he died. The official cause was heart attack. But I know—we all know—that my son was killed because he refused to keep quantum wine secret."

The auditorium went completely still.

"I have no question," Professor Moreau continued. "I simply

want to thank you. Thank you for finishing what my son started. Thank you for making quantum wine public. Thank you for ensuring that his death—and Dr Chen's lifetime of dismissal—were not in vain. Thank you for being brave enough to fight when others stayed silent."

He sat down.

Alex couldn't speak. Sophie was crying. Marcus looked stricken.

The conference chair stepped forward. "I think... that's an appropriate place to end. Ladies and gentlemen, please join me in thanking our presenters."

More applause. Standing ovation. Three hundred wine scientists honouring Elizabeth Chen, Philippe Moreau, everyone who'd fought for quantum wine truth.

Alex, Sophie, and Marcus left the stage. Backstage, they collapsed against the wall, emotionally spent.

"Christ," Marcus said. "Moreau's father. I didn't know he'd be here."

"Philippe deserved recognition too," Sophie said. "Everyone who fought for quantum wine deserves recognition."

Alex's phone buzzed. Text from Emma, watching from the audience:

> You were perfect. Elizabeth would be so
> proud. Meet you outside.

Another text. Jancis Robinson:

> Magnificent presentation. Elizabeth Chen's
> name will be in every quantum wine paper
> from now on. You've completed her
> vindication. Well done.

They stayed backstage for ten minutes, composing themselves. Finally, they emerged into the Grand Théâtre's lobby.

Emma was waiting, wrapped Alex in a hug. "You did it. You honoured Elizabeth. You made her legacy real."

"We did it," Alex corrected. "All of us. Marcus, Sophie, Jancis, Victoria, everyone who believed quantum wine was real."

Professor Moreau approached, moving slowly with his cane. Up close, he looked to be in his eighties, his face lined with age and grief.

"Ms Hartley. Ms Chen. Dr Webb. Thank you." He extended his hand. "My son died believing quantum wine would remain suppressed. But you—you made it impossible to suppress. You gave his death meaning."

"I'm so sorry about Philippe," Sophie said. "We wouldn't have succeeded without his research. Without his courage."

"He was courageous. Stubborn. Like Dr Chen." Professor Moreau smiled sadly. "He always said—if quantum wine costs me my life, at least I'll die knowing it's real. And he did. He died knowing. That's something."

They stood in the lobby, researchers flowing round them, everyone discussing quantum wine, Elizabeth Chen, the extraordinary presentation.

Alex felt something lift—a weight she'd been carrying since February. Elizabeth was vindicated. Philippe was honoured. Quantum wine was real, public, impossible to suppress.

They'd won.

Not the way Elizabeth had wanted—she should have lived to see this. Philippe should have presented his own research. Victoria shouldn't have had to hide for thirty years.

But vindication nonetheless.

"Come on," Emma said. "Let's get out of here. You've been performing for ninety minutes. You need wine and food and to decompress."

They left the Grand Théâtre, stepping into Bordeaux afternoon sun. June warmth, blue sky, the city alive with conference attendees and tourists and normal life.

Normal. But different.

Because quantum wine was real now. Officially, scientifically, undeniably real.

And Elizabeth Chen's forty years of dismissed work would never be forgotten.

## FRIDAY, 20 JUNE 2025

## SYDNEY, AUSTRALIA

Four days after the Bordeaux presentation, they gathered at the University of Sydney for a ceremony Marcus had been planning for months.

Alex had made the long journey—Bordeaux to London, a day to recover, then the endless flight to Sydney. She'd arrived Friday morning jet-lagged and exhausted, but determined to be here.

Sophie had traveled separately, taking a few extra days in Australia before the ceremony.

Professor Moreau had flown directly from Bordeaux. At his age, with his health, the journey must have been brutal. But he'd insisted. "For Philippe," he'd said. "For my son's memory."

Marcus met them at the wine science building—a modern structure on the university's Camperdown campus. Emma would have appreciated the architecture: glass and steel framed by warm sandstone, blending Sydney's heritage stone with contemporary design. Alex just noticed it was new, clean, and permanent—the kind of building that would house Elizabeth's plaque for generations.

Twenty people gathered in the building's lobby. University administrators, wine science faculty, a few students Marcus had mentored. Small, intimate, respectful.

The Dean of Sciences spoke. "Dr Elizabeth Chen never held a position at this university. But her research—dismissed for forty years, vindicated finally in 2025—represents everything we value in science. Curiosity. Persistence. The courage to pursue truth even when dismissed. We dedicate this plaque to her memory and to all researchers who fight for truth despite professional consequences."

He pulled a cloth from the wall, revealing the plaque:

*Dr Elizabeth Chen (1941-2022) Discoverer of Quantum Wine "This is the vintage that will prove them all wrong"*

Simple. Elegant. Permanent.

Sophie stepped forward, placed flowers beneath the plaque. Her hands were shaking. "Thank you. For honouring my grandmother. For ensuring her name will be remembered."

Professor Moreau stood slowly, using his cane for support. "I'd like to dedicate this plaque not only to Dr Chen, but to my son Philippe, who died pursuing the same truth. To Victoria Mills, who sacrificed thirty years in hiding. To James Wickham, who died proving quantum wine existed. And to every researcher who's ever been dismissed, destroyed, or killed for telling the truth."

Everyone was quiet.

"Science costs," Professor Moreau continued, his voice carrying the weight of decades of loss. "Sometimes it costs careers. Sometimes it costs lives. But truth endures. Dr Chen's truth endured a lifetime of dismissal. My son's truth endures beyond his death. And now—now future researchers will see this plaque and know: fighting for truth matters. Even when it costs everything."

Alex felt tears running down her face.

After the ceremony, they stood in the wine science building, looking at Elizabeth's plaque. Bronze, permanent, her name etched for as long as this building stood.

"She made it," Sophie whispered. "Her name on a university wall. Recognition from the scientific establishment. Everything she wanted."

"She deserved it forty years ago. But at least she has it now." Alex paused. "Do you think she knows? Wherever she is?"

"If consciousness can be stored in wine—if quantum information persists beyond death—then yes. She knows." Sophie touched the plaque gently. "She knows we proved her right. She knows her name will be on quantum wine research forever. She knows she didn't fail."

Marcus appeared beside them. "The university is creating a

scholarship. The Dr Elizabeth Chen Award for Persistent Research. For students who pursue unconventional ideas despite scepticism. Fully funded. First recipient starts next year."

"She'd love that," Sophie said. "She'd love that young researchers will pursue strange ideas because of her example."

They stood there for a long time, looking at the plaque that would outlive them all.

Elizabeth Chen's name. Her dates. Her greatest discovery. And her words, the ones Alex had heard in the quantum memory:

*"This is the vintage that will prove them all wrong"*

It had.

And now everyone knew.

## MONDAY, 23 JUNE 2025

## LONDON, ENGLAND

Alex returned to London late Sunday night, exhausted but content. Two weeks away—Bordeaux, Sydney, endless flights, jet lag, emotional ceremonies.

But worth it. All of it worth it.

Monday morning, she reported to the Home Office as usual. Dr Thornton's office, monthly debrief, updates on quantum wine developments.

But something was different. Thornton's expression was less stern. Almost... approving.

"Your Bordeaux presentation," Thornton said without preamble. "I watched it. We all did. The entire scientific advisory council."

Alex's stomach tightened. "I hope it was acceptable. The contracts allow—"

"It was more than acceptable. It was perfect." Thornton leant back in her chair. "You honoured Dr Chen without revealing classified information. You promoted transparent research without compromising security. You demonstrated exactly how to navigate government restrictions whilst advancing science."

Alex blinked. "I... thank you?"

"I'm not praising you for compliance. I'm praising you for showing us a better way." Thornton pulled out a document. "The Home Office is revising its quantum wine research protocols. Instead of blanket classification, we're implementing tiered access. Public research remains public. Sensitive applications—weaponisation, interrogation uses—remain restricted. But basic quantum biology research will be open."

"That's—that's what I was hoping for."

"You demonstrated it was possible. Bordeaux proved scientists can discuss quantum wine openly without compromising security." Thornton slid the document across the desk. "We'd like you to help draft the new protocols. Not just implement them—design them. Create the framework for how quantum wine research proceeds globally."

Alex read the document. Public research guidelines. Ethical frameworks. Safety standards. Everything she'd wanted when she started fighting for quantum wine transparency.

"This is regulatory building," Alex said slowly. "Not suppression."

"Exactly. Dr Chen fought suppression for forty years. You're building the structure that ensures future researchers won't face suppression. That's legacy work, Ms Hartley. That's how you honour Dr Chen—by preventing her experience from happening to others."

Alex thought about Emma's words. About architects and foundations and long-term building projects. About Elizabeth laying the foundation and Alex constructing the framework.

"I'd be honoured to help," Alex said.

"Good. Because this will be your primary work going forward. Less monitoring, more policy design. We want quantum wine research to flourish—safely, ethically, transparently. You'll help make that happen."

Thornton stood, extended her hand. "Welcome to the next phase of quantum wine development. The phase where we stop fighting and start building."

Alex shook her hand, feeling the weight of what had just shifted. Two weeks ago, she'd stood on a stage in Bordeaux and told three hundred scientists about Elizabeth Chen. Last week, she'd stood in Sydney watching Elizabeth's name being engraved in bronze.

And today, she was designing the frameworks that would ensure no future researcher faced what Elizabeth had faced.

Elizabeth had laid the foundation. Alex was building the structure. And someday—maybe soon—other researchers would build on top of what they'd created together.

That was legacy. That was victory.

That was worth everything.

## 14 / THE MASTER

THE SUMMER PASSED in a blur of government work and MW examination preparation. Three days a week at the Home Office, designing quantum wine research protocols. The rest of the time studying—memorising terroirs, practising blind tasting, refining her thesis on quantum wine implications for wine criticism.

Always, Elizabeth Chen's legacy was present. In the policy frameworks Alex designed. In the MW exam questions she prepared to answer. In every bottle of aged wine she tasted, wondering if quantum coherence might be hiding beneath the surface.

THURSDAY, 3 JULY 2025

ISLINGTON, LONDON

Two weeks after returning from Australia, Alex's life had settled into a new pattern.

Government work designing research protocols. Wine writing for Decanter. And MW exam preparation—the practical examination was scheduled for early August. Six weeks away.

Emma came home Thursday evening to find Alex surrounded by

wine books, tasting notes, and Emma's own architectural drawings—Alex had borrowed them as inspiration for understanding structure and framework.

"Still studying?" Emma asked.

"The MW exam will include quantum wine questions. I need to be ready to discuss it knowledgeably—mechanism, applications, ethical considerations." Alex looked up. "And I need to pass. For Elizabeth. To prove that wine writers who pursue strange ideas can still achieve professional recognition."

"You'll pass. You're the most qualified person in the world to discuss quantum wine." Emma sat beside her. "How's the protocol work going?"

"Good. Really good. We're creating a three-tier system. Public research—open access, anyone can publish. Sensitive research—requires ethics review but publishable with safeguards. Classified research—government clearance required, limited to weaponisation prevention." Alex smiled. "It's exactly what I wanted. Transparency with appropriate caution."

"And you designed it."

"I helped design it. Thornton's team did most of the work. But yes—I contributed. Elizabeth fought suppression. I'm building the system that prevents future suppression. That's... that feels like victory."

"It is victory." Emma kissed her forehead. "Elizabeth would be proud."

Alex's phone buzzed. Email from the Institute of Masters of Wine:

*Dear Ms Hartley,*

*Your MW practical examination is confirmed for 7 August 2025. Your research project proposal—"Quantum Wine: Implications for Wine Evaluation and Criticism"—has been approved. We look forward to your examination.*

Alex showed Emma the email. "They approved my research project. Quantum wine as an MW thesis topic. That's official recognition from the wine world's highest authority."

"Of course they approved it. You discovered it. You published the definitive research. Who else could write the definitive MW thesis on quantum wine?"

"Still. It's validation. The MW programme—the wine establishment—acknowledging quantum wine as legitimate scholarship." Alex felt tears prick her eyes. "Elizabeth never got that. Never got the wine world's respect. But I'm getting it. Because of her work. Her foundation."

"Then pass that exam. Complete the MW qualification. And dedicate your dissertation to Elizabeth Chen."

"I will. I'm going to make sure every MW student for the next fifty years knows Elizabeth's name. Knows what she discovered. Knows what she sacrificed to pursue truth."

Emma smiled. "That's the Elizabeth Chen legacy—not just quantum wine, but the example of pursuing truth despite consequences. That's what you're passing forward."


## FRIDAY, 8 AUGUST 2025

## LONDON, ENGLAND

The MW practical examination was held at the Institute's London facility—a Georgian townhouse in Mayfair that had been testing wine professionals for decades. The same rooms where legends had proven their expertise. The same rigorous standards that made MW the highest qualification in wine.

Alex arrived at 8 AM, stomach churning with nerves.

Six hours. That's all that stood between her and the qualification she'd worked towards for three years.

The examination room was austere—white walls, fluorescent lights, a long table set with twenty-four wine glasses. Twelve other candidates sat at similar tables. MW examiners moved silently between stations, clipboards in hand, expressions neutral.

## PART ONE: BLIND TASTING

Twelve wines. Twenty minutes each. Identify grape variety, region, vintage if possible. Professional tasting notes. Quality assessment.

Alex went through her ritual: appearance, nose, palate. Writing quickly, precisely, years of training flowing through muscle memory.

Wine seven made her pause. Aged Semillon. High acid, honeyed development, lanolin character. Hunter Valley? She wrote her assessment, noting the terroir markers.

Then she felt it—that other sensation. Not smell. Not taste. A feeling.

Quantum-active.

She couldn't write that in her notes. The examiners would think she'd lost her mind. But she knew. This was quantum wine. The exam had deliberately included it.

She wrote: *"Exceptional preservation of fruit despite age. Suggests ideal cellaring conditions and potentially unique terroir characteristics consistent with quantum-coherent phenolic development as documented in recent Hunter Valley Semillon research."*

Professional. Technical. Hinting at quantum wine without saying it outright.

The examiner reviewing her station raised an eyebrow. Made a note. Moved on.

## PART TWO: THEORY

Written examination. Three hours. Questions covering viticulture, vinification, wine regions, tasting methodology, critical analysis.

And yes—there it was. Question fifteen:

*"Recent publications suggest certain aged wines may exhibit quantum-coherent molecular structures capable of storing environmental information. Discuss the implications of this phenomenon for wine evaluation, authentication, and criticism. How should Master of Wine professionals approach wines that demonstrate these characteristics?"*

Alex's heart raced. They were testing her on quantum wine. The phenomenon she'd discovered, published, defended.

She wrote for forty minutes. Mechanism. Terroir requirements. Sensitivity patterns. Ethical considerations for wine critics experiencing quantum effects. The need for rigorous documentation. The importance of separating quantum experiences from conventional quality assessment.

She wrote about Elizabeth Chen. About forty years of dismissed research finally vindicated. About the responsibility of wine professionals to approach quantum wine seriously, scientifically, respectfully.

When the examiner called time, Alex had filled six pages.

## PART THREE: RESEARCH PROJECT DEFENCE

The final test. Ninety minutes presenting her thesis to a panel of three Master of Wine examiners.

"Quantum Wine: Implications for Wine Evaluation and Criticism."

Alex stood at the front of a small examination room. The three examiners sat behind a table, notebooks open, expressions carefully neutral.

She began.

"Four months ago, I experienced quantum wine for the first time. A 1986 Hunter Valley Semillon that transported me to an Australian vineyard forty years earlier. As a wine critic, I faced an immediate question: how do I evaluate this? How do I separate the quantum experience—which is extraordinary but subjective—from the wine's conventional quality characteristics?"

She spoke for ninety minutes. Presenting her framework for quantum wine criticism. The need for disclosure when critics experience quantum effects. The ethical considerations. The scientific rigour required. The importance of honouring Dr Elizabeth Chen's research whilst maintaining professional standards.

The examiners asked pointed questions:

"How can you verify a quantum experience isn't just imagination?"

"What protocols would you recommend for wine competitions that include quantum-active wines?"

"Should quantum wine be a separate category, or integrated into conventional wine evaluation?"

Alex answered each question, drawing on four months of experience, research, government policy work, and deep respect for what Elizabeth had discovered.

Finally, one of the examiners—a woman in her sixties, MW since 1987—leaned forward.

"Ms Hartley. I've been examining MW candidates for twenty years. I've never seen a thesis quite like this. You're proposing we fundamentally reconsider how we approach wine evaluation. That we acknowledge consciousness transfer through aged wine as scientifically legitimate. That's... extraordinary."

"Dr Chen spent forty years being dismissed for claiming exactly that. I'm proposing we don't make that mistake again."

The examiner smiled. "Exceptional work today. Your knowledge of quantum wine is obviously unmatched. But what impressed me most was your defence of Dr Chen. You could have claimed credit for discovering quantum wine. Instead, you spent ninety minutes explaining why Elizabeth Chen deserves sole credit for the discovery."

"Because she does. I just published her research. She spent forty years documenting it."

"That's integrity. That's what the MW qualification represents—not just wine knowledge, but ethical practice, honest scholarship, respect for those who came before us." The examiner closed her notebook. "Results will be announced in six weeks. But Ms Hartley—I think you'll be pleased."

Alex left the examination building at 6 PM, exhausted, emotionally drained, but quietly confident.

She'd done everything she could. Answered every question. Defended her thesis. Honoured Elizabeth.

Now she just had to wait.

Emma was waiting outside, wrapped Alex in a hug. "How did it go?"

"I think... I think it went well. They asked about quantum wine. They engaged seriously with the research. They didn't dismiss Elizabeth." Alex pulled back, looked at Emma. "I think I might have passed."

"You definitely passed. Now let's celebrate. You've just completed the MW examination. That deserves champagne."

They walked through Mayfair holding hands, the August evening warm and golden. Normal London evening. Normal couple celebrating a milestone.

Except nothing was normal anymore.

Because quantum wine was real. And Alex might—might—become a Master of Wine whose thesis validated Elizabeth Chen's lifetime of work.

That would be vindication beyond anything Elizabeth could have imagined.


## SUNDAY, 21 SEPTEMBER 2025

## ISLINGTON, LONDON

Seven months after the Wickham tasting. Six months after

publishing quantum wine research. Three months after the Bordeaux presentation.

Alex sat at her kitchen table, Emma beside her, laptop open, refreshing the MW results page obsessively.

Results were supposed to post at 10 AM. It was 9:57.

"Stop refreshing," Emma said. "You'll crash the server."

"I can't help it. This is—Emma, if I pass, I'm the first MW whose thesis was on quantum wine. Elizabeth's discovery becomes part of MW scholarship forever."

"You're going to pass. You were brilliant at the exam."

9:58.

9:59.

10:00.

Alex refreshed.

The page loaded. A single line:

*Congratulations to our new Masters of Wine:*

Alex scrolled down. Names alphabetically. Her heart hammered.

*Hartley, Alexandra Jane - PASS*

She stared at the screen.

"Emma. I passed. I'm a Master of Wine."

Emma screamed, grabbed Alex, spun her around the small kitchen. "You did it! You're an MW! You passed!"

Alex couldn't breathe. Couldn't think. Just stared at the screen showing her name, the word PASS, the title she'd worked towards for three years.

Master of Wine.

And her thesis: "Quantum Wine: Implications for Wine Evaluation and Criticism."

Elizabeth Chen's discovery, now part of MW scholarship.

Her phone rang. Sophie.

"Alex! Tell me you passed!"

"I passed. I'm an MW."

Sophie screamed through the phone. "Oh my God! You did it!

My grandmother's research helped you become a Master of Wine! That's—that's perfect! That's exactly what she'd want!"

They talked for ten minutes, both crying, both laughing, both overwhelmed.

Then Marcus rang. Then Jancis. Then Victoria Mills. Everyone who'd fought for quantum wine, celebrating this victory.

Because it wasn't just Alex's victory. It was validation for everyone who'd believed quantum wine was real. Everyone who'd fought for truth despite consequences.

At noon, a courier arrived. An envelope from the Institute of Masters of Wine.

Alex opened it, hands shaking.

Inside: her official MW certificate. And a letter:

*Dear Ms Hartley MW,*

*Congratulations on achieving the Master of Wine qualification. Your thesis, "Quantum Wine: Implications for Wine Evaluation and Criticism," received the highest marks of any research project this year. The examining board has selected it for the Elizabeth Chen Memorial Prize—a new award recognising exceptional research that challenges conventional wine science.*

*The prize includes £10,000 and publication of your thesis in the MW journal. We look forward to your continued contributions to wine scholarship.*

*Congratulations, Master of Wine.*

Alex read it three times. The Elizabeth Chen Memorial Prize. They'd created an award in Elizabeth's name. And given it to Alex.

Full circle. Complete vindication.

She showed Emma the letter.

"They named a prize after her," Emma said softly. "The Institute of Masters of Wine—the same establishment that ignored her research for forty years—created an award in her name. And gave it to you for explaining her discovery."

"She made it," Alex whispered. "Elizabeth Chen. Dismissed oenologist. Her name is now on an MW prize. Students will receive the Elizabeth Chen Memorial Prize for decades. Centuries, maybe. Her name will never be forgotten."

Emma wrapped her arms round Alex. They stood in their small kitchen, holding each other, crying with joy and grief and triumph.

Elizabeth had spent forty years fighting alone.

She'd died thinking she'd failed.

But she hadn't failed.

Her name would outlive everyone who'd dismissed her.

Her discovery would change wine science forever.

Her legacy would inspire researchers for generations.

She'd won.

Finally, completely, absolutely.

Elizabeth Chen had won.

*15 / THE HARVEST*




THE VINTRY, POKOLBIN, NEW SOUTH WALES

ELEVEN MONTHS after the Wickham tasting. Ten months since publishing quantum wine research. Four months since becoming a Master of Wine.

Alex and Emma stood on the veranda of The Vintry watching the sun set over the Brokenback Range, painting the sky in shades of gold and crimson. They'd arrived two days earlier—flying into Sydney on the 30th of December, driving up to the Hunter Valley on New Year's Eve, arriving at Greg's property just as 2025 became 2026.

Greg emerged from the house carrying three glasses and a bottle. "Welcome to The Vintry. Happy New Year."

He poured—Hunter Valley Semillon, ten years old, developing beautifully. They raised glasses.

"To new beginnings," Greg said.

"To new beginnings," Alex and Emma echoed.

They'd come to Australia for two weeks. A proper holiday. Time to decompress from the most intense year of Alex's life. Time to experience the Hunter Valley the way it was meant to be experienced—slowly, thoughtfully, with space to appreciate what made this place extraordinary.

Greg had welcomed them warmly when they arrived. He'd followed the quantum wine story from the beginning—read Alex's papers, watched the Bordeaux presentation online, understood what they'd accomplished. "You vindicated a dismissed scientist," he'd said when they first sat down on the veranda. "That matters. Elizabeth Chen's name will outlive all of us now."

Over the past two days, Greg had shown them his property. The Vintry itself—deluxe accommodation he'd opened in 2005, designed for wine tourism, for giving guests the Hunter Valley experience. His Shiraz vineyard, planted in 2000, growing in the red earth and limestone at the foothills of the Brokenback Range.

"Different terroir to where Semillon grows," Greg had explained, walking them through the vineyard. "The ancient alluvial sands—that's where Semillon finds its voice. Here, it's red soils, limestone, perfect for Shiraz. Each site has its own story. You don't replicate someone else's terroir. You understand your own."

They'd talked about wine. About the Hunter Valley's history—the Tyrrell, Drayton, Tulloch families who'd been making wine here since the 1800s. About Murray Tyrrell, who'd pioneered Vat 1 Semillon, who'd proved it could age for decades when everyone said Hunter whites were dead after five years.

"Murray passed away the day I finished planting this vineyard," Greg had said quietly. "Third of October, 2000. I didn't know it at the time, but when I found out, it felt significant. Like he was passing something forward. The old generation who built the Hunter, handing responsibility to those of us who came after."

Alex had understood. That's what Elizabeth had done too. Laid a foundation. Passed something forward. Built a legacy that would outlive her.

Now, on their third evening at The Vintry, they sat on the

veranda as summer heat finally broke. Cicadas loud in the eucalyptus trees. The smell of warm earth and ripening grapes.

"Tomorrow," Greg said, "I thought we could visit some wineries. Brokenwood, if you'd like—see the Graveyard vineyard. Thomas Wines for Semillon and Shiraz. Get a feel for the Valley."

"That sounds perfect," Alex said.

"And later this week—" Greg paused. "I spoke with the vineyard manager at Tyrrell's. They're starting the 2026 vintage on the ninth. Picking Semillon from the Short Flat vineyard—the same block Elizabeth Chen studied in 1986. I thought you might want to be there. To see the cycle continue."

Alex's breath caught. "The ninth. That's—"

"Six days shy of forty years after Elizabeth's harvest. As close as we can get. The vintage she predicted would prove her right."

"We'll be there," Alex said. "Absolutely."

The next few days passed in easy rhythm. Greg drove them through the Hunter Valley, introducing them to the region he knew so well.

At Brokenwood, they tasted the current release of ILR Semillon —tight, citrus, years away from its peak—and older vintages showing what Hunter Semillon could become. Honey, toast, lanolin, complexity that developed over decades. The winemaker walked them through the Graveyard vineyard, explained the ancient alluvial terroir, the winemaking philosophy that had made this one of Australia's most celebrated Shiraz sites.

At Thomas Wines, they focused on what made Hunter Valley special. Andrew Thomas poured aged Semillon and Shiraz, explained the region's geology—ancient seabeds, alluvial deposits, the mineral complexity that allowed wines to age.

"Elizabeth Chen understood this," Andrew said when Alex mentioned quantum wine. "She knew Hunter Semillon was different. That something in the terroir allowed these wines to develop in ways other regions couldn't replicate. Turns out she was right about more than just terroir."

They visited other cellars. Tasted young wines and old wines. Met winemakers who'd heard about quantum wine, who wanted to know if their wines might develop quantum coherence, who understood that Alex had vindicated forty years of dismissed research.

And every evening, they returned to The Vintry. Sat on Greg's veranda. Shared wine and stories and the kind of conversations that only happen when good wine and good company converge.

Greg never dominated. He facilitated. Shared his knowledge. Provided context. Made sure they experienced the Hunter Valley authentically.

"This is what The Vintry's about," he said one evening. "Sharing wine. Sharing experiences. Helping people understand that wine is more than chemistry. It's memory. It's time. It's the people who make it and the place it comes from."

Alex looked out at the vineyards, the Brokenback Range darkening against the sunset. "Elizabeth understood that. She spent forty years trying to prove wine is more than fermented grapes."

"And you proved she was right," Greg said. "That's legacy. That's what matters."


## THURSDAY, 8 JANUARY 2026

## THE VINTRY, POKOLBIN

A week into their stay, Sophie arrived.

She'd driven up from Sydney that afternoon—two and a half hours through summer heat, arriving dusty and tired but smiling.

"You made it," Alex said, hugging her.

"Wouldn't miss this. Tomorrow's the day, yeah? January ninth. Almost exactly forty years after my grandmother stood in that vineyard."

"January fifteenth, 1986," Alex said. "Her notebook entry. We're six days early, but close enough."

"Close enough." Sophie set down her bag. "The vineyard manager's expecting us tomorrow morning. Ten o'clock. He said they're starting the vintage—picking Semillon. Just like my grandmother documented."

Greg emerged with wine. "Sophie. Good to see you. You're just in time for dinner."

That evening, the four of them sat on The Vintry's veranda as sunset faded to twilight. Greg had prepared dinner—local lamb, vegetables from his garden, wines he'd been saving for the right occasion.

"Forty years," Sophie said quietly, looking out at the vineyards. "She stood in those vines forty years ago this week. Picked grapes. Documented everything. Predicted someone would taste the wine and experience her memory. And she was right."

"She was right about everything," Alex said.

"Tomorrow you'll stand where she stood," Greg said. "In the actual vineyard. The actual rows. Summer heat, cicadas, grapes being picked. Exactly what she experienced."

"Full circle," Emma said.

They sat in comfortable silence, drinking wine, watching stars emerge over the Brokenback Range.

Tomorrow. Tomorrow they'd complete the pilgrimage.

After dinner, Alex stepped away to the edge of The Vintry's veranda, looking out at the darkening vineyards. Her phone rang. Unknown number.

She almost didn't answer—too many journalists still calling about quantum wine. But something made her pick up.

"Alex. It's Victoria."

"Victoria."

Alex moved further from the veranda for privacy. "Are you safe?"

"I'm safe. Better than safe, actually. I'm... starting to live again." Victoria's voice carried something Alex had never heard before—lightness. Almost peace. "I saw the photos from the Sydney ceremony. The plaque. Elizabeth's name in bronze."

"It's beautiful. Permanent. She'll be remembered forever."

"I sent flowers. White roses. Did they arrive?"

"They did. Sophie cried when she read your card."

"Good tears, I hope." Victoria paused. "Alex, I'm calling because I wanted you to know—I'm coming out. Not publicly, not yet. But I'm stopping the hiding. Using my real name again. Maybe doing some quiet consulting with universities studying quantum wine. Nothing visible. Just... contributing. The way I should have thirty years ago."

Alex felt tears prick her eyes. "Victoria, that's wonderful."

"It's terrifying. But watching you fight—watching you stand on that Bordeaux stage despite every consequence—it made me realise I can't hide forever. Elizabeth fought for forty years. You fought for one year. I can at least stop running."

"You don't have to—"

"I do. For Elizabeth. For myself." Victoria's voice softened. "And I heard you're writing a book about her. A proper biography."

"I am. Starting next year. Her full story—not just quantum wine but who she was as a person."

"Good. When you do—when you're ready—I'll talk to you. On the record. Everything I remember about Elizabeth from the UC Davis years. Our early research together. What she was like before the 1979 paper destroyed everything. I owe her that much. I owe her the truth about who she was before the wine world broke her."

"Thank you. That would mean everything."

"You're in the Hunter Valley, aren't you? I can hear the cicadas."

"At The Vintry. We're visiting Tyrrell's vineyard tomorrow—the Short Flat block where Elizabeth worked in 1986."

"Stand in that vineyard for me, Alex. Feel the heat. Touch the pale sandy earth. And tell Elizabeth—" Victoria's voice caught. "Tell her I'm sorry I wasn't braver when she needed me. And tell her thank you. For proving that truth endures. Even when it takes forty years."

"I will. I promise."

"Good. Now go. Enjoy the Hunter Valley. Experience what Elizabeth experienced. That's the real vindication—not plaques or papers, but being present in the place where it all began."

They said goodbye. Alex stood on the veranda watching stars emerge over the Brokenback Range.

Victoria Mills, emerging from hiding after thirty years. Ready to contribute again. Ready to help tell Elizabeth's story properly.

Another cycle completing. Another person freed by Elizabeth's vindication.

Truth endured. Even when it cost everything. Even when it took forty years.

Elizabeth had proved that. And now everyone else was learning it too.

## FRIDAY, 9 JANUARY 2026

## TYRRELL'S SHORT FLAT VINEYARD, POKOLBIN

They drove to Tyrrell's in morning heat—already 28 degrees at 9:30 AM, climbing towards afternoon's peak.

Greg drove, Alex in passenger seat, Emma and Sophie in back. Windows down, warm wind rushing through, the smell of eucalyptus and ripening grapes.

They turned into the Short Flat vineyard at 9:50. Parked near the vineyard gate.

The soil here was different from Greg's red earth—pale sandy loam, the ancient alluvial deposits that made Hunter Semillon unique.

And harvest was happening.

Workers moved through the vine rows, picking Semillon. Bins filling with pale green-gold grapes. A truck waiting to transport them to the winery. The 2026 vintage beginning.

Forty years after Elizabeth's 1986.

A vineyard manager approached—a man in his fifties, weathered from decades working in the sun. "Ms Hartley? Ms Chen? I'm David. Been managing these blocks for twenty years."

He shook their hands, then gestured to the workers. "Started picking at 6 AM. Sugar levels perfect—20.3 Brix, pH 3.02." He smiled at Sophie. "Your grandmother wrote 11.2 Baumé in her notes —that's the same reading, just the old Australian measure. Same vineyard. Same vines. Forty years later."

Alex could barely speak. They'd timed it perfectly. Not just visiting the vineyard—witnessing the harvest. The cycle Elizabeth had predicted, unfolding in real time.

"Can we—" Alex's voice broke. "Can we walk through? See the vines?"

"Of course. Block Seven—the same block your grandmother studied. The vines were twenty-three years old in 1986. Now they're sixty-three. Still producing Vat 1."

He led them into the vineyard, between rows where workers picked steadily, efficiently, decades of harvest experience in every movement.

The vines were laden with grape clusters, leaves rustling in the warm breeze. Cicadas buzzed loud and insistent in the eucalyptus trees at the vineyard's edge.

Alex stopped walking. Closed her eyes. Felt the sun on her face.

This. This was what Elizabeth had experienced. Standing in this vineyard in summer heat. Hearing these cicadas. Smelling eucalyptus and warm earth. Watching grapes being picked.

The quantum memory had been real. But standing here now—in the actual place, in matching conditions, on harvest day—was different. More visceral. More present. More sacred.

"This is it," Alex said quietly, opening her eyes. "This is what I experienced in February. The heat. The sound. The feeling of standing in this exact place. But this—this is real. This is now. This is the cycle continuing."

Emma squeezed her hand. "You're living the quantum memory. Experiencing what Elizabeth experienced. Full circle."

Sophie walked to a vine, touched the clusters still waiting to be picked. Tears running down her face. "My grandmother stood here. Right here. She picked grapes from these vines. She documented everything. She predicted this vintage would prove her right. And forty years later, you tasted that wine and experienced her memory. You felt what she felt."

Alex pulled out her phone, showed Sophie the photo she'd saved —Elizabeth's notebook entry from 15 January 1986.

*January 15, 1986. Harvest day. Tyrrell's Vat 1 vineyard, Pokolbin.*

*Weather: Clear, hot. Temperature reached 38°C by midday. Started picking at 5:47 AM to avoid heat. Grapes perfect—sugar levels optimal (11.2 Baumé), acidity high (pH 3.04). Everything as predicted.*

*This is it. The vintage that will prove them all wrong.*

"She stood here forty years ago this week. January fifteenth. We're six days early, but the conditions are the same. Summer heat. Cicadas. Harvest happening. The vintage she predicted."

"Six days early," Sophie whispered. "But forty years. The cycle she knew would continue. The vintage that proved her right."

David approached, carrying a refractometer and a small sample of just-picked grapes. "Want to see? Twenty-point-three Brix. Perfect ripeness. We'll finish this block today, move to the next one tomorrow. By the fifteenth—your grandmother's exact date—we'll have most of the Semillon in."

He crushed a grape, tested the juice, showed them the reading. "Same vineyard. Same vines. Same parameters she documented. Forty years later, the cycle continues."

Alex knelt in the pale sandy earth between the vine rows. Picked up soil, let it run through her fingers—fine, pale, the ancient alluvial sand that made Hunter Semillon unique. Warm, ancient, the soil that had produced Elizabeth's quantum wine. The soil producing this year's vintage. The soil that would produce vintages for decades to come.

"Thank you," she whispered. To the earth. To Elizabeth. To the universe that had preserved quantum memories for forty years. To the cycle that continued despite everything. "Thank you for being real. Thank you for proving Elizabeth was right. Thank you for everything."

Sophie knelt beside her. Picked up the pale sand, let it run through her hands exactly as Alex had done. Then she pulled a small container from her bag and filled it with soil.

"To remember," Sophie said quietly. Then she stood, brushed the sand from her knees, and walked over to where David was supervising the harvest bins. Alex watched, curious.

"David," Sophie said, "would it be possible to get samples of this year's must? Before fermentation? I want to track this vintage. Document the chemistry the way my grandmother did—temperature logs, pH readings, phenolic development through fermentation and aging. If the 2026 develops quantum coherence forty years from now, someone should have the baseline data."

David studied her for a moment, then smiled. "You want to continue her work."

"I do," Sophie said. "Someone has to. She spent forty years documenting quantum wine formation, but she never got to see her data vindicated. I can't bring her back, but I can finish what she started. Properly. Scientifically. So the next generation has a complete dataset from harvest to quantum activation."

"Come back Monday morning," David said. "I'll set aside must samples for you. Temperature logs, sugar readings, the full dataset. We're doing this for Vat 1, so you'll have premium fruit. Same terroir your grandmother studied. You'll need cold storage for the samples, and a plan for tracking them over time."

"I'll arrange it," Sophie said. "Thank you."

She walked back to where Alex stood. "Forty years from now, when someone tastes the 2026 vintage and experiences quantum memory, they'll have the complete record. Beginning to end. Harvest to consciousness transfer. Elizabeth documented 1986. I'll document 2026."

Alex felt tears prick her eyes. "She'd be so proud of you."

"I hope so," Sophie said quietly. "I hope she knows I'm not just grieving her. I'm continuing her legacy."

Emma stood in the shade of a eucalyptus tree, watching Sophie's exchange with David, then Alex's embrace of her friend. Greg had stayed by the car, giving them this private moment.

"She's here," Emma said softly. "Elizabeth. In the soil, the vines, the heat. In the harvest happening around us. In Sophie's choice to continue the work. In the cycle continuing. She's here."

Greg joined them, and together the four of them followed David deeper into the vineyard.

They stayed in the vineyard for two hours. Walking the rows. Standing in the heat. Watching workers pick. Listening to cicadas. Being present in the place where Elizabeth had worked, where she'd discovered quantum wine, where she'd known—absolutely known— that she was right.

David showed them the oldest vines. Explained the terroir—the ancient alluvial soil, the quartz sand, the mineral composition that allowed quantum coherence. He talked about Elizabeth's visits in the 1980s, how she'd documented everything, how no one had believed her then.

"But you believed her," David said to Alex. "You proved she was right. You made her name permanent. That's not nothing. That's everything."

One of the harvest workers—an older man, perhaps sixty— approached Sophie. "Your grandmother was Elizabeth Chen?"

Sophie nodded.

"I picked for her. 1986. I was twenty-three. She was here every day during harvest, documenting everything. Taking notes. Measuring temperatures. Everyone thought she was mad." He smiled. "Turns out she was brilliant. Forty years ahead of everyone else."

He gestured to the bins of just-picked grapes. "This vintage— 2026—it'll be pressed and fermented this week. Bottled within months. In forty years, someone will open a bottle. And maybe—

maybe they'll experience what she experienced. Maybe they'll feel this heat, hear these cicadas, stand where we're standing now. Maybe the cycle will continue."

"It will," Alex said. "Because Elizabeth proved it's possible. Because she was right."

Finally, they walked back to the vineyard gate and climbed into the car for the drive home.

"Thank you," Alex said to David. "For preserving these vines. For continuing Elizabeth's work. For letting us stand where she stood. For letting us witness this."

"Your grandmother made this vineyard famous," David said to Sophie. "Researchers come here now. Scientists studying quantum wine. Wine writers documenting the terroir. Quantum physicists analysing the soil. All because of her. That's legacy. That's immortality."

They drove back to The Vintry in silence. Greg driving, the weight of what they'd witnessed settling over them.

They'd stood where Elizabeth stood. Felt what Elizabeth felt. Witnessed the harvest she'd documented forty years ago, happening again, the cycle continuing.

Full circle. Complete.

That evening, they sat on The Vintry's veranda watching sunset paint the Brokenback Range.

Greg brought wine—not young Semillon this time, but something special. A 1996 Tyrrell's Vat 1. Thirty years old. Developed, complex, showing everything Hunter Semillon could become.

He poured carefully. They raised glasses.

"To Elizabeth Chen," Greg said. "To forty years of fighting for truth. To vindication. To legacy."

"To Elizabeth," they echoed.

The wine was extraordinary. Honey, lanolin, toast, flinty minerality. Layers of complexity developed over three decades. The kind of wine that justified every hour Elizabeth had spent documenting quantum coherence.

"How does it feel?" Greg asked. "Being here. Standing where she stood. Witnessing the harvest. Completing the pilgrimage."

Alex looked out at the vineyards, the red earth, the eucalyptus trees darkening against the sunset. "Like coming home. Like understanding, finally, what Elizabeth was fighting for. Not just recognition. Not just vindication. But this—the cycle continuing. The knowledge preserved. The truth enduring."

"You did that," Greg said. "You made sure the cycle continues. Made sure her truth endures."

"We all did it," Alex corrected. "Elizabeth laid the foundation. I built the framework. Sophie preserved the notebooks. Marcus verified the science. Jancis validated it. Victoria provided context. You—" She gestured to Greg, to The Vintry, to the Hunter Valley surrounding them. "You keep the wine culture alive. You show people that wine is more than chemistry. That it's memory, time, consciousness."

"That's what The Vintry's about," Greg said. "Sharing that understanding. Making sure it doesn't get lost."

They sat in comfortable silence, drinking thirty-year-old Semillon, watching stars emerge.

"I'm going to write a book," Alex said suddenly. "About Elizabeth. Her life, her research, her forty-year fight. A proper biography. Make sure her full story is told, not just the quantum wine discovery but the person behind it. The scientist who wouldn't compromise. The woman who died thinking she'd failed but who actually changed everything."

"That's perfect," Emma said. "That's exactly what she deserves— her story told properly, by someone who understands what she achieved."

"When will you start?" Sophie asked.

"Next year. I'll interview everyone who knew her. You, Victoria, Marcus. Track down her colleagues from the seventies. Build a complete picture of who Elizabeth Chen was. Make sure future generations understand—she wasn't just right about quantum wine.

She was right about integrity. About pursuing truth despite consequences. About building something that lasts."

Greg raised his glass. "To the Elizabeth Chen biography. To ensuring her full story survives. To making sure no one forgets."

"To Elizabeth," they echoed.

As darkness fell, they moved inside. Greg had prepared dinner—more local lamb, summer vegetables, wines from his collection he'd been saving for the right moment.

They ate and talked and drank. Four people who'd spent the year fighting for Elizabeth's vindication. Who'd stood in the vineyard where it all began. Who'd witnessed the harvest that continued the cycle.

Normal evening. Normal summer night in Australia.

Except nothing was normal anymore.

Because quantum wine was real. Because consciousness could be bottled. Because time could be tasted.

Because Elizabeth Chen had spent forty years proving the impossible.

And because Alex had spent one year making sure the world knew.

THAT NIGHT, Alex dreamed about the vineyard. The 1986 harvest. Elizabeth Chen standing in the red earth, watching the sun rise over the Brokenback Range, picking grapes that would store her consciousness for forty years.

In the dream, Elizabeth turned and saw Alex. Smiled. Said: "Thank you. For finishing what I started. For making sure I wasn't forgotten."

"You could never be forgotten," Alex replied. "You discovered something extraordinary."

"We discovered it together. You, me, everyone who believed. That's how science works—collaboration across time. I started it. You finished it. Future researchers will build on it. That's legacy."

"I miss you. Even though I never met you."

"You did meet me. In the quantum wine. In the harvest memory. In every glass of 1986 Tyrrell's Vat 1. I'm there. Always there. Waiting to tell anyone who'll listen: wine is more than fermented grapes. It's consciousness. It's memory. It's proof that the impossible is real."

Elizabeth Chen smiled again, then faded as dreams do.

Alex woke to Australian summer morning. Emma beside her, The Vintry silent except for early birds and distant insects.

She lay in bed, watching light filter through curtains, thinking about Elizabeth. About the dream. About consciousness and memory and whether dreams were just neurones firing or something more quantum, more preserved, more real.

She'd never know for certain.

But she knew this: Elizabeth Chen had been right.

And now, finally, everyone else knew it too.

Alex got up, dressed, went outside to watch the sunrise over the vineyards.

Somewhere in Pokolbin, in rows of old Semillon vines, yesterday's harvest was resting. Grapes picked at perfect ripeness, beginning their transformation from fruit to wine. Fermentation would start soon. Cool fermentation in stainless steel, then early bottling. The transformation—citrus to honey, sharp youth to layered complexity—would happen slowly, mysteriously, in the sealed bottle over years.

And in forty years—2066—someone would taste the 2026 vintage. Experience this moment. Feel Australian summer heat. Hear morning birds. Hear cicadas. Access quantum memories Alex couldn't yet imagine.

The future tasting the past.

Consciousness preserved in glass.

Time made tangible through wine.

Just as Elizabeth Chen had predicted forty years ago when she'd stood in this same valley and said: "This is the vintage that will prove them all wrong."

She'd been right.

About everything.

And her vindication—forty years late but complete—would echo for decades. Centuries. Forever.

Elizabeth Chen's legacy: quantum wine researcher. Dismissed scientist. Vindicated genius.

The woman who proved the impossible was real.

And the person who'd shown that truth, no matter how long suppressed, eventually finds its way into the light.

Alex stood in the Australian morning, breathing warm air, feeling the cycle continue.

Elizabeth had laid the foundation.

Alex had built the structure.

And future researchers—people not yet born, studying wines not yet made—would build on top of what they'd created together.

That was legacy. That was victory.

That was worth forty years of fighting.

That was worth everything.

Wine could store consciousness.

Memory could be bottled.

Time could be tasted.

And the impossible was real.

## THE END
*of*
QUANTUM WINE: TERROIR

ALEX HARTLEY
WILL RETURN IN
QUANTUM WINE: EFFERVESCENCE

## A NOTE ON WINE

If this novel has piqued your curiosity about the wines mentioned within its pages, I'm delighted to share a bit more about them.

Semillon is one of the world's great white grape varieties, though it rarely receives the recognition it deserves. In Bordeaux—its spiritual home—Semillon is the foundation of the legendary sweet wines of Sauternes and Barsac, where its thin skins make it particularly susceptible to noble rot. Château d'Yquem, perhaps the world's most celebrated dessert wine, is typically 80% Semillon. In dry white Bordeaux, particularly in Pessac-Léognan and Graves, Semillon is blended with Sauvignon Blanc to create wines of remarkable longevity and complexity.

You'll find Semillon thriving in pockets around the world—Margaret River in Western Australia produces beautiful Semillon-Sauvignon blends, California's Central Coast is experimenting with the variety, and South Africa has old-vine Semillon that yields fascinating wines. But nowhere has Semillon found a more distinctive voice than in Australia's Hunter Valley.

Hunter Valley Semillon is genuinely extraordinary, and utterly unlike Semillon grown anywhere else. Harvested from early January through to February at unusually low sugar levels (often at potential alcohols of just 10-11%), fermented cool in stainless steel, and bottled within months with no oak or malolactic fermentation, these wines are positively austere in youth—all lemon-lime citrus and bracing acidity. Many wine drinkers taste young Hunter Semillon and wonder what the fuss is about.

Then comes the magic. Over ten, twenty, even forty years in bottle, Hunter Semillon undergoes a transformation that no one fully understands. The citrus evolves into honey, toast, lanolin, and beeswax. The acidity remains vibrant whilst the texture becomes richer. The wines develop complexity that would make a great white Burgundy jealous, yet they're made with minimal intervention and maximum patience. Jancis Robinson MW has called Hunter Semillon "one of Australia's great gifts to the world of wine," and she's absolutely right.

This unique expression is a product of terroir—the Hunter's particular combination of sandy, alluvial soils, subtropical climate tempered by afternoon cloud cover and coastal breezes, and the wine-making philosophy of picking early to preserve acidity. The result is a wine style found nowhere else on earth.

Tyrrell's Vat 1 (first bottled in 1962) remains the benchmark, but wonderful examples come from Brokenwood, Thomas Wines, Mount Pleasant, Keith Tulloch, and many others. If you can find aged examples—a 1986 if you're very lucky—do try them. The experience is unforgettable, and you'll understand why I chose this wine as the vessel for quantum memories in my novel.

Hunter Valley Shiraz is the region's other glory. Unlike the powerful, fruit-forward Shiraz of the Barossa Valley, Hunter Shiraz is more restrained, earthier, with distinctive leather, tobacco, and savoury characters that speak of the region's red soils and warm climate. These wines age beautifully, developing extraordinary complexity over decades. Seek out examples from Brokenwood's Graveyard Vineyard, Mount Pleasant's Maurice O'Shea, or Tyrrell's Vat 9.

As for quantum wine? That's pure speculation—fiction built on my fascination with both wine and consciousness. But the Hunter Valley's ability to produce wines that genuinely seem to transport you to another time and place? That's entirely real. Visit Pokolbin, taste these wines where they're made, and you'll understand why I chose this valley as the setting for Alex Hartley's journey.

The Vintry exists, by the way. If you'd like to experience the Hunter Valley yourself, you're always welcome.

Greg Mincher
Pokolbin, January 2026

Greg Mincher discovered the word "vintry" in a pub in St Albans, England in 1996 whilst studying for his Diploma in Wine Marketing at Roseworthy. The term, referring to the 13th-century landing point on the Thames where Bordeaux merchants gathered to unload wine, discuss their trade, and share stories, captured something essential about what wine means to him: a catalyst for connection, conversation, and memory.

That discovery became a vision. In 2005, Greg established The Vintry in Pokolbin, Hunter Valley—award-winning accommodation (New South Wales Tourism Awards and Hunter Tourism Awards) designed as a modern expression of that medieval gathering place. Here, guests experience wine not just as a beverage but as a medium for creating memories of time, place, and people together.

Born and raised in Sydney, Greg spent over thirty years in the wine industry before moving full-time to Pokolbin to immerse himself in writing and deepen his connection to the wine business. He owns a Shiraz vineyard in the Hunter Valley, planted in 2000. His wine credentials include Comité Champagne Champagne Professional certification and WSET Diploma studies. He has authored wine education books including *Champagne Confidence* and *Grandes Marques of Champagne,* sharing his passion for the world's most celebrated sparkling wine.

Greg's background in architecture and design informs his attention to structure and detail, whether crafting spaces for wine experiences or weaving together the complex narrative threads of a thriller. At heart, he is a storyteller who believes in mentoring and nurturing people through their journeys—an approach that extends from hosting guests at The Vintry to guiding readers through the quantum mysteries of aged wine.

*Quantum Wine: Terroir* is the first book in the Quantum Wine series, combining Greg's intimate knowledge of the wine world with speculative fiction that explores consciousness, memory, and the inexplicable transformations that happen in sealed bottles over decades. The next instalment, *Quantum Wine: Effervescence,* will see Alex Hartley return to explore the cellars and secrets of Champagne, building on Greg's deep passion for and experience with the region.

His daughter Isabella is building her own career with the same determination and independence that defines the strongest characters in his novels. The door at The Vintry remains open, always.

For more books and updates:
www.gregmincher.com

instagram.com/greg_mincher
facebook.com/gregmincher
linkedin.com/in/gregmincher
x.com/gregmincher